Junk Male

to dear Colin & Gay
see page 259
with love e gratitude

Pia Helena.

Junk Male

For a woman on her own the world is full of junk male

Pia Helena Ormerod

authorHOUSE®

AuthorHouse™
1663 Liberty Drive
Bloomington, IN 47403
www.authorhouse.com
Phone: 1-800-839-8640

First published by AuthorHouse   11/07/2011

ISBN: 978-1-4670-0852-5 (sc)
ISBN: 978-1-4670-0853-2 (ebk)

Printed in the United States of America

For John, of course

CHAPTER ONE

Edward Riverton

I look at Nina sitting next to me on the green chair. How could I tell her? I knew deep down her world was going to fall apart. Of course I love her. I will always love her. She is the mother of my children, my friend and she understands me, knows me inside out. My first love.

But I have changed. Sasha has happened and I can't turn back the clock. Just thinking of Sasha makes me happy. I am alive. For years I felt as if my blood had frozen, now it pulses through my veins again.

I look at Nina as she fusses with the coffee. Her dark hair falls around her face in thick waves, now flecked with gray. When did she turn gray? Her dress seems equally denounced by colour as if in sympathy and I notice her hips, how wide they are in that unbecoming dress, as she puts down the tray. Nina has become middle-aged and I haven't noticed until now. Her skin is coarser, wrinkles nestle around her eyes and her pink lipstick is clotted on her upper lip. Sasha has skin that I can't even touch without wanting to throw her down and make love to her. Her rosy pink nipples always swell under my eager fingers. I can't remember when I last touched Nina's blue-veined breasts.

We've been married for more than twenty years, she keeps count, I can't remember. It's been a good life, but has anyone in this family ever asked what **I** want or need? I've worked hard and made sure they all got what **they** wanted. Now, it's my turn, time for my life.

For three days Nina Riverton sat on the bathroom floor. She clasped her knees and rocked gently, moaning like a dog in pain. Grief knotted her intestines into a tangle and every time Edward tried to give her anything to eat she vomited. She must have slept, curled on the cold floor, because at the first dawn she woke up to find that Edward had covered her with a blanket. On the fourth day her wake ended and she got dressed. Edward deemed the crisis over and left.

Yet, it had all started like so many of their evenings.

The late sun painted the outside brick wall a deep gold and bathed the garden, Nina's pride, in a warm glow. The plants in their tidy beds looked almost fluorescent in the afternoon light. She admired her late-flowering tulips as she rinsed the gratin dish, scraping off gluey lasagne strands with the back of the brush. The setting sun, or maybe it was the steam, made her face pink. Wisps of dark hair curled over her forehead and with a wet hand she pushed them behind her ears.

Edward was next door, sitting in his favourite chair, waiting for his coffee, very strong, the way he preferred it. She noticed again the deeper lines drawn around his grey eyes. He works too hard, she often thought. During the last months he had come home later and later, busy with some deal. He talked about a mega-merger, but Nina was not sure what that meant. He often said things she did not understand.

Even the children, when they were around, mentioned how distracted their father had become.

"He works hard to give us a good life," she said, annoyed by their disloyalty, but secretly she agreed with her children. Nina enjoyed motherhood, a role she felt she was better at than being a wife. Her husband wanted perfection and Nina knew she could never live up to his demands. No one had ever taught her the importance of plumping up cushions or polishing door-knobs. Edward, though, wanted a home like the one he had grown up in; tidy and ready for inspection at anytime.

Edward had been distant for months and although they made love every week-end, a habit born out of courtesy rather than desire, there had been a change in the temperature. Edward had never been a passionate man. He went through the motions of lovemaking with the same ritual precision as a man shaving, a routine that never changes. Nina did not expect anything else. Her long marriage had made her believe that passion was just the heat necessary to fuse two individuals together. For Nina that weekly moment of tenderness was enough.

Nina put out two china cups on the wooden tray and poured milk into the engraved silver creamer, a wedding present from Edward's aunt. She waited for the water to boil. Strong, really strong to please Edward, thought Nina, as she spooned freshly ground Arabica into the cafetiére. She carried the tray into the drawing room, a gloomy space weighed down with inherited mahogany and Edward's aspirations.

"A mint, darling?"

Nina held out a plate with some foil-wrapped chocolates. Edward seemed not to hear. He was staring at the coffee as he stirred in the milk with rhythmic swirls. Nina repeated her question, still holding the plate. Edward jerked forward, as if woken from a dream, and the evening paper dropped off his lap. Leaning down to retrieve it, his coffee spiralled out on to the carpet. Nina nimbly fell to her knees.

"Oh, darling, don't worry," she said, half assuring, half admonishing him, "I'll get a cloth from the kitchen."

"Shut up and sit down."

Nina's stiffened. Edward had never talked to her like that before. She waited for an apology, but Edward did not move, just put his now half empty cup back on the tray.

"We must talk. We have to speak,"

"Yes, Edward, what is it you want to discuss?"

Nina looked at the mantelpiece clock, it was twenty minutes to nine. And her only thought was that they would probably miss the nine o'clock news.

Afterwards Nina could not remember what had been said. The evening had been cut from her memory. It had been like watching a bad movie and with her longing for the light to come back on. She wanted to know everything about that woman he had mentioned, but at the same time she didn't want to snoop. Still, that feeling did not stop her from ransacking his now half-empty drawers, after he left, looking for credit card statements or receipts. She was hungry for proof, but when she found something, her anger rose like boiling milk. Later she remembered with shame how she had spent several evenings sitting in her cold car outside the flat Edward had rented in town, hoping to see what Alexandra Ledger looked like. On the sixth night she saw them. Nina heard the laughter first and recognised Edward's voice as he chatted to the taxi driver. She lowered herself behind the wheel. Through the windscreen, cloudy by her own breath, she saw the two of them crossing the street, still laughing and carrying heavy supermarket bags. Alexandra looked young, blond hair swinging as she walked to the door, and when she opened it, it was with a key from her handbag. Edward took the bags from her as she fitted the key into the lock. He put his arm at her back with gentle possessiveness. The door closed with a heavy click and she could no longer hear their voices. At that very moment Nina realised with a jolt that she was eliminated, just an uncomfortable part of Edward's past.

Her anger was sometimes softened by self-pity. Raking over the past like an eager archaeologist she tried to see where she had gone wrong. Had she not shown enough interest in his job? Should she have been more exciting in bed? At other times she found comfort in thoughts of not really loving Edward. Maybe the anguish she felt so acutely was simply the pain of rejection? When had she last said "I love you" to Edward and really meant it? Was their togetherness, that Nina so cherished, just based on a shared mortgage, bleached memories and responsibility for two children? Was their marriage nothing but a comfortable old coat protecting her from the outside cold?

Her mind went blank. At times she could not remember anything. Grief often engulfed her without a cause and stopped her from breathing. She could not think clearly and at night cold sweat kept her from dreaming. Her mind needed order in this new chaos and she found it in crosswords and solitaire, pastimes that had never interested her before. The cards became a drug. Only four orderly piles with the kings atop would give her momentary relief. But then, just a memory brought Nina back and she would resume the relentless mourning over her dead marriage.

Their first meeting had been foolishly romantic, as if planned by a novice script—writer. Edward had bumped into her at the library, when she was on her exchange year at Bristol University. Her books fell to the floor and he handed her each book with outstretched arms while kneeling at her feet.

"Hi, I'm Edward, what's your name? I've not seen you here before "he asked, still on his knees.

Edward, *Edouard*, at least a name she could pronounce. She looked at his pale, long face, his lanky blondish hair falling over his forehead. So English, this face. She told him she was French, too much bother to explain her Hungarian parentage and that she saw herself as French after having lived all her life in Paris with her mother. Shyly he offered her a cup of coffee and from then on they were never apart. He had not had a proper girlfriend and he threw himself into their budding affair. He was like a pilot light waiting to be lit, thought Nina, who saw herself as experienced. She had, after all, had an affair. Her art tutor in Bordeaux had liberated her from her unwanted virginity, not out love, not even lust, but because he felt that all the A-students deserved the ultimate bonus of his love making. It was she who had to initiate Edward, guide him, massage and fondle him till he exploded in the narrow bed. Excited by their new found-skills they stayed for days in his rented room, living on oranges and wine, while exploring each other's bony bodies and feelings. Nina still stirred in Pavlovian anticipation when smelling a freshly peeled orange.

Edward had studied Classics but gave it up after the first year to study accountancy at the request of his father. Like her he was an only child. At eight his parents had sent him off to boarding school and he often told Nina how miserable he had been. But, like so many Englishmen, he set aside money so that he, in turn, could send his own son to the school he had hated so intensely.

"It did me no harm at all," he would say.

It had perplexed Nina. She wanted to keep Paul at home, but Edward had insisted.

With measured politeness Edward's parents had accepted Nina, not with open arms but with a kind of resignation. They always referred to her as French, Hungarian sounded too foreign.

Margaret Riverton, now a widow, had rushed to Wyckham Wood as soon as she found out about Edward's departure. In order to make up for what she considered Edward's unacceptable behaviour, she cooked for Nina, but even her best efforts were left on the plate. Probably hurt that her cooking was rejected, Mrs Riverton returned to her cottage in Hampshire. Sophie, just nineteen and back from her gap year, worried about Nina. She fussed, boiled eggs, made tea and turned into the mother Nina never had.

"I am phoning Dr Schultz today." Sophie declared three weeks after Edward had moved out.

"This can't go on. You're making yourself ill. You always got on with Dr Schultz. Talk to her and see if you can get some sleeping pills. I can't stand seeing you like this any longer."

"I'm fine, just run down. I don't want any happy pills."

Sophie, with that serious face you only have when very young, looked at her mother and then went straight to the phone to make an appointment. Nina had not mentioned Edward since Sophie's return, frightened that she might burst into tears in front of her daughter. Only a few days earlier a letter had arrived for Sophie. Nina recognised Edward's handwriting and had followed her daughter into the kitchen only to find a red-eyed Sophie tearing the letter into small pieces.

"So what can I do for you Mrs Riverton?" said Dr Schultz with a non-committal smile. Nina looked at the walls full of brightly coloured crayon drawings and remembered that Dr Schultz also looked after the children's clinic. She had often come home to the Rivertons, when the children were small. It was Dr Schultz who taught Nina to keep Sophie's room damp by keeping wet towels on the radiator, when Sophie wheezed through her first attack of croup, and she had sutured Paul's plump arm after he ridden his new bike through the French doors. Nina had always appreciated her calm and unfussy attitude and now, as always, she felt safe in her presence.

"I find it difficult to sleep. And my appetite is not what it should be. Maybe I'm just a bit run down?"

Dr Schultz looked through a brown paper folder, turning the medical notes.

"Any changes in your lifestyle? Any stress at home or at work? I see you work part-time at the gallery and also from home. How old are the children now? Seventeen and nineteen, well that's enough to make any woman feel stressed," she smiled.

"Any changes in your pattern of periods? The menopause can bring its own havoc. Still on the pill, I see, so it's not that then."

"Well, no nothing like that, but I've had a busy time. A bit of a family fuss, nothing serious, but . . ."

"Yes, fuss, what kind of fuss?" Dr Schultz's voice sharpened.

"My husband, well, he, no, we've hit a bit of a rough patch. We've never had that before. Maybe I am over-reacting? Shouldn't come here and bleat about my troubles . . . All I need is some pills to sleep, really that's all."

Nina's voice shrank and the professional smile of Dr Shultz died away.

"You've marital problems, is that it?"

Dr Schultz dropped the brown folder and started hitting the leather blotter with her ballpoint nib.

Nina shuddered and clasped the side of her thighs, trying to raise herself without the doctor noticing.

"Sit!" Dr Schultz jabbed the air with her biro. "I am saying this not as a doctor but a family friend. If a divorce is on the cards, make sure you get a good lawyer. Spend whatever you have on getting top class advice. Think of yourself for once. He won't be thinking of you, only himself, you can be certain of that. And as for . . . ."

"Thank you, Dr Shultz. Tell me, are there any herbal sleeping pills you can recommend, some that aren't addictive?" Nina hoped her question would stem the flow of unwanted advice.

Dr Schulz took out her pad and wrote a prescription. "I'm giving you some Prozac. Nothing else helps, believe me."

Nina grabbed the flimsy paper with a whispered thank you and quickly stepped out into the corridor. Dr Schultz did not even lift her head, but Nina could hear her blowing her nose as she closed the door. Sweat stuck to Nina's spine. She lifted her shirt by the waistband to let the air circulate and she thought everyone in the waiting room could hear her thumping heart. Sophie looked up from a dog-eared Woman's Own.

"What's wrong? There's something wrong with you, isn't there? What did the doctor say?" Sophie rushed up to Nina and put her arms around her shoulders.

Nina looked at her daughter, so fine featured like her father: a straight, thin nose, ash-blond hair that only shone like gold when lit by a strong sun and skin so pale it seemed translucent. No one could believe that this was Nina's daughter, Nina with her strong features and olive skin.

"I am fine, really fine. Let's go to the supermarket on the way home. I fancy a steak and a bottle of wine. What do you say?"

Two days later Nina got a letter from Dr. Schultz. It was a note suggesting that she should make an appointment to see Jon Lydner, a therapist, who worked closely with the clinic. "I can personally recommend him as he helped me through a tough period," Dr Schultz added on a bright yellow post-it note.

CHAPTER TWO

Jon Lydner

*I liked her face. That was the first thing I noticed about her as she
dithered in the doorway. A perfect oval with deep-brown eyes,
almost black like those Greek olives my brother loves so much.
I couldn't guess her age, her dark-toned skin looked suntanned
and there were just a few wrinkles around her eyes; as if she
had laughed a lot. But there were streaks of wiry grey in her
black hair, so maybe she was older than I first thought. She
didn't seem to bother about clothes. The navy skirt was too long
to be fashionable and seemed flecked with dog hair. She wore
dog-walking shoes and moved rather clumsily past my bike in the
hall, like a woman who doesn't believe in her own attractiveness.
Dr Shultz had told me some details of her background and I
thought she would be one of those spoilt women from the village,
who needs a therapist as a fashionable accessory. She was not
one of them and I just knew I would like her from the moment
I saw her.*

*There is something wonderfully exotic about her, the
un-Englishness, She gets enthusiastic and she doesn't hide
it behind a polished smile. No, she lights up with such a force,
strong enough to guide ships into a darkened harbour. Then she is
beautiful, but she doesn't know it.*

*Did I fall in love with her? No, but her company gave me
comfort, like the sun shining on your face on a cold day.
I'm past love, this is not an uncommon malaise among us
psychotherapists. That's what happens when you spend your
days listening to the damage unsynchronised love does to
people.*

The house was tall and narrow with two sash windows on each floor. It looked neglected unlike most of the gentrified houses around the Georgian square. The streets were lined with expensive German cars, but outside no. 5 a rusty bicycle was chained to the iron railing. The stairs up to the front door were worn by decades of heavy footsteps and a couple of un-rinsed milk bottles at the front door had been waiting a long time for the milkman.

Nina watched the house for some minutes, sitting in her car. Who would live in such a big house and not care for it, she wondered. And what was she doing here? Grateful for the Prozac, she had telephoned the number she was given by Dr. Schultz surgery and made an appointment. Several times during the last few days she had been tempted to cancel.

She rang the doorbell. It echoed inside the house. Through the dusty glass panels in the door she could see piles of yellowing newspapers on the floor.

"Hello. I'm Mrs Riverton to see Mr. Lydner ", Nina said to a young bearded man, who finally opened the door. He moved sideways in order to let her through and she passed yet another bike in the hallway.

"That's me," he said. "And you must be Nina. I'm Jon. Come in. Excuse the mess," and as Nina entered, not knowing where to go, she took a closer look at him. He seemed younger than she had imagined but unthreatening. His beard was fuzzy and the same reddish blond as his eyebrows, and the skin was pale with a dusting of ochre freckles. He must have chosen his clothes in the hope of attracting minimal attention; light gray corduroy trousers and a sweater in charcoal with stitched-on black leather patches at the elbows. "A caricature of the eternal student," thought Nina as he opened a set of double doors.

"Follow me," he said and led her into a large room facing the square. The sun fought its way in through greasy sash panes and made a filigree pattern on the worn carpet. The room was warm. Maybe it was those pale rays, as the ancient heater in the blocked-up fireplace could not possibly heat that large space?

Jon Lydner sat down on a nursing chair by the fireplace and pointed to an easy-chair by the window. On a small teak table next to the chair was a box of tissues and a glass of water. Had he filled the glass of water before she arrived? Nina looked at the tissues and wondered if he expected her to cry. She suddenly felt cold and shook her shoulders abruptly.

"Let me explain how this works," he said, as if he had read her thoughts. "You decide how often you want to come, if at all. You also decide what we shall talk about, I'm here to listen. The sessions last an hour, not a second more. I don't want any calls unless you phone to cancel, and if you don't give me three days' notice I will charge you for the session anyway." He looked serious and suddenly much older, but then he smiled and asked, with an almost girlish giggle, if Nina had any questions. She shook her head.

The room was sparsely furnished. Nina was pleased to see a mahogany grand piano in the corner, a music stand next to it and a violin case on the piano stool. There were bookshelves on either side of the fireplace and, although she tried, she could not read any of the titles, but she noted that they were old books, leather-bound. Her own shelves were now half-full with paper-backs and glossy art books. Edward had already packed up his books, heavy tomes of war and history. In the middle of the room stood an imposing round table covered in a stained, fringed cloth in wine-red velvet. It was an old person's room and did not fit in with this youngish man. How old could he be? Thirty five, maybe thirty eight, thought Nina.

"No, no questions." And as if to explain to herself why she was there, she added, "Dr Patricia Schultz suggested I should come and see you. To be honest, I am not sure why."

"I suppose Dr Schultz, who I gather is a friend of yours, thought you might benefit more from a sympathetic ear than chewing Prozac. And she has some experience herself. As you probably know, her divorce has just come through."

The outburst at the surgery suddenly made sense to Nina. The gnawing irritation she had felt since her visit to the surgery evaporated and she wanted to apologize to Dr Schultz. Yes, Prozac had eased the pain, but the pain was still there. But why did Dr Schultz think that talking to this man could help her?

She drank from the glass, hoping to find something to say. How could a stranger ever understand what another person experiences? This man knew nothing about her and he hadn't even met Edward.

"I gather you're going through a separation. How long have you been married?"

"Twenty years. And they've been twenty good years" She paused." Everyone thought we were an ideal couple. We never quarreled and as far as I know, well, until . . . neither of us ever had any affairs. It was a marriage other people envied. We both wanted the best for our children and we have no money problems to speak of. I just don't understand . . ." Nina leant forward as her voice died away. He looked at her but did not say a word. In the silence she could hear a clock ticking loudly and she counted the ticks, twenty-two, twenty-three, twenty-four, but he stayed silent. She smiled wanly and took another sip from the warmish water.

"Your marriage must be very important to you. Do you miss it more than you miss your husband?"

"What an odd question. I don't know, maybe I do. Perhaps it's because I've never seen a marriage work at close quarters. I have always been determined to make mine work."

"Your parents, what kind of marriage did they have?"

"None as far as I know," said Nina and she told Jon Lydner about her mother escaping from Hungary in December 1956, one month after the uprising. Magda had fled with Nina, then only five months old. "In a trunk, literally. My mother has, as far as I know, never divorced my father. He didn't come with us to Paris and I don't know what happened to him. My mother never talked about him, and, believe me, during my childhood I asked her a thousand times. My mother is a very private person and it is only now, as I've grown older that I realize how important her privacy is. She doesn't want to explain anything to anyone and I think it has suited her lifestyle not to be free to remarry. She often falls in love, but it never lasts very long. I grew up surrounded by *oncles,* who worshipped my mother, but they all thought of me as a nuisance, the original *enfant terrible,* a kid always in the way."

"Why do you think your mother is against marriage?"

"She speaks of marriage as an excuse for ordinary people, who prefer stability to what she calls the magic of love. And I think she equates love with desire."

"Is she a good mother?"

"She's not a **bad** mother. Maybe she shouldn't have been a mother at all. Her life has been tough, she gave up so much to get away. And she must have loved me as she did take me with her to Paris."

Nina did not say anything about the days, when she came home from the Lycee and found the flat empty. Sometimes her mother could be gone for a whole night without a word. The older Nina got, the more hurt she felt. By then she knew it was not the way other mothers behaved. She was afraid that if she told him of her lonely days, he would murmur something about neglect. Nina knew deep down that her mother did not do it on purpose, she just tended to forget about her — and that made it even more painful.

"Did you ever meet your father or any of his family? No? And when you grew up, did you miss this man you've never seen?"

"I used to dream about him. When I was young I imagined that he was a film star or a famous author, or maybe royalty, but I suspect he was just a mistake in my mother's youth. You had to marry in those days . . . and maybe he meant nothing to my mother. I certainly meant nothing to him. I have tried to find out something about him, but all I know is that he was regarded as a lay-about from quite a good family with an estate outside Budapest. I know the estate has gone and I suppose he has, too. As far as I know I have no brothers or sisters and my mother hardly ever mentioned her own family. That's why I so desperately wanted a family of my own. I hoped that my children would grow up knowing that their mother would never forget them. I wanted my home to be an oasis for them, and for my husband, a place where they could relax from the cold, a real home. And I think that's what it was, that is, until my husband met this woman, until it . . ." Nina's voice broke and her hot tears took her by surprise.

Jon Lydner pointed towards the Kleenex box without a word. Nina cursed herself for breaking down in front of a man she didn't even know. That thought made her cry even more and for the next few minutes she sobbed in uncontrollable waves.

"I don't know what came over me. So sorry. I'm really not a blubberer"

They continued to talk about her mother and it surprised Nina that Jon Lydner was far more interested in Magda than Edward. Mid-sentence she heard a sharp, shrill ring. The tick-tock she had heard was not a clock but a tomato-red egg-timer on the book shelf.

"Time's up." He signalled with his hands for her to rise as well. "Next week at the same time, would that be OK with you?"

Nina was so taken aback by the abrupt end of the session that she could do nothing but nod. "And leave the cash or a cheque on the Chinese plate on the hall table."

During the next days she came close to cancelling the appointment but dropped the telephone back in its cradle every time. The following week she was there again, meeting the same old milk bottles on the doorstep. Summer turned to autumn. Every week Nina sat in the un-dusted room and poured out her woes, hoping that the egg timer would ring and yet, wishing at the same time that it wouldn't. She talked about her mother, her children, her marriage and her fear for the future. She talked about sex, or rather the lack of it.

"I can't even imagine undressing in front of a man again. Edward knew all my lumps and bumps. Maybe that's why he left," she said wistfully.

"You mustn't do yourself down. There's nothing wrong with you." Nina felt that Jon Lydner regretted the words as soon as he'd said them.

He never spoke about himself. If she did not want to speak, or answer his questions, he would sit quietly and wait for her to collect her thoughts. When Nina thought the silence was unbearable she would think of just anything to say just to get her thoughts back on track, but he seldom broke the silence. She felt at home in this musky room and noticed that there were different sheets of music on the music stand every week. Who did he play with? Was there a Mrs Lydner? Certainly no children, Nina would have noticed signs of them with her trained maternal eye. These sessions were her anchor. She worried about her dependence on this uninteresting man and what it was that made her feel cleansed inside after she had seen him.

～

Late in August Nina saw an advertisement for a concert with the famous Hungarian violinist Karoly Szabo. He was scheduled to play at the Festival Hall. Last year she had met him at a Hungarian charity do she had helped to organize at the gallery. They had found themselves at a dinner afterwards, where a posse of hangers on accompanied him. She was on her own. Maybe he took pity on her, but he had asked her to come and sit by his side. Nina had never heard of him before and that seemed to amuse him. They ended up talking about food, in his eyes just as much an art form as a violin concerto.

"I often get homesick on these world tours. When I do, I try to find a Hungarian restaurant and, then, with a bowl of black cherry soup or steaming goose with fat little dumplings in front of me I am suddenly back in my mother's kitchen," he said as he crunched a fresh radish between his yellow teeth. He had made her laugh and Nina wanted to thank him for that happy laugh with her applause at the Festival Hall.

She still hated going to any event on her own, but she knew she had to get used to it. Neither Tessa nor Jen, her two closest friends, would contemplate a concert unless it was The Rolling Stones or Status Quo. Nina ordered a ticket for one.

JUNK MALE | 19

"Name, post code . . . and number of your house," said the efficient voice at the other end of the telephone. Nina could hear the girl's fast fingers clattering over the keyboard and after a short silence, "Oh, yes Riverton, 45 Wardell Drive, Wyckham Wood, of course Mrs Riverton, you have ordered with us before," she said in a different tone, as if Nina suddenly was a long lost friend. It was only when Nina replaced the receiver that she realized that the transaction had been debited to Edward's Visa account. A ray of satisfaction replaced her initial sadness.

Entering the Festival Hall, a building she disliked for its angular brutality, she suddenly felt at ease. All through the rain sodden drive to South Bank, accompanied by the rhythmic see-sawing of her windscreen wipers, she fought back her wish to turn back, home to her fire. "It's all right to be here on my own," said Nina to herself as she with long, sure steps crossed the foyer. Here she had spent many happy evenings with Edward. Now, when looking back, those days felt as if they belonged to some other Nina, a woman she could just vaguely remember.

The Violin Concerto by Bruch made her catch her breath. She listened as the music sent arrows through her flesh before they came to rest in an almost painful point in the middle of her chest. She wanted to close her eyes, let the sound pull her away from the pale panelled walls, the worn-out cloth on the seats and the heavy breathing from the old man sitting behind her. She couldn't. Her eyes were fixed on Zsabo and the way he allowed his own playing to fill his body. He was swinging backwards and forwards in slow motion and Nina suspected he was humming as his lips moved with the music. She noticed that the first violin, a pale girl in the customary long black dress, looked at him with admiring eyes.

At the end of the Concerto there was a second-long silence, — to Nina it seemed like minutes, — before the applause cascaded down the tiers. The clapping rose like a giant wave of sound. With an almost balletic grace, Szabo bowed to the audience and then flashed his yellow smile at the pale girl, who clasped her violin in her arms like a lover. He bowed again to the audience and then turned to the girl and clapped while turning gently in her direction. A sharp dart of jealousy surprised Nina.

"Mrs Riverton? Nina?"

A voice came to her from behind. She couldn't place it. She turned around and there was Jon Lydner, walking across the aisle, as always in his gray corduroy.

"I didn't know you were interested in music. Did you enjoy it? Isn't Szabo just fantastic? What a musician. I'm sure Bruch would have loved it, this must be how he wanted it played. Oh, how rude I am. Would you like a drink? I am going to the bar and I would be very happy if you . . ."

"A glass of white wine would be lovely". Nina was relieved to have some company but at the same time almost frightened by the torrent of words from Jon Lydner.

"I got some Chablis, that's OK isn't it?" He handed her a glass of greenish wine as he returned from the bar and they sat down at a small table in the foyer.

"Have you been crying?" he asked suddenly.

She dabbed her eyes hoping that her mascara had not run.

"Silly, I know. It was just the beauty of the music. It moved me. I usually don't cry," she added, but then she thought of her weekly weeping sessions at his house and smiled. "Apart from when I see you, of course. Maybe I'm just allergic to you and somehow felt that you were in the auditorium."

As they drank the cool wine Jon told Nina that he played the violin and his brother played the piano. "We meet as often as we can, to play together. My brother is a very good pianist, almost up to a professional standard, while I'm just an eager amateur. I love music, both to listen to and to play. It's, I suppose, my form of therapy. I always end my day by playing for an hour or so. And I try to go to concerts as often as I can. I come here several times a month. Do you come here often? Oh, my God, I sound as if I am chatting you up, don't I?"

During the second part of the concerto she smiled. Maybe it was the wine, maybe it was Jon's sudden verbosity. When the concert was over and Nina had clapped until her hands ached, she gathered her coat and bag and there was Jon Lydner at her side again, this time dressed in a yellow plastic mac.

"I would offer you a lift, but I only have my bike."

"And I can't offer you a lift either, because I would never get your bike into my small Honda."

She thanked him for the drink and both said good bye without looking each other in the eyes.

~

No one looked at the women sitting in the smoky corner of the wine bar. During the last ten years these three had gradually got used to the idea of being invisible to those much younger. Nina assumed that Tessa and Jen still smiled at their reflections in the mirror each morning. Nina certainly didn't. She avoided direct eye contact with her own reflected image. The face she sometimes caught a glimpse of was one she hardly knew. She hated her hair turning gray but could not be bothered to dye it. Nor did she know what to do with those blotchy shadows under her eyes.

"We thought it was high time you had an evening out as you'll be joining Jen and me as a single woman soon. No, not single, that sounds too sad. Let's just say we happen to be between men. And a bloody fine trio we are, if you ask me," said Tessa, her voice veiled by too many Marlboros. "The wine's on me tonight. My lawyer has assured me that I got as much out of Jack as I possibly could. He's a bloody good lawyer, Nina, and with him on your side Edward won't know what hit him."

Nina looked at Tessa with her golden halo of thick hair, her smart raw silk suit in an equally golden hue. She stroked her own reliable tweed skirt as if to press it into style.

"Thank God I've been spared the rigmarole of a divorce and the more I see of marriages the more I see what a sensible decision I made years ago never to marry. If I had, I would probably have ended up paying some faithless bounder alimony just to get rid of him." Jen lifted her glass and held it up to Nina, "and you, you must not let Edward get away with it. You should be properly prepared and let Tessa's lawyer deal with it all. Oh, by the way Tessa, with your track record, do you get a discount?"

"You would have thought so, especially when you see that it's always the damned lawyers who get the most out of any settlement. But in my case I must say Joshua Greene paid for himself. And he'll do the same for you, Nina. You deserve all you can get after having given Edward your best years."

"Well, actually I think I got the best years out of Edward," Nina said almost in a whisper.

The Sauvignon was going to her head. The brain finally stopped repeating the sad mantra, "where is Edward now, what is he doing, will he come back." She looked at her two friends, so unlike her, the glamorous Tessa and clever Jen.

Both of them had helped her through the black days; Jen with soup and advice, Tessa with wine and laughter.

"I'm worried about the future. I mean, how can I cope on my own after all these married years? I can't see myself having affairs. And if I wanted, how do I meet any men? Look around this room, there is not one man here that I would like to share a drink with, let alone a bed. It might seem odd, but I've not fancied another man since I met Edward. I don't even know how to flirt any more. You must help me because otherwise all I can look forward to is bridge parties and becoming a grandmother."

"Sure, we'll help you. We really have had different experiences of life, haven't we? Tessa, you marry again and again . . ."

"Oh, come off it, only three times, so far."

"and you, Nina, so utterly innocent. And me, I suppose I'll fall somewhere between the two of you. I have my precious career, my fought for partnership in Lovett Page and a good income. I can do what I want, when I want. So Nina, what kind of help do you think we can give you? Tessa'll tell you that wide-eyed admiration goes far when trying to catch a man. Just let them talk. Still, I suppose you'll be surprised by what you'll find out there in the land of singledom. A lot of junk male, that's all I can say, but enjoy the ride and don't let them invade your life and take it over like you allowed Edward to do."

"Are you two happy with your lives? Is that what it's all about, a fine career or new husbands at regular intervals?"

Jen stared into her now empty glass and Tessa lit another cigarette, pulling the smoke deeply into her lungs.

"My God, the bottle's empty. If we're going to discuss the deeper meaning of life we need another one." And with an elegant wave Tessa managed to attract the attention of the young waiter immediately. As she always did.

"Nina, darling," she said, when her glass was refilled and yet another Marlboro lit, "don't you see that you've got something we haven't. Both Jen and I would have given up everything for a family. Sometimes I wonder if my eternal search for Mr Right isn't because I still cling to the hope that the next husband would provide me with a brood, yes, I know, hopeless in my case. Stepchildren are not the same. Tried that. Jack's ghastly daughters hated me with an intensity, which was matched only by my dislike for them. I look at you Nina and that great relationship you have with Sophie and I become green with envy."

Jen looked at Tessa, as if she had not heard this before and she smiled.

"For me it was all work. A career's is what I always wanted and now when I have one, I wonder. Is this all there is? Dealing with high-powered deals and finding new ways to charge our clients? In twenty years time when I retire with a golden handshake, what do I have to look forward to? Saga cruises with other old bags, who will show me photos of their grandchildren? What can I show them? Copies of successful contracts?"

It was past midnight. Nina fiddled with the key in the lock. Had she not double locked the Yale? On the hall table she found a note, written on a yellow foolscap paper, the sort Edward always used.

Dear Nina,

I came to talk to you tonight, but you were obviously out. I have now got a lawyer. You might remember Tony Oliver from Dickson Oliver. You can send all household bills to him. He will deal with them—within a limit. The insurance is paid on your car until March next year. Before you turn on the central heating you must air the radiators. The radiator key is kept in the orange tin on the top shelf in the cellar.

Love to you and the children

Edward

Edward must have kept the keys. Was that not a good sign? She regretted her evening out, her breath soured by too much wine. She should have been at home. They could have talked, but her wistfulness soon turned to anger. How dare he think he could still walk in and out of the house as he pleases. Tomorrow she would phone Tessa and ask her to set up an appointment with her lawyer. And she would get a locksmith to change the locks. She took the note, crumpled it into a ball and threw it in the bin.

Next time Nina went to see Jon, only a few days later, he did not mention their meeting at The Festival Hall and Nina was too embarrassed to bring it up during their session. As she was fumbling with the money to put on the plate in the hall, she shouted

"Thanks for the drink the other night. It was very kind of you. I really . . ."

Before shad finished the sentence Jon was out in the hall.

"Nina, I really enjoyed it, too. I would love to do it another night, but as you are my patient, it wouldn't be very professional. O, heck, I'm not awfully good at this. I'm going to the Purcell concert on Friday at The Festival Hall and if you also happen to be there, we could meet for a drink in the interval. I don't think that's breaking any ethical rules, do you? I usually sit at the upper level next to the entrance to the bar."

"I don't know what I'm doing on Friday. The children might be around. Paul is coming home from school." She felt a twitch in her chest, almost like a pain, and she knew she would be there.

Nina went through her wardrobe. There was nothing there, yes, clothes, but nothing to wear. The midnight blue dress was far too serious. She had worn it last time at Edward's annual company dinner. The silk still reeked of corporate boredom. The black trouser suit was too business-like and would make a man in corduroy feel underdressed. She tried on a long skirt with appliqué flowers, swirled in front of the mirror and quickly took it off. The trusty tweed skirt and a green polo neck with Magda's jade pendant would have to do.

She waited until Friday before she phoned the concert hall, this time giving her own credit card number. If it was sold out, fine; if not, she would go.

"I am so glad you could come."

He must have waited for her. "I was hoping you would come early so that we could have a drink. Do you like Purcell.? I adore his music and I think Anthony Neville-Smith is a brilliant conductor Where are you sitting? Did you have any problems getting a ticket?"

Again, this rush of words. Nina laughed and put her autumn cold hand on his.

"Let's go and have that drink and then I'll show you where I sit." It was like dealing with an overexcited child.

Nina was swept away by the mixture of Purcell's foot-tapping joy and his plaintive melodies. Her eyes closed and she thought about Edward, but slowly his face dimmed as if in a milky cloud and instead she saw Jon waving to her from the other side of the aisle. He was dressed in his usual gray, but this time he had a new white shirt. Nina noticed the sharp folding creases from the packaging. She was touched.

"I love the counter tenor. There is something about that voice, so pure, so naked. You feel the emotions in spite of the formality of the singing."

"Or maybe we sense the passion so strongly because of that formality, "replied Nina. "Maybe I shouldn't be telling you, with all your training, but I believe that sometimes by hiding the emotions behind an armour, they come across much stronger."

"You mean that the stiff British upper lip can convey feelings after all? I don't know why we English have a reputation for coldness, while you Hungarians are meant to be full-blooded and strong like your wine. We seem to cope with our cultural differences by turning them into caricatures."

"Maybe Hungarians are more showy with their emotions. We have a saying that when a Hungarian kisses your hand, you'd better count your fingers afterwards. And as you know, I grew up in France, where the worst thing you could say to a Frenchman is that he is a lousy lover. That wouldn't bother an Englishman too much, he'd be far more upset if you called him a bad driver. That would be like telling an Italian that he's singing off key."

"Well, I'm safe then. I don't drive and I can't sing."

The bell rang and they went back to their seats. After the concert they met in the foyer. People were rushing out into the night, chatting noisily as if to make up for their two hours of imposed silence. The lights on the other side of the Thames promised glittering evenings. Her own cold salad at home didn't inspire. She wanted wine in fine glasses, candles and starched waiters. Many an evening, alone at Magda's flat in rue de l'Universitée, she had stared through misty windows on the family in the flat opposite. The *maman* serving steaming food to her family seated at a round table, properly laid with a tablecloth and sometimes flowers. For Nina it was magic because it was unattainable. She wanted to fly through her window and join them, sharing their meal and laughing with the children.

"I didn't take my bike today" Jon looked down at his shoes. "I thought maybe we could go somewhere for a pasta. That is, if you're not in a hurry. We can get a cab into the West End or just go across the road to the Archduke."

"I would love to, across the road is fine," said Nina, both to his and her surprise.

They shared mushroom pasta, half a bottle of red and the bill. No coffee. Nina remembered that the car park closed at 11.30 and after maneuvering her car out, just in time, drove Jon home to his house, the milk bottles now looking golden in the yellow porch light.

Next Wednesday neither of them mentioned the concert until Nina was out in the hall, about to leave.

"Thanks for a lovely evening. I really enjoyed myself."

"No, no. It is I who should thank you, for the company and the lift home. Next Friday there is a Brahms concert at the Festival Hall. That new Chinese violinist Cho something is meant to be very good. I'll be there. Maybe it is something you might like to hear as well?"

"Who knows, Jon. My plans are up in the air at the moment." Yet both of them knew that she would be there and that neither of them would mention their concert evenings during their sessions.

It became a pattern. On Wednesdays Nina would talk for her allotted hour, and the man sitting in the nursing chair would have no connection, in her eyes, with the man she spent her Friday evenings with. Each concert would be followed by a simple pasta and some wine before Nina drove Jon back to his dark-windowed house.

They would talk about books, his un-named clients but mostly about music. Jon seemed to know so much about music and he taught Nina about the composers, the importance of the conductors and her enjoyment grew with each concert. One Friday while waiting for the bill—they had been to roughly ten concerts by this time—Jon looked at Nina and folded his napkin into a tight wad.

"My brother is coming to London next Friday. Would you like to hear us playing for a change? He's not only a brilliant pianist, he's also a good cook. We can have some dinner afterwards. Say you can come. My brother really wants to meet you."

CHAPTER THREE

Tor Lydner

I don't have much in common with my brother and when I'm in London I sometimes stay with him. We get on, not that we're close, but we share a love of music and we enjoy playing together. I was a bit surprised when he asked if we could invite this woman to dinner, to hear us play, as he explained it.

She had something, I don't know what it was, but she appealed to me. Obviously, she was older than me and she struck me as an unhappy woman. Yet, every little thing done for her seemed to please her. She was so easy to please, it was almost embarrassing. Not much of a looker, though. Still, I appreciate some company during my visits to London, and she didn't ask for much. And I certainly have not got much to give.

I think Jon is quite taken by her, but then he likes homely women.

"Hello, I'm Tor, Jon's brother. Come in. We've been expecting you." Nina looked at the tall man, dark-haired and with an almost military posture. This could not be Jon's brother, they were so different, Nina thought, as he led her into the room she knew so well.

"So this is what you look like," he said and guided her to a tray with bottles on the round table, now without its fringed cloth. "I've heard so much about you and your concerts. Jon tells me you have a very good ear. No wonder we both feel a bit nervous about playing for you. But first, let's have a drink. What can I offer you?"

There was polite warmth in his voice, which she didn't see reflected in his eyes. He turned hic face towards her and she saw that it was covered by a web of fine lines. Nina hoped they were caused by laughter rather than too much sun. His long-fingered hands made her want to touch him and she let her hand brush his as he gave her a glass of red wine.

"Welcome to this evening of Schubert and supper." Jon had so far not said a word.

"Is there anything I can do to help you two?" Nina needed a task.

"We're more or less ready," said Tor, "but let's finish our wine first." They emptied their glasses in silence.

Tor sat down at the piano while Jon tuned his violin. They started with a Schubert sonata. Every note, every pause was dictated by Tor, and Jon looked at his older brother with a mixture of admiration and fear. Tor's long fingers danced over the keys and Nina closed her eyes and let the music pull her away from her discomfiture. Jon's stubborn silence made her feel like an uninvited guest.

Nina clapped her hands, quietly to start with and then louder.

"I really enjoyed that. Thank you; I'm so spoiled having a recital for one."

Tor smiled and nodded to Jon. "Now we can relax. Let's go down for some dinner. You must be starving."

Nina followed Tor downstairs. The large kitchen covered the whole basement. In the middle of the dining area there was a large table surrounded by simple pine chairs. She could smell some ripe-smelling cheeses. A scent of herbs and garlic mingled with the steam from the old-fashioned AGA.

"I've made a broad bean risotto," said Tor as he pulled a large ironware pot off the range. "I try to fit in with Jon and his vegetarian ideas. I assume you share his convictions?"

Nina was just about to admit that she had no idea that Jon was a vegetarian, but she kept quiet and thought about their post-concert meals. Of course, he always picked a pasta or a salad, how stupid of her not to notice.

They ladled their plates with creamy risotto and sat down at the table. Nina ate far more than her hunger dictated. The wine bottle was emptied and another one opened to accompany the cheese and salad.

The food and wine loosened Nina tenseness. Jon was quiet and busied himself by clearing dirty dishes off the table.

"I love cooking. It's not often that I have a chance. I travel a lot in my work and spend most of my time eating in hotels. But when I'm here I spend hours in the kitchen. Jon likes his food but can't cook at all, never has shown any interest, have you, Jon? We often share a meal after some music. This is actually the first time we've invited a guest, I mean one we've actually played for. No, no, don't think of it as an honour. We're just desperate to have an audience and somehow we hope that you'd look more kindly on our musical offerings if we tempted you with some food and wine in return."

"I do cook, occasionally," said Jon, "and tonight I'm in charge of the coffee, at least."

He stood up and collected a tray with coffee cups and a cafetière identical to hers.

Tor smiled as he watched his brother.

"Has Jon told you that this is our parents' home? Our father's an accountant and for the last five years our parents have been living in Gibraltar, where he runs the finance department of a small off-shore bank. He's threatening to retire and come back here in a few months' time. And then my mother . . . . well, first of all, she'll put a stop to my cooking. She's very territorial and the kitchen's her private domain."

The discussion stalled. Nina asked about Tor's work, a trick she knew helped when dealing with Edward's clients at company functions. Tor told her that he inspected oil wells in the Middle East and he managed to make it sound quite uninteresting.

"They would pay me much more if I stayed out there on a regular basis, but I need London, to go to concerts, see plays and, well, if nothing else, to look after my little brother." Nina could hear Jon shuffling his feet under the table.

"I somehow manage to cope when you're not here," he said tartly.

The wine warmed Nina and she smiled at Jon in an attempt to cheer him up.

"Where's the egg—timer?"

"The what?"

"My sessions with Jon are timed by a plastic tomato," Nina explained.

"You're not a . . . what's it called . . . a patient . . . of Jon's? I had no idea."

"Does it make any difference?"

"No. It's just that I thought Jon only dealt with troubled souls and you seem anything but."

"Well, there you are. Jon has obviously worked miracles with me." Nina blushed.

Nina looked at her watch. It was past midnight.

"I must go. Look at the time. I've had a fantastic evening and I can't remember when I've enjoyed myself as much as I did tonight. Thank you, thank you both."

Jon looked at her, as if to reproach her, but quickly Tor took her hands in his.

"So have I," he paused for a second. "We, I mean. Jon and I have really enjoyed your company. You must come back. We'd love to see you again. Wouldn't we, Jon?"

~

At her next session Nina was uncomfortable. She had little to say and the silence felt heavier than usual. Jon did not mention the evening, nor his brother and it was only when Nina was leaving that she shouted her thanks from the hall. Jon rushed before she had time to close the door and grabbed her by the arm.

"What did you think of my brother? He liked you. Say you will come and hear us again?"

Nina gently shook his hand from her arm and made a fuss of putting on her gloves as not to upset him.

"Of course, I'll come again. Yes, I did like your brother. He's totally different from you. And I loved hearing you play, made me feel like a princess, being an audience of one, but now I must rush."

Nina shivered in the cold car. She could see that Jon was watching her through the window. She started the engine and moved away from the kerb, pretending not to see him.

A week later Tor telephoned her from Dubai. She didn't even know where it was. That embarrassed her and after the call she looked it up on the large Atlas Edward had left behind.

"I'll be in London the week-end after next. Can I persuade you to have dinner with me on that Saturday? Great, let's say The Savoy at eight. I'll pick you up at 7.30. And, Nina, I don't think we need to mention any if this to Jon."

"No, of course not," she said and already regretted her Yes.

The Savoy. Nina had been there a few times, once for Edward's mother's 70th and only last year with a client of Edward's. It was smart, very smart. What could she wear?

At seven thirty she was ready. Nina had changed her outfit three times ending up in the one she first tried on. The dress puckered around her now much slimmer body — not having to cook every day had its advantages — but she couldn't, no, wouldn't spend money on a new outfit until she knew what she had to live on. She hadn't yet phoned Joshua Greene, Tessa's lawyer. Somehow she still hoped that Edward would come to his senses and that this nightmare would end. For now Nina was left worrying about the leaky ceiling and the ever-growing pile of windowed envelopes.

The doorbell rang at 7.35 by which time Nina had looked out through the windows at least six times. Should she ask him in for a drink? A tray with a sherry decanter was put on the side table in the living room.

"Mrs Riverton? I've come to collect you and take you to The Savoy. Mr Lydner is expecting you."

The car was not an ordinary cab. The uniformed driver opened the door for her and she sank into cream leather seats. Nina allowed herself to enjoy the ride, accompanied by soft music from the car radio. When they arrived at the hotel, Nina pulled out her purse, dreading what it would cost her.

"Mrs Riverton, no problem. It's on the account. Enjoy your evening!" Did she imagine a wink?

Nina stepped out among the crowd waiting to get into the Savoy theatre. Cigarettes glowed in the dark and the air was full of American voices. Tor waited for her in the foyer and led her across to the cloakroom.

"Shall we start with a drink in the American Bar? It's my favourite bar in London. The bartender makes superb Daiquiris."

Nina followed him like a puppy and in the distance she could hear the gentle clinking from a well-tuned piano. *Night and Day*, an old favourite. Her spirits rose and the frozen Daiquiri melted her fears. There was nothing to be worried about. She was going to enjoy herself, no matter what.

"I once visited the hotel in Havana, where they invented the Daiquiri, La Floridita it's called. But I can assure you the Daquiris, that Ben mixes here are far superior to the original ones."

Tor wore a smart dark-blue suit. "Cheap to have them tailored in Dubai," he replied, when she complimented him, as they sat down for dinner. Tor tried to make her feel at ease as several waiters hovered around their table. There was a constant," would madam like this, or would madam prefer", and after a while Nina just smiled and felt that she deserved this service as a matter of right. A napkin in starched linen was folded on her lap, pats of butter lifted on to her side plate and the tiny bread roll was served with silver tongs as if any touch of a human hand would sully its golden crust. Everything at the table sparkled and Nina hoped that the gleam was reflected in her eyes.

Tor and Nina talked about concerts, art and travel. They did not talk about themselves. Nina tried to make Tor open up by asking him questions but he managed to deflect them and always brought the conversation back to a neutral ground.

"You're very different from your brother. Tell me some more about your family? Do you have any sisters or more brothers? And what about you, do you have any family?"

"How kind of you to ask, but believe me, I'm not very interesting. I live on my own and I am still trying to figure out if it's by choice or not." He smiled and waved his hand to attract the attention of the waiter. While the waiter poured some more wine into Nina's empty glass Tor looked intently at her. She smiled back and felt herself softening, allowing herself the luxury of a sensuous stir. He gripped her hand.

"Nina, such a pleasure this is. The car is picking you up at eleven, so that gives us just time for a quick coffee."

He helped her into her coat and led her out into the courtyard. The car was there. Nina leant forward to accept a kiss from him on her cheek, the expected gesture after such a fine dinner. Tor stood still and gripped her shoulders with very straight arms.

"May I phone you before my next visit to London? I would very much like to see you again."

Nina whispered yes, but her joy of being asked was marred by her disappointment of not being kissed, not even on the cheek. Tor stepped back and opened the car door. Through the back window she could see him walking back to the foyer without turning,

"Had a good evening then, Mrs Riverton?"

~

Nina tried not to think about the evening at the Savoy. It had been a mistake and she found Tor's aloofness as yet another sign of her lack of allure. It hurt her, but just now her leaking roof was far more of a concern. These were matters that Edward had always dealt with. She turned to the Yellow Pages in order to explain about leaks and missing slates. The first firm mentioned in the directory had a man answering calling her Dearie and she knew instantly that she would be ripped off. The second man, this time chosen randomly, sounded gruff and slightly more professional, the third had a secretary and that to Nina was a sign of a reliable business.

Mr Chalmers of Roofs-R-Us turned up in a battered van next day and after having climbed over her roof, sucked in air and tutted while shaking his head from side to side.

"Dear, oh, dear," followed by more intake of breath, "this **is** serious. The whole roof needs relaying. You're suffering from nail fatigue and that's why the slates fall off. We're talking serious work here, Mrs . . . Whats-yer-name-again" He then mentioned a sum, which was not much less than Edward had paid for the house eighteen years ago.

Edward was not interested in the leaking roof.

"Your lawyer has informed me that you want the house, well, then you pay for the house. And if you can't cope, take in a lodger or two. The house is certainly big enough with the children away." Edward's tough response shocked her and when the phone rang immediately after she had put down the receiver, she was sure it was Edward phoning to apologise.

"Nina? Tor Lydner. I'll be in London on the 23rd. Are you free for dinner? There is a concert at The Barbican, Tokyo

Symphony Orchestra playing Brahms, and then we could have supper afterwards at the Savoy. You seemed to like it there. Great. I'll make sure the car is with you by seven. Bye then."

Not a word about his week, no small talk, it was more like setting up a business meeting. Again Nina had a feeling of being used, but for what?

The same car with the same chauffeur came to pick her up on the Saturday as agreed. Was it wrong to enjoy the luxury of a chauffeur-driven car? Nina certainly did not think so and at the Barbican she admitted to herself that she felt proud to have a handsome, well-dressed man sitting next to her, in very good seats. Her new dress was just right, and worth the money.

"You look really lovely in that shade of blue."

It was the first time that he had complimented her. She liked it. Edward had never noticed what she wore, never given her compliments except for her cooking. Looks were something Edward didn't think worth discussing. His lack of any interest made Nina realise that whatever effort she put into looking good was entirely for her own confidence rather than pleasing him. She lacked her mother's touch. Magda was always chic. Her almond-shaped nails were painted a gleaming red and each week she visited the hairdressers where her auburn hair was turned into an elegant chignon. Magda never spent a fortune on her wardrobe, but she could just tie a silk scarf around her neck and look stylish, a trick Nina never managed.

Magda would have approved of the blue dress. Tessa had come up with Nina to London and after lunch Tessa had taken Nina into a small shop behind Oxford Street. There were only a few racks of clothes to choose from and the shimmering midnight—blue silk immediately caught Tessa's eyes.

"That's the one, and it's your size. You must try it on"

It was deceivingly modest. The three quarter sleeves gave the dress an air of afternoon tea while the deep V-neck indicated cocktail time. The dress was perfect, but that was before Nina saw the price tag.

"It really does something for your figure," said the slim sales assistant as Nina walked out of the cubicle. Nina bristled. The girl's remark, served with cold contempt, made Nina think of her figure as a helpless victim that could only be saved by designer wear.

Back in the cubicle Tessa took one look at Nina's sensible white underwear and smiled.

"Honey, you'll never catch anything with those knickers. I'm going to take you to Aimant for some proper underwear and it's my treat."

Sitting next to Tor she wondered if he knew that she had pale blue silk underneath her dress. Tessa had been far too generous and Nina had tried not to look at the bill, but the underwear had come to more than the dress. The silk made her move in a different way, as if she were caressed.

As they stepped in to the foyer of the Savoy she felt she belonged as the coat slipped off her shoulders onto Tor's waiting hands.

"Why don't we start with a Daiquiri as usual?"

When they entered the bar the pianist began playing *Night and Day*, as if he recognised them, and he nodded to Nina on Tor's arm.

When she returned home, driven back by Brian, now on first name terms with Nina, she could not decide whether it had been a good evening or not. Tor had laughed at her story of Mr. Chalmers of Roofs-R-Us and his insistence on Hobnob biscuits as part of their negotiations. She had even told him about the shopping at Aimant, where most of the customers seemed to be men.

"And I wonder what they thought about Tessa and me, as she picked up the bill?"

Yet, Tor had not said one word about himself. He was polite, thoughtful and good company, but the distance was there.

"How do you spend your evenings in Dubai? Do you have a chance to hear any music? Do you socialize with other ex-pats? Can you drink there? Do you . . ."

"Hey, Nina. So many questions. Are you interviewing me? Dubai is really quite boring unless you like shopping and you have just told me that you have little interest in that pastime and I personally can't think of anything more boring. Of course, I have some friends there, but most of my life in Dubai revolves around work. My only breaks are when I come to London. Still, I enjoy what I do, so I don't have time to feel lonely."

"When did you move to the Middle East?"

"You're still interviewing me, aren't you? Believe me, my life in Dubai is not very interesting, nor am I, come to think of it," he added with a smile.

Nina folded her napkin neatly, just to unfurl it again.

"It's so funny. You and your brother never talk about yourselves. It seems I do all the talking."

"Maybe it's because our father constantly tells us it's best to let the women do the talking while we do the thinking. No, honestly, I am far more interested in hearing about your life and your adventures with Tessa and Mr Chalmers."

Nina looked across the damask and smiled. She was getting closer to him, she could sense it.

"Nina, it's been another wonderful evening. I've looked forward to it. The car is outside and it is almost midnight."

"I am not a Cinderella, you know. Tomorrow is Sunday and I'm not in a hurry." She held her breath. "Actually, why don't you come back with me, I am not far from Jon's house, for a cup of coffee?"

Tor's face stiffened. He pulled back and stood up, his back straight as a rod.

"Nina, that's very kind of you. I really appreciate it, but I've just arrived from Dubai and I'm staying at the Savoy tonight as I'm mentally still in another time zone. Next time, perhaps . . ."

Before stepping into the waiting car he touched her shoulders with straight arms and this time Nina did not proffer her cheek for a kiss. When she undressed in her bedroom and put away the blue silk she felt both cheap and soiled. Edward and his indifference, so hurtful at times, now seemed like a comfort to her. Naked, she ached of loneliness.

She had another two evenings with Tor during the late autumn. Concerts followed by dinner, not only at the Savoy, he had also taken her to Claridges. Smart, impersonal places which never invited intimacy and but where Nina thought she had to whisper as not to attract attention from the other diners. She knew that it was no good expecting a good night kiss or inviting Tor home for a night cap. This relationship was obviously meant to be chaste and she enjoyed it for what it was, a night out.

Coming out of Claridges, Brian waited outside with the car and Nina said her usual goodbye, not even expecting a handshake.

"Would you mind if I shared the car with you? I'm staying with Jon this week-end."

"Of course not. I'll be glad of the company."

Inside the car, Tor closed the glass partition behind Brian. Frank Sinatra sang softly through expensive loudspeakers and the only light was the bluish gleam from the dashboard. Without a word Tor leant forward in the darkness and kissed Nina hard on the mouth, his tongue separating her lips. She was so surprised that she didn't even pretend to hold back. The scent of his aftershave, the leather in the car and the soft music made her feel safe and she kissed him back, moving her thighs closer to this. He pulled her to his suited chest and his hand came to rest on her upper leg. Without even thinking she opened her legs to allow his hand to touch her. Not a word was said.

Nina saw red traffic lights change colour through her closed eyelids, she heard a burglar alarm go off somewhere, but her whole being concentrated on the nearness of Tor. She had not kissed another man except Edward for years and the sensation was infusing her with blood-pumping heat. Breathing became difficult and she only came back to reality, when Brian coughed and declared that they had arrived at Nina's house in Wyckham Wood. Tor signed a chit and sent Brian back to wherever he came from and then watched Nina fumble with the keys.

There was no talk about a coffee or a night cap. In the hall, Tor took off her coat, unzipped her dress and then pushed her upstairs, holding his hand on her lower back. Inside the dark bedroom, he grabbed the silk and tore the dress off her and almost threw her on the bed. Although she longed to give in to his all-over kisses Nina still made sure that they did not veer over to what she still thought of as Edward's part of the bed. First when on her side did she allow herself to respond to his kisses and his brusque caresses. Tor's strong body made her feel flayed by desire and she cried out as he without tenderness plunged into her and pressed her hard into the mattress. He held her thighs apart as if to keep a distance between their hot bodies. His eyes were closed and he did not seem to notice her soft sounds as he pinned her with his thrusts. The pain was part of her pleasure and his detachment both excited and frightened her. Afterwards she shuddered as if an inner string had broken and she burst into tears. Moving closer to Tor she put her head on his shoulder.

He pulled away brusquely and began to dry himself on the corner of the sheet. Nina pushed her hand onto his back and gently stroked his spine. "Tor, darling Tor," she whispered. He shook her hand off by shaking his shoulders and turned to switch on the bedside light. There was no softness in his eyes, just cold boredom.

"Oh for god's sake. This is what you wanted, isn't it? Just a fuck. I really shouldn't have come home with you. God knows why I did it." He patted her absentmindedly on her naked shoulder. "Where's your bathroom? And do you think you could order me a cab?"

His unexpected rudeness made Nina feel lonelier than ever, and dirty. She pulled the dampened sheet around her cold body and picked up the phone. Her tears were burning behind her eyelids. From the bathroom she could hear him gargling as if he wanted to get rid of the taste of her. They waited in ghostly silence for the cab to arrive. Tor's back was turned as he slowly dressed, he behaved as if he were frightened to face her. Each shirt button took seconds and he unfolded the trousers he'd so carefully put over the back of a chair, and then stepped into his shoes, which he gave a quick polish with the damp corner of the sheet. He shot a glance at her dress left in a heap on the floor and she could see his contempt. Finally the doorbell rang. Tor ran down the stairs without a word and picked up his coat. Nina followed, still draped in the topsheet. She couldn't even say goodbye to him, just saw his shadow through the hall window as the car disappeared down the road, two red menacing lights in the dark.

Not a word from him. Nina circled around the telephone all Sunday, still not getting dressed. She wanted to talk to him, explain that, of course it didn't mean anything, it was just sex, but that was not true. She wanted it to mean something. As the day passed, she knew he would not get in touch and she did not want to phone him at Jon's and, anyway, by then it was too late.

The next Wednesday she was back for another session with Jon. The sun was low and warming up the room. Suddenly the heat was unbearable. She pulled off her cardigan. Jon looked questioningly at her

"Tor's my brother and maybe I shouldn't tell you this, just let you find out for yourself eventually. But I feel I have a responsibility for you. You've put your trust in me. You may think I interfere, or that this has nothing to do with me, but . . . well, I have to ask. How far have things gone between the two of you? Tor came back last Saturday and I have the impression that your relationship with him has changed. Am I right?"

Nina's armpits dampened and she swallowed hard.

"We have no relationship. And if we did, it's certainly none of your business. We've been to a few concerts and that's all," she said.

"Nina, I know how he operates. God, I shouldn't be saying this. He uses women, no, not for sex but for some kind of emotional kick. He wants women to fall in love with him and when they do, he loses interest. Has Tor told you anything about himself? No, I thought not. He married quite young, a lovely girl we all thought, but she left him after only a few months and I think it unhinged him. It's almost as if he wants every woman to suffer as a revenge for what his wife had put him through. Yes, I know it sounds like cod psychology, but maybe it's because it's not unusual for people to react to emotional pain in a set way. Nina, I'm telling you this, because I don't want you to get hurt. You're just finding your feet . . . ."

"I don't want to discuss this. Your brother and his love life are of no interest to me and what I think has nothing to do with you."

"Listen to me. He's my brother and I suppose I love him, but I don't like him. I."

"You worship your brother. I've seen you. Jon, I think this is some form of envy. He gets the girls and what do you get?"

"You know nothing about me, or my relationship with my brother." His face was reddening and his soft voice had a new edge, a sharp, cold tone and he pronounced every word as if he was dictating to an inexperienced secretary.

"You see, I did get the girl. We're talking years ago. Maureen, a sweet girl and I adored her. We married young. We were both politically active and dreamt of creating a better world, the way you do when you're in your early twenties. Tor was already abroad and he didn't meet Maureen until we'd been married for just over a year. I wanted him to like her. She felt so hurt by my parents' coolness and we both hoped he'd accept her for what she was, a lovely, warm-hearted girl. Yes, you're right, I have always admired my brother. Admired him for his brain, his education, a first from Oxford, and his good looks, yes, I admit that."

Nina squirmed in her chair, knowing what was coming.

"Maureen had always loved the theatre," Jon said wistfully. "I think, if she'd had a chance, she'd tried for drama school, but she left school at sixteen and when we met she was working for the local council. She had talent, though, real talent."

"You say" had "as if she's dead," asked Nina in a rather petulant tone.

"I haven't seen her since . . . . well, Tor **did** like her and we were both thrilled. When I had late sittings at the council he took her to the theatre. And I was pleased, idiot as I was, so bloody pleased. Well, you can guess the rest. She left me, said that Tor understood her in a way that I never could. As soon as she left me, he lost interest and after a while she moved north to Leeds, where her sister lived. Our divorce was a fact a year later. I lost interest in local politics. I wanted to help on a more individual level. So I started studying in order to become a psychotherapist."

"Well, that happened to your ex-wife, what makes you think it's happened again? I'm not even a girlfriend . . . ."

"No, but he knew that I cared."

Nina looked at Jon, so achingly childlike. She felt an almost maternal urge to comfort him, but she held back. Suddenly it all became clear to her, as if cold water had cooled her overheated brain.

"Jon, I certainly don't want to become embroiled in your fraternal dramas. As a matter of fact, I've been planning to say this for a long time. I am, as you said, ready to stand on my own two feet now. I want to move on and now is as good a time as any."

Nina rose and wondered if she should shake hands or kiss him. She did neither, just turned and left the room. She paused at the Chinese dish in the hall and dropped three ten pound notes in its shallow bowl.

"Nina, no, no please . . ."

She ignored his pleas and opened the front door. The sun was warm and she could hear children laughing in the private garden square. Life continues, thought Nina and as she turned she saw through the window the shadow of Jon, shoulders crumpled.

Chapter Four

George Solyom

Nina is part of the family, well, not by blood, but by ties of years and background. I've known her mother since before Nina was born and she is the daughter I should have had. She has none of that strange reserve which corset the English, just look at her husband, never could stand him, so tight and correct. Nina has an inner glow, which Edward never saw. Until he dashed off with that blonde I always suspected he was a closet gay, but then that's my view of most ex-public school men. They all seem so damned uncomfortable among women. I love the company of women. Too much, maybe.

Nina is true to her Hungarian roots. She's always put her family first and she cooks like an angel. I've always felt welcome in her home although I must admit I'm happier there since Edward moved out. And I loved our last Christmas together, Nina's first without Edward. We all gathered at Magda's flat in Paris. Nina busied herself in the kitchen most of the time and Magda seemed quite quite overwhelmed by all of us invading her privacy. One evening I took them all to my favourite restaurant off Boul' Mich' and Nina laughed until she wept as the waiter tripped and the oysters clattered on to her lap from his up-ended tray. I'll do anything for that girl – and Magda. They are the most important people in my life.

Nina could not stop thinking about Tor and his behaviour. She remembered how she, still in her dressing gown, had torn the sheets off the bed and scrunched them into a black bin liner. In the dark she had pushed the sack into the dustbin and clamped the lid with a hard bang. Since that night her feeling of rejection was like the constant pain of a broken tooth. She could hardly concentrate on her most pressing problem; the bills. Finally she thought she had an answer.

It was staring at her from her bedroom wall. Her Russian icon. For years it had been stashed in her wardrobe. Edward had never liked it. Magda gave it to her, when she married Edward, "a piece of your background, now that you'll settle in that cold, new country". Nina remembered gazing at it as a child. It was one of the few things Magda had brought with her from Hungary and for Nina the icon became a door to that unknown country and family she knew nothing about. It was also an image of loving motherhood, equally unfamiliar to Nina. She admired the innocence of the Madonna, her almond-shaped eyes caressing the infant on her lap. Behind her the azure sky was dotted with stars laid with gold leaf that intensified the blue. Magda had told Nina that it was a valuable piece, early 17th century. Could Nina part from it? That was not a question any longer. The leaky roof had to be paid for and there was no cash available. Edward had been adamant. And Joshua Greene had warned her that she had to be careful with her expenses before a settlement was reached. His warning had come with a hefty bill for his own services.

George Solyom would help, of course he would. George had been part of Nina's life since her childhood. He had been her only contact, when she first came to England for her studies. He was Magda's oldest friend and he still made a point of always seeing her on his many trips to Paris. George was not a handsome man, yet women seemed to flock to him, adoring his small eccentricities symbolised by his English, word perfect, yet still burdened by Balkan vowels.

"Why should I change my accent? Women adore it and it has put me in more beds than I care to admit," he said as Paul or Sophie used to laugh as George strangled yet another word.

It was certainly not his body that attracted the women. George was potbellied but looked slimmer in his well-cut suits, paid for only when his tailor threatened to sue. His shirts were always professionally ironed and his ties, of the finest silk, were obviously chosen by lovers. His features were heavy as if drawn by a caricaturist; damp dark eyes glinting under eyebrows that grew bushier each year. Nina loved to kiss his jowly cheeks always scented with old-fashioned lemon cologne.

He never brought any of his conquests to the Rivertons. Occasionally George mentioned some woman, often with a sigh.

"She just doesn't understand that I'm not the marrying kind."

Like Magda he was unable to form a long-lasting relationship and Nina thought that was the reason why he and Magda had remained such staunch friends.

"Magda and I did jump into bed once in our youth, but we soon realised that we liked each other too much to be lovers." Nina remembered how Edward had laughed at that notion and later told her that both Magda and George suffered from giant egos — "no relationship would be big enough for those two" — and secretly Nina had to agree.

George had left Hungary at the same time as Magda, but he had gone to London, where he managed to get a job as a runner at one of the smaller auction houses. He was later taken on as an assistant at the Russian Arts department at a grand auction house, where one director noticed that he had an arts degree from Budapest and spoke fluent Russian. The clients loved him, certainly more than the directors did, and fifteen years ago he had set up on his own and moved into a shabby office above a boxlike shop in Bond Street.

"Oh, Nina, I know it's a horrid office," he would say as he shuffled away piles of catalogues, "but it's the address on the stationary that matters in this poncy art world."

As a thank you for Sunday lunches in Wyckham Wood, and Nina loved cooking for George and his rewarding appetite, he often reciprocated with lunches at The Gay Hussar. He never asked Edward. He knew that Edward did not approve of him and he, in turn, never made a secret of his dislike of Edward.

He would ply Nina with sweet Tokaj and, as his eyes filled, he would tell her about the grand country houses near Lake Balaton, where he first met Magda.

"Such a beauty she was. We all wanted her, but she was determined to go her own way, to choose her own man. But she was never good at picking men, dear Magda. Your beautiful Maman."

Nina did not mind the tears, she loved hearing about her mother. Magda never mentioned her youth, as if talking about her life in Hungary would remind her of what she had lost. And like Magda, George never mentioned Nina's father. "He came on the scene after my little adventure with Magda. I know nothing about him," he said with a tone that always put an end to that strain of the conversation.

It was a cold February morning, when Nina phoned to say she needed George's help. The day after her call she turned up at his unheated office with the icon, wrapped in brown paper and thrown into a Sainsbury bag.

"Darling Nina, couldn't you at least packed it in a Fortnum & Mason bag? An icon of this quality deserves the best," said George. Nina knew he had admired the icon since he first saw it in Paris.

"Are you really sure you want to sell it, my flower. All right, but how much do you want for it? Well, tell me first how much have you insured it for?"

"Nothing, I mean, we have not insured it all. It's been kept safe in my wardrobe until Edward left. So it's on the general household insurance."

Nina suddenly realised that she was talking down the price and added," but I know it is valuable, Magda has told me so. By the way, I'd be grateful if you didn't tell, her if we come to an understanding, that is if you offer me a temptingly good price."

George looked at her but didn't say a word. A small smile warmed his face.

"You tell me what you want, petal."

She thought of the bill on her desk from Roofs-R-Us, four thousand pounds.

And she remembered the other bills as well — and she needed room for negotiation.

"I think a good price would be six thousand pounds."

"Nina, my petal, because it's you I'll do better than that and give you eight thousand pounds and I'll do it this week, so you don't have to wait until it's sold. Can't be fairer than that, my angel."

Nina dropped the empty orange bag and ran across the un-carpeted floor to George, who had already opened his arms.

"Now this calls for a glass of Tokaj and some almond biscuits."

He walked up to a grey metal filing cabinet and out of the top drawer came a bottle. With an elegant gesture he dusted two crystal glasses with an immaculate silk handkerchief and totally ruined the effect by putting the two glasses on a pile of newspaper clippings. Slowly he poured the golden drink into the glasses, lifted his and said "To our first little deal, darling."

A week later Nina got a call from Edward. He did not phone often. Her cheeks went hot and her tongue grew in her mouth. Did he know about Tor, that she had been in bed with another man? Nina prayed that he didn't and at the same time she wanted him to know that other men, or at least this man for a short time, had found her attractive.

"Nina, I am saddened to see that you are selling off your inheritance. Is it really necessary?"

"What do you mean? I'm not selling anything. I have nothing to sell, as you well know."

"Well, I happened to walk past George's rather scruffy shop in Bond Street yesterday and saw what looked like Magda's icon in the window. For God's sake it's the only thing that Magda has ever given you of any value."

"Oh, that." Nina felt a wave of relief. "I needed to sell it to pay for the repair of the roof, as you wouldn't help me."

"Have you had the roof laid with marble? I mean twenty six thousand pounds is a lot to replace some slates. A heck of a lot and I think this unexpected revenue from the sale should be mentioned to our lawyers . . ."

"What do you mean, twenty six thousand."

"Well, that's what George wants for it according to that dotty girl, who works there. I can only assume he's selling it on commission, Fifteen percent or what? I should hope less as you're almost family."

Nina swallowed. George would never cheat her. It must be a mistake.

"Are you sure it's mine?" Her brain was aching and she felt nauseous.

"Nina, have you, or have you not, handed over your icon to George?"

She shivered. She always shivered, when Edward spoke to her in that tone. She had been so proud that she had managed to get such a good price, now her hard-won business victory felt hollow.

"Yes, I have," she whispered.

"And what agreement did you come to?"

"I got eight thousand pounds, a cheque," her voice was hardly audible.

"Oh, for heaven's sake, Nina. Sometimes you're so stupid, so bloody stupid. Did you ask for a second opinion? Did you talk to someone at Christie's? Now you go back to George and tell him the deal is off."

"I can't and besides I've already spent most of it. The roof came to four thousand and there were some other bills, and then the fee for the lawyer . . . ."

"Nina, can't you do anything right? You undersold your icon and you've been had by the roofing firm. It should have been less than half of that to replace those slates and besides, you have the insurance. Didn't you speak to the insurance company? It was storm damage after all, and that's why we have insurance. Can't you do anything right?"

His sharp voice mellowed, he sounded now as he talked to a small child. Tears dropped on to Nina's hand holding the receiver. He always managed to make her feel useless. But was she really? She had trusted a family friend, that was all.

"Edward, I'll deal with this tomorrow. There must be some mistake. I'll sort it out with George. Don't you worry." And with a polite "Thank you for phoning", she put the phone down.

Sitting on the bench by the window she wept. Edward was right. She could not look after the house on her own. But she would show him. She reached for the telephone, still damp from her clenched hand.

"George, Nina here. Fine, thank you. No, that's not the reason I'm phoning. I need to talk to you. No, today. I can be at your office by six, all right, by seven then."

She was still shaking as she put the phone down. As always when Nina was nervous she headed for the kitchen. With a J-cloth in her hand she polished the workbench until it shone. It soothed her nerves and while rubbing she rehearsed what she would say to George.

By six she had played out several different scenarios and she felt well prepared for her showdown with George. Dressed in her severe business suit in grey she set off for Bond Street. On the 38 bus she went over what to say, determined not to let George charm her out of her well-earned anger.

The evening light made Green Park look magical. Edward's office was just around the corner in Stratton Street and Nina remembered all the times she had packed a picnic and travelled to London to meet her husband in the park. He would take off his jacket and roll up his shirt sleeves and sigh with pleasure as he relaxed on a hired deck chair. They always met in what they called "their place", not far from Birdcage Walk. By seeing each other in the middle of the day, their meeting took on an illicit tinge and Nina felt more like a mistress than a wife. She had once suggested to Edward that they should take a room at a nearby hotel. Edward mumbled something about a meeting and, besides, they had a perfectly good bed at home. Nina never suggested it again.

And it was to their special place they had gone when Nina had been told that she expected Sophie. She had bought a bottle of champagne, but she had forgotten glasses and she remembered how they sat on their knees, glugging straight from the lukewarm bottle. How happy I was then, thought Nina as the bus stopped at The Ritz. She looked at the park, now a place for other people creating their memories.

Walking past jewellers, fashion shops and elegant picture galleries the self confidence she had built up since talking to George seeped away for each step she took. George's office was on the second floor and his tiny window at the street level was empty, her icon gone. A plain door, leading to George's office, was half hidden next to the main entrance. Nina rang and after a buzz pushed the door open. Nervously she walked up the narrow stairs.

"Darling Nina, how wonderful of you to come."

Nina heard his voice before she saw him. How typical of George to make it sound as if she had come on his invitation. He obviously expected her to behave like a well-mannered guest. She let him take off her heavy coat and he rested his arm on her shoulder.

"You look more splendid than ever. Single life suits you, or does that glow come from a new man? You can tell old uncle George, well?" He put her coat on chair by the window.

"George, I have come here to discuss my icon . . ."

"MY icon" he quickly interrupted her, "remember I bought it from you and paid a good price for it."

"I had a phone call from Edward and he said you were selling it for twenty six thousand pounds, so how can you say you gave me a good price? Come on, that doesn't sound like a good price to me."

"Oh, petal, do you really think I got twenty six thousand for that icon? Edward knows zilch about the arts trade. As a matter of fact I've not been able to get even half of that. Even you, my dear, must realise that you start off with a high price, which allows the buyer to haggle and thereby ending up with a sum that he sees as a bargain and me getting roughly what the object is worth. It's that simple."

"I want it back George, or I want a higher price for it. You didn't give ME a chance to haggle, did you?"

"How can I give it back to you? I've just told you that it's been sold. I just made a teeny, weeny margin on it, which just about covered the cost of having it properly valued, cleaned and photographed. I also had to provide some kind of provenance for it as you asked me specifically not to speak to Magda. Not easy, but I wanted to respect your wishes, petal. Come on, we both did well on our little deal."

George smiled. His scent of lemon calmed Nina down. It was, of course, the insurance company she should speak to. They should pay up for the roof repair. Why had she not thought of that before Edward mentioned it?

"Nina, my sweet, I have a table reserved at The Gay Hussar for eight o'clock. Come on, let's have dinner together and forget about Edward and his insinuations."

Why not? She would enjoy a dinner in good company.

"Must just make a call. Sit yourself down."

Nina heard him dial a number and then talk quietly into the mouthpiece.

"Yes, petal. Big client, interested in buying a major piece. So am I, sweetie, very disappointed, but you know work goes before pleasure in these tough times." He chuckled down the line at the same time as he winked at Nina.

As they stepped out through the door on to the deserted Bond Street George put his arm through hers and smiled.

Tessa was waiting at the Adelphi, their usual wine bar near Lavender Grove. Yet another evening when two women tried to convince each other how great it was to be single while both dreading the return to their empty double-beds.

"Did you get the extra money out of George?" Tessa asked even before Nina had sat down. "I mean, are in for a night of vintage or will it be the usual plonk?"

"No such luck. George said he'd only got a little bit extra over what he paid me and that just covered his expenses. He said, and I use his words, that Edward knew zilch about the world of arts. Still, I'm hoping to get something back from the insurance company for the storm damage. Thanks to several packets of Hobnobs and some tears I got Mr Chalmers to write a very nice letter to the insurance company and they are looking into it. So here's hoping. I just want to show Edward that I can cope."

"How is the old charmer?"

"Edward?"

"No, silly, George, of course. Haven't seen him for years, well since last Christmas, when we had a very jolly dinner at the Gay Hussar. I still can't get over the way he ditched me. He's such a gentleman. I didn't even notice that I was being dumped. He made me feel as if he was doing me a favour and now, thanks to his diplomatic finesse, we can both look back at our affair with unconditional pleasure."

"If the banquettes at The Gay Hussar could speak, George's reputation would be in tatters. He took me there last week, I suppose, to make up for Edward's interference. He had already booked the table and I heard him cancelling his dinner date with some woman over the phone. He is unique and although I know he's a rogue I can't help adoring him. Let's drink a toast to the ever charming György."

Tessa stubbed out her cigarette and looked at Nina.

"Listen, I've asked you to come here tonight because I have an idea. I know times are tough for you now, both emotionally and financially and I have a business proposition. No, don't say anything until I've told you what it's all about. You know all that lolly I managed to get out of Jack, and God knows I deserve it, well, I thought I'd buy a small mas in Provence. Jack insisted on keeping our lovely house in Cannes and I miss it, really miss it. My French is almost non-existent and you, you're a native. It really would make life easier for me, if you'd help me dealing with all those lawyers and agents. I couldn't negotiate myself out of a bag and I'm sure those crafty French would make me pay double. We can combine the house-hunting with a spot of sun-worshipping and in return for you dealing with the bureaucratic nightmare of French house buying I'll pay for your board and lodging. So it would be help for me and a holiday for you. What do you say? You told me Sophie is settled at her uni and Paul's on his gap-year, so come on. Either Provence or being stuck in Wyckham Wood."

Tessa combed her gleaming hair with her hand, a large diamond still on her finger, the one Jack had bought for their engagement. Nina thought about her own ring, which she had put away saving it for Sophie. It was a thin band set with a row of diamonds, exactly what an accountant would buy. And what Nina had pointed to as Edward had pushed her into the inner sanctum of Gerrards & Wainwrights. Prices had not been discussed in front of her, but she knew that the rings on the first tray they were shown cost more than Edward earned in a year. A second tray was proffered by the unctuous salesman from below the counter and Nina saw it first. Plain and simple, just what she wanted. Edward's mother had already offered a spindly ring with an emerald surrounded by a row of tiny diamonds.

"It's been in the family", Mrs Riverton had said as if it were an heirloom. Later Edward admitted that it had been given to his spinster aunt by her married sisters for her 60th birthday, when, no doubt, she had given up hope of an engagement ring of her own.

Nina rubbed her empty ring finger.

"Tessa, it sounds marvellous. Let me think about it. I must first get some money together for the kitty, before I contemplate a holiday, even a working one."

"Wine's on me today" said Tessa and gracefully waved her hand in he air. Within seconds a waiter stood by her side. Nina envied that ease of Tessa's and thought of how she always had to flap her arms, use the napkin as a flag, even shout in order to get some attention in the Adelphi.

The wine made them talk but still Nina could not tell Tessa about her night with Tor. Tessa would not understand her anger, not so much with Tor as with her own lack of judgement. And the memory of that night only confirmed Nina's feeling of abandonment. The wine helped, bandaged the wound, and after the first bottle of house white Nina agreed to come to Provence in May and after the second bottle she looked forward to it.

The next day Nina woke with a woolly brain and promised herself to go easy on the wine. She admitted with some shame that her wine consumption had become a Prozac substitute rather than a pleasant accompaniment to a meal. During lonely evenings, and they were now more frequent as friends thought it was time for Nina to cope on her own, the wine bottle became her company. Never so much that she was drunk, but enough to give her a deep and sweaty sleep always clouded by dreams. Edward would be there in her sleep, they would meet and often kiss or make love, but then Alexandra, or Sasha as Edward called her, making her sound like some Pushkin character, would turn up and smile winsomely as she dragged Edward away. Nina would wake and find the pillow wet and her eyes swollen. The sadness of her dreams would follow her all day, until her night time wine blotted it out.

Work was her blessing, not only because the money was useful, but also because it kept her thoughts focused. For the first time in her life she had to sell herself, telephoning publishers and ask if they needed any Hungarian translations. She worked for two advertising agencies and also for a couple of publishers of art books. It didn't pay well, but Nina enjoyed the work. And in order to leave her cluttered desk and see people she continued her unpaid work at the local Art Gallery, the showcase of a rich philanthropist's collection.

It was at the Gallery she had met Tessa for the first time. Tessa in her former role as a rich man's wife looked after fund-raising events. She had clippety-clopped into the lecture room on her high heels, where Nina was trying to inspire a group of rowdy six year olds to copy a marine painting by an unknown Dutchman. The sailing ship was just about to leave a sandy harbour and in the forefront some lazy fishermen gazed at the sails, drooping from the mast in want of some wind.

"Where's the engine, miss?" asked a freckle-faced boy with surprisingly black hair for such a pale face. From the back of the room came a throaty laugh. Tessa had brought in a journalist to show him how the Gallery made use of the public funding it received in return for teaching the children from the neighbouring council estates the value of fine art. An uphill struggle, but one that Nina enjoyed. Once or twice she saw a light being switched on in someone's eyes and then saw it transported to the cheap white drawing paper she handed out.

The children turned around to see who laughed and they saw a thin woman, tall as a Nordic birch and with a helmet of golden hair.

"You must be Nina Riverton. I'm Tessa Kingley-Havers, in charge of fundraising events, and this is John Price from the Kent Herald. He has promised to write a very supportive piece on how we spend our paltry subsidy from the Council and the even smaller one from the Lottery Fund in order to spread some culture to the local population. Do tell him something about the work you do for the Gallery."

"I take two mornings a week and it's usually this age group, five to seven year-olds. We select a painting in the Gallery and then we talk about it and try to copy it. The groups are chosen by the schools in the area . . . ."

"Miss, where's the bloody engine?" The freckled boy was not giving up his quest.

"There were no engines in those days, they used sails in the 17th century and that is when the painting was done. They're waiting for the wind and then . . .

"No engines, what's this? I'm not gonna paint an old boat without an engine. I wanna paint a super-fast rocket ship and . . .

64 | Pia Helena Ormerod

Tessa sent Nina an approving glance and then gently led John Price out of the room. "As you can see we really inspire the children . . ." her laugh echoed down the corridor.

After the session Nina found Tessa waiting for her outside to apologize for the intrusion.

"Come and have a drink with John and me and tell him more about the Gallery, from your point of view. I have bored the poor man to tears with visitor statistics and the spiralling cost of insurance. We're just going across the road to the Pen and Paper for a sandwich and a glass of wine. It's on the Gallery, part of my PR and Promotion budget. Do come."

John Price did not get a word in over the PR-promoting Chablis. Within minutes Tessa had found out that Nina knew Jen, the formidable lawyer, and that brought on a welter of Jen-stories. Mr Price chewed his pen hoping, no doubt, that Nina would leave him alone with this glamorous blonde. Later Tessa and Nina were congratulated by the Director of the Gallery for the two page spread in the Herald, full of praise for the fine contribution the Gallery did in allowing the children access to the riches of the collection. Tessa appeared in several of the photos and in one overshadowed the Rubens in the background.

It didn't take long before Tessa invited Edward and Nina to dinner in her Georgian home on the Green with Jen. After a polite return match in Wardell Drive, the dinners stopped, as it was clear that Edward and Jack did not get on. Tessa's husband had made his millions on a chain of beauty spas and his robust enjoyment of his wealth irritated Edward. After that the women met without their spouses and when Edward left Nina, Tessa and Jen took it in turns to keep her from sinking into the comfort of self-pity.

~

"Six thirty is an ungodly hour, one that I haven't faced since school", sighed Tessa as they met at Waterloo Station.

"But there's only one direct train a week to Avignon and we don't want the bother of having to change in Lille. At least they serve champagne in first, so we can soon go to sleep. I hate the tunnel, the thought of all that water sloshing over my head."

Tessa leaned against her almost trunk-sized valise, on top of which she had a matching vanity case and in her hand she made a fan of the two first class tickets.

Nina had been up since four packing her new wardrobe. Thanks to some unexpected translation work for a French building firm and the money back from the insurance company, but only after Edward had intervened, Nina had enough money to buy some clothes for Provence. It wasn't Bond Street like Tessa's outfits, but at least there were a couple of sundresses, a pair of sandals and even a new swimsuit as the old one was far too baggy. Sophie had helped her choose the clothes in a steamy cubicle and when she complained that the dress Sophie had selected was far too young for a woman her age, Sophie laughed and said "for years you were lamb dressed as mutton, now it's time to be mutton dressed as lamb." Nina was not sure it was a compliment or an insult, but she was relieved to have her daughter's blessing and why shouldn't she wear bright red?

They did serve champagne with the morning coffee, Tessa fell asleep and missed the dreaded tunnel. The silence was welcome after the early start and Nina stared out through the picture window on the landscape flying by, dotted with woolly sheep and silver-coloured lakes. Her book remained unread by her side. She had never travelled with Tessa before, as a matter of fact, she had never travelled with anyone but Edward. The children had told her some weeks ago that Edward and Sasha had spent Easter in Florence, the city, where she and Edward had spent the first part of their honeymoon before travelling on to Amalfi. Now she could not think of Florence without a greasy film covering her memories. Had they stayed at the same hotel, not far from the Uffizi? Had they made love in the same bed . . . ? Everything she did was overlaid by her thoughts of Edward and Sasha together. It was like an echo reverberating through all the sounds of her everyday life.

A holiday would do her good and she looked forward to sixteen days in Provence.

"We don't have to lift a finger. A housekeeper is included in the rent. The house belongs to a friend of Jack's and he's quite happy for this woman to have some proper work to do rather than being paid for airing the rooms and binning the junk mail. That means we'll have all the time in the world to find the perfect house for me."

Chapter Five

Jacques Debrel

Do I see it as a perk of my job to sleep with the women, who ask me for help? Perhaps. I am not married and if I find a woman attractive, why not? I thought Nina was quite attractive, but she lacked something. I think she still hankers for her husband to return. Women never forget men, who leave them. For me, when it's over, it's fini, tout fini.

I certainly didn't want a serious affair, nor did I want a permanent partner, but the weather was hot, the wine cool and one thing led to another. Little did I know that it would change my life. I'll always be grateful to Nina and I hope she understands that.

"Let's see what we can do for you. After all those years you deserve a proper pay-off. Remember it is only your right as you don't have a pension." Joshua Green had not wasted time on social chit chat. He was in it for the kill.

"I want you to provide me with a list of all your bank accounts, your husband's tax returns, a valuation of your property in Wyckham Wood, any other assets, second properties, shares yes, even antiques. And what about the size of his pension? I am sure that his firm sits on a pension fund worth millions. Does Ms Ledger work? And what about her property?

Nina flinched, as she always did when Sasha was mentioned.

"Oh, I see, you've not discussed that with your husband. Well, if she has a property it does change the equation — and to your advantage. And then there are the children to think of, their education."

Nina's head was spinning as she sat in Joshua Green's leather clad chair. In the window, facing her, was a photograph of a rather sullen, black-haired woman and two young boys, both dressed in a school uniform vaguely familiar to Nina.

"The children, they look so sweet in their school uniforms."

"Well, I thought your daughter was at University by now . . . ?"

"No, I mean those children, the two boys." Nina pointed to the silver framed photo.

"Oh, my sons. Yes, they are, aren't they? I don't see enough of them. They live with their mother."

He turned to his papers, shifting them on to another pile on his desk.

Nina did not know what to say, she wanted to apologise, instead she just smiled.

"They're lovely at that age."

Joshua Green unscrewed the top of his claret coloured fountain pen and wrote, rasp, rasp against the yellow legal pad.

"There's no blame apportioned any more in the break up of a marriage. We must just see it as any business deal, where we come to an agreement, which both parties can accept and live with. But the law still acts as a gentleman. It tries to make sure that the interests of the woman are met in the first place. Your husband has many years of good earnings to come, your income I regard more as pin money."

Nina looked down on her folded hands, smarting from his comment.

"It is the further education of the children I am interested in. As for myself I can always cope . . . . on my pin money," she said sharply.

"Now, now Mrs Riverton. It's you I'm thinking of. I want to make sure, absolutely sure, that you can continue to have the same life style as the one you had, when you were married to Mr Riverton. Your income is all derived from free lance projects and they can dry up at any time, isn't that so?"

Nina nodded, still not placated by his unctuous explanation.

"I need a list of all your outgoings, everything from household expenses to money spent on holidays, clothes, beauty treatments, bang it all in."

Finally Nina had put down the cost of the ticket to Provence.

~

The train sped through France, following the arc of the sun. Green fields were morphed into maize-yellow acres and as the afternoon turned golden, lavender rows gave a new colour to the landscape. Grey granite of the north was replaced by the golden stone and terra cotta tiles took over from moss-green copper roofs. Nina's worries about sixteen days away from home shrank by each mile on the smooth journey south. She had given the children Tessa's mobile number, but hoped they would not phone. She wanted to forget about Wyckham Wood, roof-repairs and bills from the lawyer. And most of all she wanted to forget about Edward and Tor.

"Prochaine Avignon. Next stop Avignon."

Tessa leant forward and applied some fresh lipstick. "This will be fun, Nina."

Nina nervously gathered her travelling debris, unread magazines, the Saturday papers and the complimentary first class gift, a lip balm tasting of chemical cherries. Nina helped Tessa by boxing one of her heavy valises down the steps and was met by a wall of soggy heat. By the time she had pushed her own suitcase down the steps, she was damp all over. The station was crowded by queues of passengers waiting to board the train on its return journey and the shock of sun-blistered flesh on proud display made Tessa and Nina feel overdressed. They smiled at baguettes sticking out of newly bought woven baskets in bright colours and at the clink of bottles, as bags were shuffled along the floor of the concourse.

"I've booked a car through Hertz. We must look for a Monsieur Rapelli. With a name like that, he must be dark and with a bushy moustache."

"Madame Kingleee-'Averse?"

"Dear me, clean-shaven and blond, didn't get much right there, did I?" said Tessa with a champagne-sodden laugh as they followed Mr Rapelli out to the car park in front of the Avignon city walls. There a grey Peugeot estate car waited for them. Nina filled in all the papers, showed her French driving license and asked him to point out the best way from Avignon to St.Remy.

"Did you get that? I didn't understand a word, but then Jack always did the driving when we were in France. Can't get used to driving on the wrong side of the road."

"That's the right side for me. Don't forget. I learnt to drive in France," said Nina as she tried hard to maneuvre the large car out of the parking lot. The France she loved and remembered from her childhood had disappeared, now she looked in horror at the ugly shopping bunkers painted in garish colours nestling behind signs promising rock bottom prices. Nina sighed and opened the sunroof to catch the last rays of the sun and to her surprise the air was scented with lavender and thyme. The warmth of the day lingered as a promise of heat to come.

Just outside St. Remy they passed stalls selling lavender, honey and fruit.

"Let's stop to buy some fresh apricots. I suspect that the housekeeper, Madame Galine, has brought in enough food to feed us for a week, but I just love the scent of fresh apricots. Get a kilo, please," Tessa handed over her bulging purse.

As they spat the apricot stones out of the window Tessa suggested that Nina kept the purse. "I have a few notes in my handbag for things I might want, but I want you to keep count of the money and buy what we need. OK?" Nina put the purse into her bag and nodded. The sun was sinking fast and by the time they left for St. Remy it was nearly seven and time to put on the headlights. Nina turned off the main road, when they saw a small painted sign saying Brehet. A gravelled drive took them to an imposing wrought iron gate surrounded by climbing greenery. Nina stepped out of the car, happy to stretch her legs and pressed the bell.

"Madame Galine? Madame Kingley-Havers ici" said Nina guessing that the French woman answering would not know her name.

She heard an electronic purring sound and then slowly the gate opened. Nina stepped into the Peugeot and drove through a formal hedge of bushes cut into identical balls. At the end of the drive was a short woman, dressed in a bright red skirt and a blue top. She was waving her arms over her

head showing Nina to drive forward and it was then she
saw the house. A low slung house in honeyed stone with a
door big enough to take a carriage and on each side of the
door six deep windows with pale blue shutters, all open.
The roof was covered in Roman tiles of different hues and
set into the roof there was a mansard window opening to a
small balcony with a wrought iron railing.

Madame Galine was in her late fifties and her grey hair
was knotted into a small bun at her nape. Her brown skin
was etched with fine lines from too much sunshine and
her reddened hands showed that she did more than air the
rooms and bin the junk mail. Nina recognized the hard g in
her "*biengvenue*" as that of the area. Madame Galine quickly
gathered most of their bags and ran indoors while chatting
excitedly, how lucky they were with the weather and how
was Monsieur Dickson, the friend of Jack? Dinner would be
ready in an hour, "time to freshen up and for an aperitif on
the terrace."

Tessa picked the master bedroom, the one with the balcony
and Nina was shown to a whitewashed room with a view
of the swimming pool at the back of the house. She had her
own bathroom and she danced with girlish pleasure as she
unpacked her wash things and placed them on the dressing
table. In the wardrobe she found a clean bathrobe in softest
towelling. It took her twenty minutes to unpack, wash up
and change into her linen trousers and a T-shirt.

Before going down to the promised drink Nina bounced on
the bed. If only Edward was here, no, no more thoughts like
that, she admonished herself. It was more than a year since
Edward had left.

～

The sunray sneaked through the ivory linen curtains and
like a shy lover crept across the stone floor towards the bed.

Gently touching her sleeping face, it forced Nina to climb from her dark dreams to meet the generous light.

It had been a late night. The food Madame Galine served was enough for four but after a day sitting still on a train the two women had still managed to work up an appetite. There were vegetables, lightly grilled and served with a garlic scented mayonnaise, to accompany the chilly vin rosé and then veal with creamed potatoes followed by salad and a plate of cheeses before finally an apricot tart.

"Tell me she's bought it," sighed Tessa. "I can't bear it if she's made this cake herself. We'll not be able to stop eating and we'll return like two lard balls."

The dinner was served on the terrace under a canopy of vines, not yet in fruit, and in the background, rising from the plain, were the pleated grey mountains, Les Alpilles, with their jagged peaks. The air was heavy with chirruping noises from the cicadas — and later on from the clinking of ice cubes to freshen up the wine.

The distance from their normal lives made it easier to talk.

"How come you don't seem affected by your divorces? I am shattered by just one and can't imagine what it would be like to go through all this again."

Tessa looked at Nina, whose face was in part shadow from the lit storm-lanterns.

"Oh, Nina. Do you really think I wanted to leave Jack? He left me because he just wanted to trade up to a better model. But what can I say? It's exactly what I did when I married him. I traded up. He wanted someone to match his bloody beauty spas and I wanted the life that came with his millions. It's all bartering . . ."

Nina suddenly shivered in the soft evening heat.

"And my first divorce, well, I never told you about Richard, did I? We were married for seven years and I loved Richard, really loved him. We met in our early twenties, like you and Edward. I was in some play and he was hanging out with some of the other actors, or pretend actors. We fell in love and bed immediately and I never fell out of love."

"You still love him?"

"Yes, no, it's love itself I love. That excitement of first passion. I still dream about Richard now and then and if they play that old Beatles song *Norwegian Wood*, I weep. We used to play it again and again.

"What went wrong?"

"Wrong? Nothing. He just fell out of love with me and into love with another girl, as simple as that. I tried not to show him how hurt I was, always the cool Tessa and in a way, that protective shield I put on then is what I still hide behind. When I finally got over it, no, that's not true, you never quite get over it, I knew that I would never allow myself to be vulnerable like that again."

"But you always told me that one does get over it," Nina said with a petulant tone.

"No, sweetheart, you inflict pain on some and others do it to you. And those you leave will never get over you — that is the only true eternal love. We've all changed. In the old days, women had to put up with lousy marriages, unless they had money of their own. Now we work and change husbands with the same ease as we change jobs — you know, we just get tempted by a better offer."

"I can't believe you're that cynical." Nina reached for the wine bottle and poured Tessa some more wine, as if hoping that would soften her sharp tone. "I always believed that Edward and I would be together for ever, we often spoke of it. We even talked about where we wanted our ashes scattered. Now all those promises we made seem distorted, like looking through a kaleidoscope, fragments turning, making new pictures but never a whole one. Everything I trusted and believed in turned out to be nothing and I wonder if I can ever trust anything or anyone again?"

"You can, but you'll always be wary. And that's not a bad thing. Do you remember how we used to trust our parents and the pain, when we realised that they have clay feet like everyone else? It's the same with men, you trust them because you're in love, but every time you're hurt or betrayed, a little bit of that trust is knocked off like enamel on those tea mugs we had as children and after a while the rust sets in. You can still enjoy the tea, but you you'd rather have a new mug."

"I don't want a new mug. I rather like my old rusty one."

"Well, Edward doesn't want you, so you'd better face facts and if you still want a man, look for a new one."

"Well, I did, and it was a catastrophe."

As the evening cooled Nina told Tessa about Tor and their single night. To Nina's horror Tessa burst out laughing.

"Darling girl, I know the type. There are some men who simply can't cope with the fact that they have sexual urges and they hate the women, who lure them to bed. They probably think we have teeth in our vaginas and that we want to devour them. Now that you know what he's like, promise me you won't see him again. Don't for one moment think that you can change him. He doesn't want to be changed. He'll just hate you in the end."

Madame Galine had cleared up in the kitchen and it took Nina some time to find the coffee to refill the cafetiere. There was no kettle so she had to boil water in a saucepan.

"But what about Jack? You always seemed to get along so well," asked Nina as she returned with the hot coffee.

"We gave each other what we needed and wanted. He wanted a representative wife, someone with a bit of class. Having come to money quite late in life he realized he couldn't buy class but he could marry it. Also he had no idea of how to spend all that loot and that's where I came in. I have practice. Unfortunately, money makes a man very attractive, and soon young girls on the make were after him, flattering him and when you have the Ferrari and the yacht, a new girl is about as exciting as it gets. And of course he would fall in love, eventually. I knew that and in a way I was prepared."

Nina blew on the hot coffee to cool it.

"You make it sound like a business deal."

"You'd be surprised how many marriages are just that. Of course, they all pretend that it's "luuuv", but often there is more love in arranged marriages."

"You know, Tessa, sometimes you sound exactly like my mother. You must meet Magda. You two would really get on."

~

Next morning, after strong coffee and warm croissants, Nina went into the kitchen to talk to Madame Galine about the evening's menu. The discussion was one-sided as Nina only nodded smilingly to the suggested dishes. Nina was dressed and ready, but through the window she could see Tessa, stretched out on a lounger by the pool, a book open on her bikini-clad chest. Her own morning was going to be spent touring the six estate agents that had been recommended by the local chamber of commerce. She wanted to prove to Tessa that she was worth the outlay.

First on the list were three agents in the centre of St. Remy. She drove the heavy Peugeot into town and found it almost impossible to park. Worse than London, Nina thought, as she slowly circled the main streets. Then she saw that it was market day. The square and all the streets leading to the square were full of stalls selling fresh produce and everything from bric à brac to those pottery garlic graters in gaudy colours that seem to be sold all over Provence — yet Nina had never seen one in use. Eventually she found a parking space as an English registered Mercedes pulled out. By now it was twelve and she would only be able to see one agent before lunch.

Gustave Poiret Immobilier had an elegant office on one of the side streets from the main square and Nina walked in through double glass doors. In the window were photographs of expensive villas in golden stone with turquoise swimming pools in the foreground. The prices in euro made Nina wince, but she knew what Tessa wanted and what Tessa was willing to pay.

Madame Poiret, the elegantly coiffed wife of Gustave, welcomed Nina and when she heard what Nina wanted, she literally licked her fuchsia lips.

"Madame, such luck you came to us. We have the absolutely best selection of top properties in this area. Well, our customers, between you and me, are not only members of royal houses but we also have company directors and, of course, the French nobility. And several film stars come to us in order to find the perfect villa in this most perfect part of Provence. I just know that we shall find you a most heavenly house."

Nina shrank away from this torrent of self-laudatory sales talk and asked Madame Poiret to send her suggestions of houses care of Mas de Brehet.

"Ah, Mas de Brehet. I know the house well. Charming in its own way. Sold some years ago by Monsieur Decasse. No, not through us, but I am sure we could have got a better price for it, but there you are."

After a simple salad at a small bistro called Les Alpilles, where the size of the bill was larger than the amount of calories consumed, Nina brought out her map to find the other two recommended estate agents in town. The first had nothing on the books and was honest enough to admit it, the second was willing and helpful but warned Nina that houses in the vicinity of St. Remy cost double of those in the surrounding area.

"And, if you are willing to consider the area north of Route Nationale 10 the prices plummet."

Nina knew what Tessa wanted and she wanted St. Remy.

Next day Nina visited the other three on the list and found to her surprise that she rather enjoyed stepping into the swish offices and explain that she was looking for a house with at least three bedrooms, three bathrooms, swimming pool and garage all for a budget of around 900,000 euros. At the mention of the sum, smiles widened and she was immediately offered coffee, in one case delivered from the café next door. At the last agent, called simply St. Remy Immobilier, she was welcomed by a man in his late forties, who turned out to be the manager as well as owner.

"I suppose you got our name from the Chamber of Commerce. They know we sell a lot of properties to foreign clients, but in spite of your English name I assume you are French, n'est pas? Do you plan to return home?"

For a moment Nina paused and then, and she would later not know why, she said with a smile.

"I have always loved Provence and I felt I needed a bolthole."

"Listen, I have many properties on our books that I think might be of interest to you. When would you be willing to start looking at some of our houses?"

"Tomorrow would be fine. I'd like to see as many as possible of those we select today. I can be here in the morning at ten, if that suits you?"

He handed over his card, the name Jacques Debrel printed in midnight blue on a white card. Stylish, thought Nina, compared to the over-ornate card given to her by Madame Poiret, but then she found Jacques Debrel rather stylish, too. He was slim and well toned without looking bulky and with his blue chinos he tried to look causal but the sharp creases showed that he preferred a more formal style. His short-sleeved cotton shirt was immaculately ironed and there was something wholesome and clean about his appearance, even his sun-lined face looked scrubbed.

As Nina returned to Mas de Brehet after a full day with agents, she was met by a glowing Tessa.

"I've just had Jack on the phone. He's down in Cannes at our, no, blast it, HIS house now, and he wants me to come down and see what I want. His new girlfriend has brought in a decorator, so if there is anything of the furniture I want I should get it now or he will just sell it all. Do you mind if I leave you here for a day or two, while I go down to Cannes? You'll be busy with looking at houses and Madame Galine will look after you. And you have enough cash, don't you?"

Madame Galine was informed that evening of Tessa's departure. She winked at Nina and promised to look after her properly.

Next morning Nina dropped Tessa off at Avignon for her train journey down south.

"I'll only be a few days at the most and by the time I come back I hope you have found at least three houses for us to look at and that one of them will be the perfect one."

Nina was ten minutes late as she entered the office of Jacques Debrel. The morning sun was dancing on the street outside and made the groundfloor of the small townhouse look almost dark inside. Nina took off her sunglasses in order to adjust her eyes.

"Bonjour, Madame Kingley-Havers. I have here a list of the houses we discussed yesterday and I have spoken to the owners. One is abroad, but I have the keys and the other two can see us this afternoon. I suggest we set off now to see the first one, which is the one you seemed to like the most. It's about thirty minutes drive from here."

Nina nodded and Jacques Debrel turned to an older woman, Nina had not even noticed. She sat in the corner, half hidden by a computer screen. He told her that he would be out most of the day but that he was available for important calls on his mobile phone.

"I suggest we take my car as I know the way and then you can just sit back and enjoy the scenery." Outside he elbowed her gently towards his Peugeot parked outside and Nina liked the touch of his cupped hand. The comfort of his silence put Nina at ease as she looked at the particulars of the three places. The first one was a villa just outside St. Remy. The house was a renovated farmhouse with a swimming pool and a separate loggia with a barbecue area, parking for several cars and its own little vineyard. And just above the 900,000 euro limit, "don't worry, we'll negotiate him down" ensured Monsieur Debrel. The photo showed the view from the terrace, sweeping down over fields of lavender in bloom with grey mountains in the background.

The interior looked rustique with dark stained wooden beams against the white plaster and stone floors. Yes, that looked absolutely right for Tessa.

Nina leafed through the other two particulars, one looked more like a Bauhaus chalet and totally out of place in the Provencal landscape, the last one, an old school house had what estate agents called possibilities, it needed much money and work spent on it, and she wondered if Tessa was willing to take on such a project? Jacques Debrel was a calm driver, still Nina felt a slight turn in her stomach as the road became steeper and more vertiginous. She looked down and the fields of ripe lavender blue were now just a shimmering haze and the noise from the main road had turned into a distant hum.

"This is like another world and yet only minutes from St. Remy, Monsiuer Debrel."

"Please call me Jacques, we are after all going to spend the day together. OK?" Nina nodded.

"And what is your first name, Mrs Kingley-Havers?"

"I am Nina, well Christina actually, but everyone, even my mother, calls me Nina"

"That's not a very French name, Italian?"

"No, it's actually . . . , well, it has nothing to do with Italy at all. My mother admired a Swedish painter who was called Christina and I was named after her". Nina wondered why she had not yet told him her own surname. Was it because she did not want to bring up the whole background of Magda and the flight from Budapest? Or did she secretly enjoy playing the part of the well-off woman, who could spend a million on a second home?

"Well, I think it is a very pretty name."

He smiled at her and she suddenly knew that it was going to be a pleasant day. The vertigo had gone and the morning sun shone through the windscreen high-lighting Jacques' hands on the wheel.

They drove through a little village, a square in front of a golden stone church topped by an iron-lace bell tower and flanked by two cafés, both empty apart from two dogs who slept under one table. Opposite there was the mairie with the tricolour hanging listlessly above the door.

"Do you want a café crème? It is after ten now and I think it is time we talk. I did promise to be quiet but there is so much I want to ask you"

Nina laughed.

"And the dogs could do with some company."

Two wet noses nuzzled Nina's unstockinged legs and she suddenly thought about Larry, now in kennels in Sussex. Her own life, her lonely life seemed unreal, sitting here in the sun in a tiny village in Provence nursing a decent coffee.

"So what is it you want to ask me about?"

"Why Provence, well, you come after all from London and you mentioned that you spent your university years in Bordeaux, so what brings you here?"

"Every one in England seems to regard Provence as the best of France. I want," Nina suddenly interrupted herself, maybe now was the time to be more truthful? "I want to be here, to share a house with one of my very best friends and she knows people in Bonnieux and in Goult, yes, they are all British. It would be difficult for us to come here and not know anyone. We have both split up from our husbands quite recently and need time to readjust to being on our own."

"Was yours a painful divorce?"

"Aren't all?"

"Most, perhaps, but my wife and I managed to do it without too many fights, but then we had no children, that makes a difference, I think."

"How long ago did you divorce?"

"Five years ago and I have not remarried. My wife has. Nice guy and she seems happy, so it must have been the right thing" His smile looked forced.

"And you? Are you planning to remarry?"

"Heavens no. I am still at the stage with lawyers and I find it all so distasteful. Maybe that's why I find it such a bliss down here. I don't have to think about lawyers or how to split the pension pot."

Jacques insisted on paying for the coffee and Nina patted the two dogs lovingly before they went back to the Peugeot. In the car Jacques concentrated on the driving and Nina was glad that she did not have to talk. There were so many questions she wanted to ask him, yet somehow she knew that some of the answers would come before the day was over.

They reached the first house. Jacques pressed the electric key pad and the iron gates slid open with a gentle hum.

"The house is very secure, with electric fencing all around the perimeter and the house itself is protected by an alarm system, which means that when you are away a guard will look in at regular intervals and they'll come immediately the alarm goes off. You'll be safe while you're here and you won't have to worry when you're in England."

The gravelled drive up to the front door was raked into straight lines and the flower beds were almost too perfectly tended. More alarms had to be turned off before they entered the house. There was nothing musty about this house, a fresh smell of polish and, yes, lavender was the first impression.

"A cleaner comes in regularly even though the owners are not often here."

"Why do they want to sell? Such a lovely house."

"The wife suffers from rheumatism and they want more sun. I think they've found a house on Mauritius."

Nina looked at the downstairs, perfect. Tessa could move in straight away. The livingroom was sparsely furnished with billowing sofas on either side of a stone fire place. The dining room had blue-painted cane chairs around an oval table, dressed in a quilted Provencal tablecloth in matching blue. The kitchen was a cook's dream, not that Tessa would ever cook. Jacques must have read her thoughts.

"Apart from the cleaner there is also a cook able to stay on if you would like her to."

The upstairs with its bedrooms and bathrooms were all spacious and obviously done up by an interior decorator. There was hardly any sign of the owner's own taste.

"It's very impersonal," Nina said.

"Well, they let it sometimes to friends or acquaintances. In the summer you can easily get 4,000 euros a week for the place. We often help with the arrangements for the owners.

And we would of course do the same for you if you want to let it."

Nina shook her head. "Tell me about the neighbourhood. How close is the nearest super marché and what about restaurants? It is quite some way from the village, but then the stunning views make up for that. It is just lovely"

"Might you be interested?"

"Definitely, but I want to show it to my friend first. She is down in Cannes for the moment."

Jacques look pleased and for a minute Nina suspected he thought about his commission.

"Anything more you want to see, or shall we set off for the second house down in the valley. It's quite some way from here."

In the car Jacques leant over and handed Nina the map.

"See if you can find some village off the main road, where we can stop to buy some provisions. It's such a fine day. I suggest a picnic rather than popping into some bistro. What do you say?"

"I think it's a wonderful idea. I just love picnics." Nina remembered all the picnics she had organised during the years with Edward and the children. They never shared her enthusiasm for outdoor eating. In her view everything tasted better when eaten al fresco, but Sophie and Paul always complained about her seeping egg and cress sandwiches, they preferred a burger from some smelly café and Edward hated not sitting at a table—and drinking out of plastic or paper cups. It had been tough even to get him out in the garden for a meal. "Why carry it all out just to carry it all back in again?" Edward used to say.

Turning the map sideways Nina tried to find out where they were, with her nail she followed the red line of the main road.

"Ah, there is quite a big village at the next crossroad, turning left, then if we follow that road for about four kilometers we'll hit it. It's called Bonlieu and I'm sure with such a pretty name we're bound to find everything we need there."

Nina was excited. In her mind she started to plan the picnic; must have some black, glossy olives marinated in herbs and garlic, then some cold ham, fresh baguette from the bakery, some ripe goat cheese and some tomatoes and then to finish it off, some fresh apricots. She must not forget water, paper cups and napkins — and would there be some cheap cutlery in the village to buy. And wine? Or maybe Jacques did not want to drink as he was driving. Nina's mental shopping list was done as they reached Bonlieu. It was the quietest village she had seen that day. Even the flies outside the butchers' were sleepy. No one seemed to move in the midmorning heat.

"Stop here, I'll ask if they have a delicatessen" said Nina as they approached the village square with parking for a handful of cars.

"They have one speciality food shop just behind the church and two bakers. And there's a wine merchant next to the estate agent."

The bell clattered thrillingly as Nina opened the door. Her face fell. It was a mini-super-marché with a small counter for cold meats and some rather sad-looking patés. The vegetables had lost their fraicheur and on one shelf there were loaves of sliced bread, wrapped in waxed paper. A woman dressed in denim and with a dragon tattooed on her arm looked up from behind the counter, still with a magazine on her lap.

"Madame, et vous cherchez?"

The accent grated.

"You're English?"

"Yeah, and you, too. What can I help you with?"

"Some food for a picnic please. Olives, cold meat and." Nina's voice tapered off as the woman plucked a tin of stoned black olives from the shelf. This was not going to be a gastronomic feast.

"How long have you been here and why Bonlieu," Nina asked as she scoured the shelves for something to eat.

"Just over a year. You know, it's mostly Brits living in this village. Great, isn't it? We play cricket on Sundays and there's a pub just around the corner where we can get decent beer. And we have quiz nights there. You'll love it. Are you on hols?"

At that moment Jacques came in to the shop with a bottle of vin rosé and a paper bag. "The wine merchant offered us some glasses, we can return them on the way back. How are you getting on with the food?"

On the way out of Bonlieu Nina told Jacques how the British had invaded the village.

"There's even a pub serving decent British beer. And a cricket team."

"Two things I could easily live without," Jacques gladly admitted.

"Me, too, me too," laughed Nina and when she looked at him, still laughing, she experienced that gut-wrench she had felt as they climbed the vertiginous road up to the house.

The sun was reaching its zenith, shining through the windscreen and Nina felt the heat dampening the inside of her legs. Slowly she moved them apart and as she did Jacques looked across and looked at her legs then at her. His eyes lingered at her hand as she was flapping the hem of her skirt to get a cooling draught. The simple movement suddenly seemed charged, an invitation. Nina's face reddened.

"Oh, it's getting hot," she said trying to disguise her blush.

"Do you feel it's time for some lunch? I'm getting quite hungry," Jacques replied, as if he wanted to assure her that he had not noticed her gesture. "And a glass of wine would be welcome. I think there is a parking lot in the next village. It doesn't sound very elegant, I admit, but it has a great view and you can spread out the picnic on the parapet. I also know that you can get a decent coffee there. Only two weeks ago I sold a tiny house in that village to an English playwright. He said he needed to get away from his wife in order to write. Somehow that made me feel quite sad; that you have to live like a monk in order to get your work done. Can you understand that?"

"Yes, I can. When I do my translating work I must close myself off from my ordinary world. I dawdle, tidy my desk, anything rather than getting on with it. And once I get going I hate being interrupted. I move onto another level and live with the text, chew on each word, hoping that it will give me the true flavour, so that I can do it justice. I often wonder if it's not easier to write than to translate. At least when writing you're in your own head, when translating you have to move into someone else's mind."

"I used to write when I was at University. I suppose I saw myself as some kind of young Sartre. I loved it, but I was never any good. I AM good, though, at selling houses. And fulfilling people's dreams of a place in the sun is very satisfying. It doesn't always work, sometimes people don't know what they really want. We have a lot of English coming over hoping for some kind of glossy magazine happiness, where the sun always shines and the wine is always chilled. They forget that the winters here can be pretty cold and nasty and that the mistral is a bloody headache. But worst of all is the loneliness. Many of them don't speak much French, a problem you won't have, of course, and they become isolated."

The car sped up a steep hill and within minutes Jacques had parked just off the main square. Nina rushed to the protective wall and a quilt of green and lavender spread out beneath her. Orderly rows of vines were on parade and in between the fields were golden stone houses, some with bright turquoise pools glittering in the sun.

"You can see the Mont Ventoux from here, Look there." Nina's eyes followed his index finger. "It still has snow on its peak, while down here we pant in the midday heat."

Together they carried their paltry bags from the car. The wine was tepid and had a rather tangy aftertaste but the bread was fine and the paté tasted better than she had expected.

"There wasn't much of a choice" said Nina as if she wanted to be forgiven for not having served up a feast."

"I'm sorry, I should have found a better shop for you. But listen, let's make up for it. Will you allow me to take you out to dinner tonight? I know a decent place just outside St. Remy and I promise to drive you back home to Mas de Brehet. Deal?" His hand rested on Nina's shoulder and he gave her a gentle squeeze as she nodded.

Why do I feel so comfortable with this man Nina asked herself, as they continued their journey to the next house. Is it because I am back in my own language? And by speaking French it is as if I've eradicated my English life and come back home, both physically and mentally. I feel at ease, Nina thought and she smiled at Jacques as if he had read her thoughts.

The two houses they looked at were very different from the one in the morning. The first one belonged to a German industrialist and he had turned the inside into a minimalist haven. There were no curtains, no squashy sofas only white leather and steel. The kitchen had clearly never been used and the master bathroom had black tiles and a copper basin. The second one, the old schoolhouse, was big but had only two small bedrooms upstairs but with plenty of space downstairs but it would need much money spent on it. Yet, the position was wonderful with a view over a steep valley. It even had a small garden, where flowers were drooping in the heat and laden apricot trees desperate to shed its fruit.

"What is it with the English. They always want a garden, even when they are surrounded by the most magnificent landscape." Nina laughed and thought of her own garden in Wyckham Wood and the hours she spent weeding and pruning. The French would never understand the charm of a mixed border, they preferred order and straight lines in their gardens.

It was nearly five o'clock when Jacques returned her to Mas de Brehet. She was tired and sticky and wanted nothing more than a shower. "I'll pick you up at eight, is that okay?"

"We can have an aperitif here, if you like" but then Nina remembered Madame Galine, who would call her Mrs Rivington and she wanted to keep that anonymity, her English self at bay and she quickly added: "Maybe not. Maybe another day. Today I don't want to be too late. See you at eight."

Madame Galine came through the hall and in her hand she had freshly ironed towels. "Did you find the ideal house for Madame Kingley-Havers? She has phoned and said she would phone again tomorrow. When would you like dinner tonight?"

Nina shuffled her feet like a schoolgirl.

"I'm so sorry but I have been invited out to dinner tonight by Monsieur Debrel. We have some matters to discuss and I do think that we have found the perfect house for Madame Kingley-Havers. It's near St. Remy, only fifteen minutes from the outskirts and it's lovely."

Madame Galine did not look pleased.

"I wish I had known. I have made a daube, but I suppose that can wait until tomorrow." She made a sigh worthy of the stage and walked to the staircase carrying her towels in front of her as if they were a treasure.

For the next three hours Nina rested, showered and tried out what to wear. In the end it was the red dress that Sophie had chosen. She plucked her eyebrows and some stray grey hairs that now had become a daily arrival in her black hair. Nina even painted her toenails and then took it all off again as the colour clashed with the red of her dress. Was this a date or just a polite way of handling a prospective client, Nina wondered as she brushed her hair into an electric fuzz.

At five to eight she wandered down to the gate, she did not want him to meet Madame Galine and exactly at eight she saw the gleaming eyes of the Peugeot. Nina clicked the gate open as Jacques stepped out of the car and opened the door for her. She loved his manners. And she was pleased to see that he had changed; a pale blue shirt, dark blue trousers and a bright red sweater, which was draped over his shoulders.

"My favourite colour. You look great in red", he said as she sat down in the car. There was a scent, clean but still with an undertone of musk. She made a sniffing noise, "nice smell. I like it."

He drove in silence. She did not know what to say and fingered the handle of her handbag. After some minutes they reached the main road and she was surprised that there was so much traffic. The swishing sound of passing cars made her feel sleepy and she closed her eyes. When she opened them she saw that they had turned off the main road.

"We're soon there. It's a small place but I know the owner and I promise you that the food will be good. It's difficult to get a table, but he owes me a favour. I hope you won't be disappointed."

He was right. It was a small place. There were only six tables and four of them were taken. A grey-haired man rushed forward and kissed her hand.

"Madame, I am Julien. An honour to have you here and with my good friend Jacques. Sit down and I hope you will have a glass of our local wine with my compliments."

He fussed and cooed over her, folding the napkin in light beige linen over her lap. Two minutes later he returned with two small handwritten menus and two glasses.

"May I suggest the coquilles St Jacques, of course in honour of our friend, and then the lamb?"

The voices of the other guests receded, as if a volume knob had been turned down. She took a deep draught of the golden wine and it went straight to her head. Frothy clouds entered her blood stream and Nina leant against the back of her chair.

"What a welcome. What a place. If the food is just half as good as the ambiance . . ."

"I don't think you'll be disappointed."

There was something in his tone that made the sentence as thrilling as a caress.

Nina enjoyed the meal, one of the best she'd ever had, and she got used to Julien, who popped up by her side all through the evening making sure everything was to her liking. Jacques was a considerate host. He entertained her by telling her about the famous clients he had helped to find homes in Provence.

"You must have heard of the English writer who wrote about his year here. He had to leave the area because he found coach loads of Japanese tourists trampling through his garden. His readers felt that they had the right to see his house and garden for themselves, they had, after all, bought his book. Then there was this big American actor who wanted a house so isolated that he could enjoy some privacy, but he still insisted that everyone in the village paid homage to him, whenever he turned up."

Nina let Jacques do the talking. He seemed to enjoy it and for her it was a pleasure to just listen to his French. The hours sped and when she returned from the lavatory he had already settled the bill and thereby avoided the embarrassment of her having to see money changing hands. As they were leaving Julien came running after them holding a small glass jar.

"Nina, this is for you. Foie gras, cooked by me. It is a specialité de la maison. With my compliments."

He took her hand and brushed his lips kissed against her hand and Nina made a fake curtsey and kissed him on both cheeks.

"Jacques, I'm not sure what favour he owes you, but tonight couldn't have been nicer. And we haven't spoken one word about the house . . ."

In the dark of the car Jacques took the glass jar from her hand and then he kissed the inside of her wrist and suddenly Nina could hear her pulse throbbing so loudly that she thought Jacques must have heard it, too. She felt his lips moving up towards the crook of her arm. "Like silk," he whispered and drew her closer, still kissing her arm. His other arm went around her shoulders and suddenly they were face to face and his hands cupped her chin. He didn't say anything, just looked into her eyes and Nina knew then that it was too late to say no. His other hand lowered onto her breast and in a swift movement he had freed her breast from the elastic lace and gently rubbed her nipple. Red hot strings were drawn from her breast down inside her and she had to control herself when he kissed her stiffening nipple. The pulsating ache, which had not been eased by the dreadful night with Tor, tightened her throat and she found it hard to breathe. Her other breast came loose and she leant back on the seat. Her hand fell on his lap. She was pleased, no, proud that he had a firm erection and slowly she opened his trousers. His left hand left her and she heard a clicking noise and suddenly the front seat fell backwards. He folded his body over hers and lifted her up on the seat and put his hand under her bottom. Gently he pulled off her knickers and touched her. She was wet and panting. He writhed out of his trousers and lifted her onto him and she rode him without control, thinking only of herself, until she cried out in the sweet pain of release.

"Oh, Jacques," she said with a purring laugh, "I don't think I've ever made love in a Peugeot before". She leant forward to retrieve her soggy knickers and expected to feel ashamed or embarrassed, but she was just happy. An uncomplicated surge of pure joy filled her and she wanted to sing, instead she kissed him gently on his eyelids.

It was past midnight when she was delivered back to Mas de Brehet. He would come to collect her next day for a proper picnic, which he promised to arrange and then they would look at yet another house in the area.

"My darling, darling Ninette. I'll pick you up here at twelve—and thank you for a most wonderful evening. He kissed her earlobe and that pulse started beating again. She quickly whispered goodbye and opened the door. Madame Galine must have gone to bed, it was all quiet. Nina was relieved. Anyone looking at me now, she whispered to herself, would see that I have been freshly laid.

CHAPTER SIX

Magda

My life did not turn out the way I expected it. Am I bitter? No, not really. I do wish, though, that I had been closer to Nina, but she was always such an independent girl and I had my own life to lead. I never thought I'd be a single mother and it was not easy in those days. We are so different, she's so English and middle class, living only for her family in that dark, gloomy house in Wyckham Wood. I can just about stay there for a week before I feel throttled by that goodness of hers. She's always at the stove as if she felt that love was best expressed through cooking. Sometimes I can see why Edward left, there was no excitement in that marriage. I never heard them quarrel, nor showing any passion for each other. Very English.

Of course I love her. She's my daughter. And I chose to bring her with me to Paris when I left. But I just wish she was a bit less, well, less English.

"You're in France and you haven't even bothered to phone me." Magda's voice had an angry rasp, which made Nina shrink inside. The sun making a pattern on her arm through the open French windows suddenly felt cold. Magda continued without giving Nina a chance to answer. "I could not get hold of either Paul nor Sophie and George didn't know where you were, so in the end I had to phone Edward at his office in order to find a number for you."

"Maman, please. What is it that's so important? And why did you have to bother Edward? I'm only here for a few days with a friend helping her to find a house."

"Nina, I want you to come to Paris. *Immediatement*. I have just come out from hospital. Breast cancer. No, no, it's all fine. But I need help. They sent me a bloody nurse, but she was useless. Hardly spoke French. Whatever your friend needs you for, that can wait, but I really need your help."

Nina shivered. Her mother had never asked her for anything or admitted that she needed help. As a child Nina would have been touched if Magda had just once said that she needed her. That would, at least, had been some sign of them belonging to each other. Now Magda told her about the diagnosis after a routine mammogram and the operation that followed. Words of horror for Nina, that made her reach for her own breasts.

"I'm very weak", Magda said with a thin voice.

"Why didn't you phone before?" Reasoning took over from her fear. "Why didn't you let me know? I would have come over immediately."

"Didn't want to ask you, you know I hate fuss of any kind. And besides I looked such a mess and a friend helped me." Again Nina felt excluded, not one of Magda's circle.

"Dear Maman, everyone looks a mess after such an operation. You'll soon be back into shape."

"Well, not quite, will I? I'm maimed now, not me anymore." Magda's voice had been replaced by a tearful whisper

"I'll get a train today from Avignon and I'll be in Paris before tonight. Don't worry, I'll look after you."

Nina replaced the receiver. Standing absolutely still she started crying. Was it for her mother or for having to leave Jacques? Guilt snaked through Nina's intestines. For once she was happy and then this had to happen.

Madame Galine tutted kindly but Nina suspected she was probably pleased to see her go. She had hardly been around since meeting Jacques. After the first evening she spent the nights at his place. It was a small flat, dark with heavy stone walls that made Nina feel she was imprisoned.

"It's close to the office," he said as if he sensed her discomfort and then added, "I had a house once, but now my ex lives there with her new husband. Well, she moved in when we married and before that I had lived there for five years with my former partner. She left, when I met Denise. Love is like musical chairs, isn't it? If you're lucky you have somewhere to live, if not, you have nowhere to stay when the music stops."

Three nights were all they had managed before Magda's call. She had not yet told him about Tessa and that she was acting on Tessa's behalf. Somehow the right moment never came. Now, though, she had to tell him and over the phone.

First of all she had to arrange a ticket, then telephone Tessa, and then, yes, then she would get in touch with Jacques. She was hoping that all the airlines would be booked and the trains cancelled just to give her one more night with Jacques. She remembered their second day. Again they set out to view a house, but Nina was sure that his choice was based on its position rather than its suitability. The owners were back in the UK and had decided that they wanted a place back home, nearer to the newly arrived grandchild. The house was far too small, but the garden had a terrace under a laced canopy of pale-green vines and there on a stone table Jacques unpacked all the things she had put on her unfulfilled shopping list the day before; black olives, a paté covered in a gem-glistening jelly, fresh radishes, bread and cheese. In a paper punnet there were some apricots. After lunch the wine and heat made them lie down on the sharp grass. His love-making was languid and generous, this time giving her time to enjoy it rather than rushing for the much wanted orgasm. She shook in his arms, clinging to his damp shoulders, her legs tangled up with his.

"Darling Ninette," Jacques said with his lips to her neck, "if only we could stay like this, live here and forget about the rest of the world."

Nina smiled. She loved being called Ninette, it confirmed her newfound feeling of being young again.

In the evening he had picked her up and offered her dinner at his flat and she had enjoyed watching him cook. With a large knife he was cutting up the onion so quickly and deftly that she could hardly see his fingers move. He threw the chopped onion in a pan, added two steaks and poured some red wine over it all. With his hands he sensuously massaged some fresh salad with dressing and for a moment she hoped he would be equally gentle with her later on. This time Nina was prepared, a tooth brush was in her handbag and she thanked her lucky star that she was still taking the pill.

Tessa was more or less finished down in Cannes. "As I don't know where I'll end up I've taken most of the stuff, I can always sell it later and I've arranged to have it put into one of these self-storage places until I, or rather you, find my perfect house."

Nina told her about her mother and that she had to leave immediately, but that she had found a perfect house and she would ask the estate agent to show it to her as soon as Tessa returned.

"I know you'll love it and I think you'll quite like the agent as well. Very nice."

"You're a star. And I'm so grateful. If you need a break after having nursed your mother, please fell free to come down. I'm planning to stay another ten days to get the feel of the place. I've got Madame Galine to look after me but I'd love your company."

"I really don't know how much time I need to spend with Magda. I've never heard her sounding like this before."

Nina circled around the telephone for ten minutes before she forced herself to dial Jacques's number. His secretary answered and told her that he was out with clients and would not be back until after six. "Can I leave a message for him?" the secretary asked in a bored voice, as if she did not really want to bother. "Or you can try his car phone?" Nina did not want to speak to him if he had clients in the car. "Tell him that I had to go to Paris and that Mrs Kingley-Havers will contact him later about the house. If he wants to get in touch with me I'll be at this number in Paris, no wait, I'd better phone him." Nina hoped it made sense to the gloomy secretary, it hardly made sense to her, but she did not want him to phone her in Paris and maybe disturb Magda. No, it was not just consideration for Magda, she just did not want to explain about Jacques at this stage.

The rain ride from Avignon was uneventful but the stress of leaving made Nina's head ache and she decided to take a taxi rather than the Metro to Magda's flat at rue l'Université. She boxed her large suitcase into the tiny lift, which cranked itself up to the fifth floor. She knew the house so well, as a young school girl she had skipped down all those stairs, each step worn hollow in the middle after decades of heavy feet scuffing the stone. The smell was the same, that rich scent from the oil that was used for the lift mechanism, likewise the sound of the inner iron gate as it unfolded like a concertina and then the click of the gate lock, all stirred memories from Nina's childhood.

The brass name plate at the door of the flat was unpolished, had Magda's cleaner given up? Nina rang the doorbell and heard the sound echoing across hall. Then steps, heavy steps and finally the rattle of the chain.

"Geoge, but George, what are you doing here?" She threw herself into his arms, again that lovely scent of lemon.

"I've just come over. She phoned me in London trying to get hold of you, but she didn't tell me how ill she was. It was only days later, when I phoned to see if she got hold of you I realized how ill she was and what she's been through. She is very weak."

George took Nina's suitcase and through the dark corridor he led her to Magda's bedroom. Her mother looked like a stranger, resting on freshly puffed up pillows. The chignon was gone, just tufts of uncombed hair covered the skull. The eyes were shadowed in veiny blue and had sunk into their hollows. The white lawn cotton nightdress covered bandages around the chest and from it a plastic tube was connected to a bottle with red fluid on the floor. Nina could not say a word. This was not Magda, this was a woman ten years older.

"Nina, you don't need to say a word. I can see it on your face. Only George has been allowed to see me. They've maimed me, my hair, my breast, it's all gone." The dark eyes filled with tears and George let go of Nina's arm and rushed to the bed. He murmured softly to Magda, like a mother comforting a frightened child. Nina moved forwards, she tried hard to find something to say but no words came to her and she fell on Magda's bed, hugging her quilt-covered lower legs.

"Oh, maman, poor, poor maman." she said without looking up into Magda's face.

"Your room has been made ready for you by George. Why don't you unpack and then have a cup of coffee with us? George will make us a strong cup of his special brew."

With a feeling of relief she left the room with its cloying odour of medicines and an unaired bed. She walked into her small bedroom, the one that had been her refuge during her childhood. After she left home Magda had turned it into a combined dressing and guest room. The wardrobes were full of Magda's too good to be discarded clothes, voluminous hatboxes and shoes with matching handbags wrapped in silk tissue paper before being put into soft linen bags. Nina's old desk, a French escritoire, was now full of unwrapped stockings and lacy underwear. Magda had never taken to tights. Among the underwear were empty perfume bottles that her mother always saved "for the drawer" and the stale scent of Carven's Ma Griffe and Rochas's Femme hit Nina's nostrils with such a force she wanted to cry. George knocked on her door and she quickly closed the drawer.

"Nina, my petal, come and join me in the kitchen while I brew some coffee. Or you might want something stronger? It must be a shock to see Magda in this state. It certainly shook me and I thought very little could do that nowadays."

He pottered in the kitchen, finding his way in Magda's cupboards with an ease that surprised Nina.

"Actually, I think I could do with a gin and tonic," Nina said. Was it only hours ago she had left St. Remy?

"Me, too. I'll just prepare some coffee for Magda. She's not allowed any alcohol, not even a glass of wine. Coffee is all she can have and I try to make it as delicious as possible. Are you hungry? Magda has no appetite at all, but I've got some steaks for tonight and some cheese. Please say you're hungry. I hate eating on my own."

Nina smiled.

"I'd love some later".

He poured generous slugs of gin into two tall glasses and added some lemon and tonic.

"You find the ice and I'll go and give Magda her coffee."
Two minutes later he was back with the untouched tray.
"She's asleep. Just what she needs."

The living room was untidy. "Is Juliette no longer with
maman?"

"Oh, no she left months ago, couldn't cope with the journey
from Neuilly any more. Didn't Magda tell you?"

"No, but then she didn't even tell me about her cancer . . ."

"She is a very private woman, your mother, very private. I
suppose she hasn't told you that I have asked her to marry
me either?"

"What? Oh, George, but why? You're friends!"

"And friends can't marry? Is that what you think?"

"No, of course not, but at your age . . . sorry, you know
what I mean"

"Don't worry, petal, she said no. But I'll go on asking until
she says yes."

George took a long sip from the iced drink. Nina shook
her glass and the bell-like clink of the ice cubes covered the
heavy silence.

"The prognosis is not very good. I think you should
know. I have spoken to Dr. Bernard and he says they tried
everything, but the cancer cells have spread to the lungs.
They hope they can manage it, but I think you should
prepare yourself." George's face crumpled and his smooth,
olive eyes reddened.

"I'm trying to prepare myself, but I can't. I just can't." His
voice dimmed and he drank greedily from his tall glass.

"What do you mean? Surely they wouldn't send Magda home if they didn't think she'd be all right? Magda is so strong, she's never been ill, not properly ill."

"Do you think she looks strong? No. She's lost ten kilo and she's in mourning for her good looks. I try to tell her that she is beautiful, still the Magda we all admire and that in my eyes her beauty is undiminished. I tell her she's my amazon, ready to fight and ready to survive, but I don't think she hears what I say. She's given up, Nina, and that's why I persuaded her to phone you. She only did it because I said I'd have to leave. I hope your presence will cheer her up."

Nina was trying to disseminate the words but nothing made any sense. Was George telling her that Magda was dying?

"We must have the best doctors for her, George. Has she had a second opinion? I have a friend whose father is a professor of oncology at the American Hospital. I'll get in touch with her tomorrow. Dr. Bernard has been her doctor for almost thirty years. He has no idea about new developments." Her voice got shriller. "And who was her doctor at the hospital?"

"Nina, trust me. Both her surgeon and her oncologist are the best. Professor Gallecourt, the oncologist, is a friend of a friend and I have spoken to him several times. He's been marvellous, and I think he's quite taken by Magda. They're doing everything they can for her, but she's losing her strength. I'm so sorry to have to tell you this."

"Have they given any indication of when. I mean, how long . . ."

"No. Nina. It's all in the lap of the gods, whatever that means. Now, don't mope. That won't help either you or Magda. How are the children? Is Sophie doing well at Newcastle and what about Paul? And what were you doing in France?" The questions came tumbling as if George wanted to make sure that there would be some time before they had to return to Magda and her uncertain future.

After two gin and tonics Nina felt better. George made her laugh when describing the nurse, who had turned up.

"She hardly knew any French at all, nor had she taken the precaution of learning an alternative language. She was Malaysian and God knows what her native tongue was. She might well have been an excellent nurse but poor Magda could not make herself understood at all. When she asked for some coffee and coffee being the only drug she enjoys now, this woman turned up with a cup of cocoa. And the food she cooked was all spices. Your mother couldn't eat it at all, but the nurse wolfed it down. It was when I heard about the nurse I decided I'd better look after Magda, but it was Magda who sacked her. She seemed to perk up at the thought of getting rid of her and for a brief moment I saw a bit of Magda's old self again."

A quiet voice reached them from behind the doors

"Nina, please come to the bedroom."

Nina stood up and went to the double doors leading into her mother's room. She knocked.

"What are you and George talking about?"

"He just told me about your nurse. Why would they send you someone, who can't speak French?"

"There aren't any left, darling. The French girls would rather stay behind the perfume counter at Galleries Lafayette than emptying bedpans, and who can blame them? Now I want to hear about my darling Sophie? Do you think she might want to come over? I'd love to see her before . . . . before it's too late."

"Maman, don't speak like that. You have the best doctors looking after you and everything is going to be all right."

"Don't be so naïve, Nina. You've always put your head in the sand. Now's not the time to pretend. You and George. You're just the same. Did he tell you that he wants to marry me? He thinks that will cheer me up, but all I want is some peace. I don't need sugary lies." Two red blotches appeared on Magda's pale face.

"I'm tired of lies, so tired."

Nina sat down on the bed and leant forward to grasp Magda's pale hands.

"Tell me what you want me to do and I will help you."

"I want to see Sophie."

"And Paul?"

"No, just Sophie!"

Again Nina felt the rejection of Paul as if it were of her.

"All right, then. I'll talk to Sophie tomorrow. We can share my room."

It was past midnight before Nina went to bed in her old room. George had cooked the steaks and opened one of Magda's bottles of Egri Bikaver. Nina prepared an omelette for Magda but she hardly touched it and at nine, when George and Nina started their dinner, Magda was asleep. George talked about their days in Hungary and his voice had a softness Nina had never heard before.

"You know, I always loved her, but she never wanted me. When we were young, years ago, I was so sure that I'd finally won her over, but she just looked at me with those wonderful eyes and said she hoped that our little interlude, that's what she called it, an interlude, wouldn't ruin our friendship. Interlude, I looked it up, it means a breathing space between games."

Nina thought about all the lovers she had seen pass through those double doors. Magda loved the chase but never stayed for the kill. Men were ejected before they had time to feel hurt and some had remained friends. But George was her best friend, always there for her — taking her to the theatre when she was in London and to fine restaurants when he was over in Paris. Magda mentioned his name with a mixture of delight and contempt. She had few women friends, actually Nina could not think of a single woman, who was close to her mother. And was she close to her mother? There was only one answer. Nina hardly knew the woman, who was slowly dying in the next bedroom.

Just before drifting off to sleep Nina remembered that she hadn't phoned Jacques. She was surprised that she hadn't missed him at all.

~

Nina had to admit that although Magda might not have been the best of mothers, she was a loving grandmother to Sophie. It was as if she had saved all the love she had held back as Nina grew up. There were times when Nina felt shameful stings of jealousy as Magda held Sophie in her arms and sang Hungarian lullabies to her baby granddaughter. As Sophie grew up impractical silk shirts arrived folded in finest tissue paper from Parisian stores for her birthday, Paul got a cheque for his — if Magda remembered. Nina's were always ignored. Sophie received letters, long letters written in Magda's neat stylish hand and as Sophie got older, she responded more often to her beloved "Gramma" than she wrote to her own mother.

"Gramma understands me. Why can't you be more like her?" These were rebukes that Sophie used to throw in Nina's face after having spent weeks of her summer holidays with Magda in Paris. She had never asked Paul. Only once did they all have a holiday together, when Edward rented a house in Brittany for three weeks in order to improve his own French as well as that of his two reluctant children. He had invited Magda to spend some time with them and Nina still shuddered to think of that summer. Magda and Sophie rejected all suggestions made by Edward and Paul, who thought trips to the famous Casino in La Baule for afternoon tea were a waste of time. Nina spent all her energy on keeping the two camps apart. When Magda left, some days earlier than planned, Sophie, then eleven, asked if she could accompany her grandmother back to Paris. And after that summer Sophie often went across on her own to see her grandmother. Edward never invited Magda to share a holiday with them again.

Nina could not get hold of Sophie during the day and she was relieved. She knew Sophie would be upset, more so than Nina was. Sophie had never had to deal with death in the family. Edward's father had not been close to the children and Mrs Rivington's fussiness created a fence between her and her only grandchildren. Her house was full of fragile bibelots on spindly tables and every time the children touched anything Mrs Rivington would complain of sticky fingerprints. "Why can't they be in the garden?" she asked when they came to visit, but then complained about the mud they brought in. It wasn't really her fault, Nina thought, Edward had been such a placid child, never one to make a mess.

George and Nina took turns to watch over Magda, who seemed better after a good night's sleep. She even ate some pasta and salad for lunch. In the afternoon Nina went out to do some shopping for supper and just to get away from the musty quiet of the flat. She and George whispered as not to disturb Magda and they continued to speak in hushed voices even when she was awake.

The street had changed so much since Nina left twenty years ago. The coal merchant was gone and in its place was a trendy shop selling fancy tassels and velvet covered waste paper bins. The old dairy, which had sold wonderful cheeses and home churned butter, had been replaced by a jewellery designer and next door was a modern Moroccan brasserie. She turned the corner into avenue Bosquet and was caught up in the rush of busy Parisians on their way home, carrying baguettes and shopping bags. Cars were hooting and behind the tables on the pavements tired café owners were enjoying the lull before the evening rush. Nina sat down on a wicker chair and ordered a coffee. She was trying to delay her return to the flat and Magda's sickbed, but more than that, her call to Sophie.

"No, I can't come," said Sophie with a determined voice. "I've got things on. I'll come later, when the term is finished. Tell Gramma that I'll write and give her a big kiss and . . ."

"Sophie, Gramma is very, very ill and this is important. She's specifically asked for you to come."

"Can't Paul come for now and then I'll come later?"

"Gramma doesn't want Paul, she wants you".

"Don't be so dramatic. You make it sounds like life or death."

Nina drew her breath, she did not want to be accused of pushing her daughter.

"And George is here, he would also love to see you."

The presence of George seemed to make Sophie change her mind and after promises of a plane ticket and extra pocket money Sophie agreed to come. When Nina told Magda she smiled for the first time since Nina had arrived.

"Thank you for organising that. I want some time with Sophie. That'll give you and George a break."

Nina was calmer after having arranged Sophie's travel plans and finally she picked up the phone to call Jacques. Still no Jacques. His secretary answered and promised to forward her message and her telephone number in Paris. After a light dinner Nina sat down with a book and waited for his call. At nine the telephone rang. She threw herself on the receiver, hoping the ring would not wake Magda.

"Nina? It's me, Edward. Sorry to phone so late but I had a call from Magda some days ago and now I hear that Sophie is coming over. I just wanted to make sure everything is all right?"

Her disappointment that it wasn't Jacques lasted only for second. She was touched by Edward's concern and told him about the prognosis.

"Would you like me to come?"

Nina fought against the tears, hot and burning behind her eyelids. Whatever had happened they were a family after all.

"Strangely enough Sasha and I have planned a long week-end in Paris. I can get away and come and see you and Magda. I'd like that"

Nina straightened her back and gripped the receiver with a firm hold.

"Don't let Magda's cancer interfere with your plans. George is here and he has been here for the last week and Sophie is coming on Tuesday. No need for you to worry. I'll keep you informed, but thanks for ringing. Must go now. Bye." The tears were streaking her cheeks before she even had time to replace the receiver.

During the night Tessa turned and turned in her narrow bed. Unlike the night before, when the three drinks had lulled her into a deep sleep, she kept thinking about Jacques, Edward and how these two men made her feel more lonely than ever. She woke with a foggy headache to find that George had placed a tray next to her bed with fresh bread and some coffee.

"Doctor Bernard is coming at eleven this morning with a nurse, who will change Magda's bandages. It means we can go out for lunch as the nurse has been booked to spend a couple of hours with Magda. I've reserved a table nearby at a small bistro, it's usually very quiet at lunchtime."

Nina dressed as if she expected the doctor would reprimand her for looking too casual with a sick mother around. She washed her hair and then tidied up the flat in a furious haste. She sent George out to buy fresh flowers and he returned with sweet smelling freesias, Magda's favourite, and some yellow roses for the living room. Nina washed Magda's emaciated body with a flannel dipped into water scented with cool cologne. Blue veins covered the pale skin around Magda's bloodstained bandages. Nina tried not to let her repulsion show, but she couldn't stop thinking of the breast that had been cut off.

Magda surrendered herself to Nina's hands and Nina gently stroked her mother's face. Although Magda had lost weight, the drugs had puffed up her cheeks and she looked as if she was wearing a mask of flesh. The skin felt dry and papery.

"I've told George to take away the mirror. There's not much I can do. I haven't even got any hair left to brush, it's just like a thin layer of gorse all over my head." Nina patted the grey tufts, which was all that remained of her mother's thick auburn hair.

"Would you like me to put some lipstick on?" Nina asked, hoping it would make Magda feel better. Magda nodded and Nina returned from the dressing room with a pale pink lipstick, the most neutral shade she had found among the dark berry — reds usually favoured by Magda.

It was when Nina put the colour on to her mother's scrunched up pout, trying so hard to stick within contour of her thin lips that Nina realised that Magda knew she would die. She would never have allowed anyone to come this close to her if she were not dying. This was an act of incredible intimacy but also of surrender. Nina's hands were shaking as she held onto the golden case, the faint chemical smell of the lipstick sticking in her nose.

"That's much better. Doctor Bernard will be pleased to see you looking so well," she said with the tone she used for recalcitrant children in her art groups. With a brush she caressed her mother's remaining tufts into a blanket of wiry grey and then evened out the counterpane of the bed with gentle strokes.

When Nina and George returned after lunch they were both weary. The doctor had no more news, no more hope to give them and the nurse's impersonal efficiency left them feeling inadequate. She taught Nina how to turn Magda in the bed and how to check the new bottle by her side.

"If she is in pain, give her two of these, but not more than two pills every four hours." She spoke as if Magda was not present, or just an inconvenience.

Nina slept in the afternoon, the quiet of the sick room made her exhausted. George snoozed in the sofa and it was after six when Nina woke up, befuddled after odd dreams, which stuck in her brain. She tried Jacques again, no answer.

Maybe it was time to speak to Tessa, but Madame Galine answered and said, with a detached coolness, that Madame Kingley-Havers was out, yet again, for dinner and was not expected back until later. Nina left her telephone number.

Next day both George and Nina were busy preparing everything before Sophie's arrival. Nina spent the morning buying food and wine, George went to the airport to pick up Sophie and Magda forgot that she was not really eating and seemed to enjoy the cold chicken soup.

"In my top drawer there is a leather box. Please Nina will you give it to me. I have only some few pieces that are worth anything. Most of the jewellery I brought with me from Hungary was sold during those first tough years. I want you and Sophie to pick out what you want, nothing is very valuable."

"Please Maman. Don't talk like that. You're going to be all right. And Sophie doesn't want to hear that kind of talk, when she arrives."

"And then there's an envelope I have given to George to give to you if something happens to me. I want you to read what's in it and then talk to Sophie and Paul. I don't have much to give you, but at least you have the icon. I'm so glad that's safe."

Nina had completely forgotten the icon and prayed that George would never tell her mother. She had no idea it meant so much to Magda.

Chapter Seven

SOPHIE

Sometimes I feel like I'm my mother's mother. She can be a bit of a drama queen. Like all this with Gramma. But Mum insisted that I'd come over. No problem, really. I love Gramma, I've always admired her. She's so chic, so elegant. Mum used to look more like a big sheep in her woolly skirts. But now, since Dad left, she has made more of an effort and having lost weight, she looks better. I keep telling her she needs to do something about her hair though, why go grey?

I'm glad that I'm at Uni now, the atmosphere at home has not been the best since Dad rushed off with that woman. If it weren't for me I don't think Mum would've coped. That's what I mean with me being like a mother. We had Christmas with Gramma and I suppose it was all right, but Mum only laughed once during that whole week. Gloomsville all around. So I thought it a brill idea that she went to Provence with Tessa, even helped Mum to buy some decent clothes.

Nina had forgotten how beautiful Sophie had become. As she entered the flat followed by George carrying her suitcase Nina looked at her daughter as if she were a stranger. There was no physical resemblance between the two. There were certain traits that reminded her of Edward, but she could see nothing of herself in Sophie. Her blond hair contrasted with Nina's unruly dark mane, now speckled with grey and Sophie's hazel eyes were just as unfathomable as Edward's. Gone was her teenage *rondeur,* now replaced by muscled curves, which were both feminine and athletic. A soft cotton top was draped across her bust and the slim hips were hugged by denim. She walked across for a welcoming embrace, not running as she used to, and there was a languorous quality to her movements Nina had not noticed before. Her thoughts were interrupted as Sophie disentangled herself from her mother's arms and demanded to see her grandmother immediately.

Nina brought her into the sick room. Magda's eyes filled with tears as she pressed her granddaughter to her maimed chest. Sophie did not seem to notice the blood-filled bottle or the change in Magda's appearance.

"Gramma, darling Gramma. Everything's gonna be all right. You look fine and now I'm here to look after you — just like in the old days." Her enthusiasm seemed to cheer Magda up and she waved an impatient hand at Nina, who knew she was being dismissed. After a while Nina and George heard laughter from behind the closed door.

That night they all gathered in Magda's room to eat dinner. Magda had regained her appetite and even sipped a glass of claret after Sophie had told her to ignore the recommendations of "that old fusspot Doctor Bernard". The colour was returning to Magda's face and her eyes had lost the opaqueness that had so worried Nina.

"I knew it. Sophie being here is the best medicine," George said, sadly aware that Nina's and his presence had made no difference at all. "She's always had a soft spot for Sophie."

George offered to wash up to give Nina and her daughter a chance to speak after Magda had finally said her good nights and kissed them in turn.

"I can only stay a day or two. I've changed my ticket to an open one. I really need to get back."

"Are there exams still to take?"

"Yes, no, not really, but I want to be back in Newcastle on Saturday. There's this party . . ."

"Party? You worry about a party, when your grandmother is dying." Nina regretted the words as soon as they were said. It was as if her hurt of being dejected by Magda blanked out her own maternal feelings.

"It's a special party, end of term one. And, well there's this guy I've invited. I can't then not be there, can I?"

"And who's this young man?" Nina could hear how prissy she sounded.

"You don't know him. He's called Peter, runs a record store in the town centre. It's his own shop. I've helped out there a couple of Saturdays, you know, for extra money. I know I told you about that. It's great, I even get a discount. You won't believe how different he is from all the boys at Uni. I mean Peter has achieved something, his own business."

"That's impressive, darling. How old is he?"

"Thirty five, actually, but he's no old fart. He loves the same bands as I do and we're off to Glastonbury later this summer. I know you'll like him. You'll meet him. I've asked him to stay the night in Wyckham Wood, when we're down in London to see the Bratz Boys. That's OK isn't it?"

"Is this serious?"

"Serious, what do I know? But he's so different. You'll see what I mean, when you meet him. That's why I've got to be in Newcastle this Saturday."

Nina paused. There had been boyfriends before; some pleasant but often rejected by Sophie as "booooooring", some less attractive and a few that Edward had kicked out either because they were drunk or did not fit his jealous-ridden criteria of what he considered suitable for his daughter. Sophie had always regarded boys as an added bonus in life but not a necessity in order to have fun. Somehow that seemed to attract the young men. Nina knew Sophie was not a virgin, a discreet search of Sophie's sponge bag before she set off for Newcastle had revealed not only contraceptive pills but also a packet of Durex.

"We'll discuss your travel plans tomorrow, when we know more about Gramma and what she wants. That's why you're here, after all. Now, time for bed. Say good night to Uncle George. You go first in the bathroom."

It was midnight. Nina looked at her sleeping daughter with pride—and worry. Would she manage to keep her innocence? She touched Sophie's unlined forehead. Then Nina thought of her nights with Jacques. Why hadn't he been in touch? "I'll phone again, yes, tomorrow."

Magda was clearly better. Sophie spent the whole morning with her and as soon as George or Nina entered the room the two went quiet, like two naughty schoolchildren caught out. Magda was not a giggler, but here she was laughing in happy gurgles. Her appetite returned and Nina and George found it reassuring to discuss menus rather than nursing regimes.

"With both of you here I feel I can return to London to check my desk. There are a few things I must do. I thought I'd leave tonight if that's OK with you. I've talked to Sophie and she wants to return to England on Friday, so I'll be back by then." Nina kissed George's cheek. "I told Magda. She didn't seem to mind. Actually, I have a feeling she's bored having me around."

The flat was empty after George's departure. His big body had filled the tiny rooms and now they grew, just like the furniture, back into normal size again. Sophie wanted to go shopping and Nina looked forward to a quiet afternoon. She was determined to get hold of Jacques – and also to find out if Tessa had approved of the house, they'd found for her.

"Monsieur Debrel is with a client. Can I take a message?" The tone was cold and distant. Nina left her number and this time stressed that it was important. Tessa, on the other hand, answered immediately and her voice reassured Nina that her Provencal adventure had not been a dream after all.

"Darling, love the house, absolutely perfect. There are some searches to be done and incredible amounts of papers and forms to fill in, but Jacques, the estate agent, is helping me. His English is not bad, actually. Oh, Nina, what a find!"

"Well, I thought the house would suit you."

"No, not the house, sweetie. I'm talking about the estate agent. Jacques!".

"Well, he's rather nice, too." Nina giggled nervously. Something was wrong.

"Nice is not the word, I'd use," Tessa said and laughed, "He's bloody gorgeous. Today he took me for a picnic up among the mountains near Roussillon. Said he wanted to show me the neighbourhood, well, that was his excuse. A bit odd as it was miles away from the house. Anyway, I'm seeing him tomorrow to sign the contract and he's promised to take me for a dinner at some special place afterwards. It's owned by a friend of his just outside St.Remy. I'll tell you all about it when we meet. You **are** coming down aren't you?"

"I'm afraid my mother . . . oh, it's not good news. Excuse me Tessa, I'll have to phone you back later. When I know more." Nina's throat ached as she tried to swallow.

"Sophie, Sophie, *viens ici, ma petite*". Magda's voice sounded weak. Swiftly Nina put the receiver back on its stand.

"Where is Sophie? Tell Sophie to come here and keep me company." It sounded like an order and Nina felt useless as she often did with her mother, and the tears she had held back after talking to Tessa, came in an uncontrollable burst.

"What's the matter? Why are *you* crying? You're not in pain, are you?" Magda, petulant as ever, examined her daughter through semi-closed eyes.

"No, Maman, I am just tired. And worried about you." It felt good to lie. Her mother wouldn't understand about Jacques and what was there to understand any way.

She put her arms around her mother's thin shoulders and rested her head against the damp pillows.

"Just so tired . . . . , but nothing that a good cup of coffee won't cure. Can I make you one, too?"

"Where's Sophie? I didn't hear her leaving."

"She didn't want to wake you up. She came in to say goodbye." Another lie. All these endless lies Nina told in order to keep the family together. "She told me to say that she'll be back by dinner time. She wanted to know if there was something you wanted as she was going down to Boulevard St.Germain to buy some art books."

"Sweet girl. I'm so glad Sophie is happy, that she has found a man she admires. That friend of hers, Peter wasn't it, seems the right kind for her. She needs a mature man. I hope it'll work out. Life's so difficult at that stage. I remember you falling in love with your art tutor when you were at university. Oh, all those tears. Endless tears. You were such an innocent. Sophie seems much more balanced. No doubt we will hear all about this Peter, when she returns after the end-of-term party on Saturday."

"Sophie is coming back?"

"Yes, I've asked her. That'll give you some time to go back to Wyckham Wood. No doubt you have things that need your attention. What about your divorce?"

Her mother shook her shoulders in order to dislodge Nina's clinging arms.

"Yes, of course I do. But are you sure? I'll speak to Sophie tonight."

~

Next day Sophie spent the morning reading to her grandmother. Nina used the free time to replenish the larder. As soon as she returned Sophie beamed at her and said now it was her turn to go shopping. She skipped through the hall and closed the door with a bang.

Nina had put an egg flan in the oven and was shaking a salad dressing in a jam jar, when she heard the key turn in the front door. Sophie was back and laden with satin-glossy carrier bags.

"Gosh, I'm tired. Any of that soul-reviving coffee going?"

Sophie threw a pleading glance at the percolator. "I've forgotten what it's like to shop in Paris. Such fun and much more to choose from. I've got the dress for Saturday. Will you believe it, Gramma gave me a whole wodge of money, said I deserved it. So I bought her some flowers. Look, she loves freesias." She held them out for Nina to smell. The scent was almost too strong and Nina recoiled.

"She shouldn't have scented flowers in her room. It's not good for her." Nina snapped.

"But I'm sure she'll love them," she added with a forced smile.

"Now, what do you think about the dress I've bought." Sophie pulled out a black and white dress from one of the bags. "Just you wait till you see it on." In a flash she dropped her jeans on the floor, stepped out of them and dragged her T-shirt over her tousled blonde hair. The beauty of her long limbs, like a prize-winning foal, stabbed Nina with a mixture of pride and envy. The dress, once slipped on, turned her gangly daughter into a twirling model. It fitted perfectly and the thick grosgrain silk fell in heavy folds from the tight waist and left her shoulders bare.

"And there are shoes to go with it, matching silk, but God knows, how I'm going to be able to dance in these heels . . ." Sophie put her bare feet into the strappy shoes and pranced around the kitchen floor.

"Is Gramma awake? I want to show her. And here, here's a shawl in softest wool to go with it. Isn't it lovely?" Her face shone as she continued to dance, now in the direction of Magda's bedroom.

Nina lifted the empty bags from the floor and found a receipt for the dress amongst the rustling tissue paper. She looked at it as if transfixed. In her mind she translated the numbers into pounds, not once but three times: close to six hundred pounds. Nina had never owned anything at that price. Nor did she think that Magda had, but then Magda could turn a cheap dress into something special by adding a silk *foulard* or a belt. With a sting Nina realised that Magda had never offered to buy Nina something as expensive. But for Sophie there was no holding back. Anything for Sophie.

Nina folded the bags neatly and put the freesias in a vase, she finally found at the back of the china cupboard. A mess, thought Nina, and promised herself to clean the shelves whenever there was a spare moment.

Nina carried the flowers into Magda's bedroom. Sophie was doing her twirl again and again and both were laughing happily as Sophie tried to cope with the heels.

"You'll be the belle of the ball, ma petite. Your young man won't know what's hit him."

"Gramma, I don't know how to thank you. It's absolutely lovely." She threw her arms around Magda, who opened them to receive the embrace. Tears made silent rivulets along Magda's pale cheeks and she smiled over the shoulder of Sophie at Nina. There was such pride in her eyes, that Nina felt it almost like an intrusion to watch them.

"Oh, my flowers. They're for you, Gramma. I *know* you love freesias, but Mum says they're no good in a bedroom . . ."

"Nonsense, they'll do me a lot of good and they're my absolute favourites. So sweet of you to think of me." Magda looked at Nina for a second.

"You can put them here on my chest of drawers. No, more over here so I can see them properly."

Over dinner Magda and Sophie made plans for the next week, "when I'll look after you Gramma." The evening sun slanted through the louvred windows as the evening closed in. Nina was too tired to leave the table to switch on the light and besides the dusk suited her darkening mood. Sophie would leave the day after and although George's doting hand-holding at Magda's bed irritated Nina, she found herself longing for his quiet company. Her yearning for Jacques had become distant, as if she was not quite sure any longer that those glowing days down in Provence had happened. She missed her son more acutely. She needed an ally. He had, on Nina's instigation, written a Get Well card with gaudily printed flowers to his grandmother and his undisciplined handwriting had touched Nina. "All that money you spent on fine schools and he still writes like a ten-year old," Magda said with a mock-angry smile handing the card back to Nina.

It was past ten when the telephone broke the silence. Sophie sat in the sofa reading a glossy magazine, another purchase from her shopping foray. Nina had found an old issue of *Figaro Madame* and tried in her mind to translate the measurements for a double-cooked cheese soufflé into English. Not that she would ever cook one, but she was too tired to grapple with the novel she had brought from Provence. She nodded to Sophie, indicating wordlessly that she wanted her to answer the ringing telephone. Sophie sighed, something she managed to do with her whole body, and slouched over to the table by the door. She picked it up, suddenly smiling, maybe she thought it was Peter. "*Oui, qui parle?*"

"It's for you, Mum, it's Tessa. She says she has some good news for you."

Nina unfolded her legs and sat up.

"What was all that about?" asked Sophie as Nina returned the receiver to Sophie. "You look like a thunder cloud, couldn't have been all that good news, not the way you look."

"No, it *is* good news. Tessa liked the house I found for her near St. Remy. You remember I told you about it. She has just signed the contract and she phoned from the restaurant, where she's having a celebratory dinner with the estate agent.

"She sounded very jolly . . ."

"Well, they had cracked open a bottle of champagne to seal the deal and now they were on to the brandies."

"She must be very pleased with you. She's got what she wanted and you got a free holiday, win-win, isn't it Mum?"

"Yes, my darling, win-win, I suppose that's what you call it." She put down the magazine on the sofa. "I'll just look in to see that Gramma is OK and then I'm turning in. Will you manage on your own?"

~

The sheets were stuck to Nina's damp body as she awoke at first light. She had dreamt of Jacques, how he had left her at the square in Bonlieu and as he walked away, Tessa came out of a doorway, swinging her blond hair. They rushed towards each other and embraced, Tessa's silky dress crumpling against Jacques' thighs. Nina could not shake off the sadness of her dream, not even after she had drunk a glass of water and washed her sticky face. She remembered how Tessa and she had discussed dreams that first night in Mas de Brehet. Nina had confessed that she dreamt of Edward almost every night, that he was coming back, but that somehow he could not let go of Sacha, yet he admitted he loved her and missed her. The same dream almost every night. "It's crazy, I know, but feel happy because I'm close to him in my dreams and I forget all about the divorce and the pain for hours, sometimes for days." Tessa had smiled and then told Nina that she still dreamed about Richard, "happy sexy dreams and then I wake up and I'm sad, really sad that it's all over and that I'll never be that happy again. And sad that he left me. It's like an ache. How different we are."

Before Sophie was leaving, Magda insisted that Nina should take a photograph of her in the black and white dress, "and put those lovely shoes on, too". When Sophie had brushed her long hair and painted her lips ready for the camera, Magda called her to her bedside.

"There's something I want to give to you, something for that dress." She picked up a Chinese lacquer box and fiddled with a miniature lock and key. From it she pulled a smaller, leather case. She opened it and inside, shimmering against the black velvet, nested a pair of diamond earrings.

"I was given these by your grandfather a long time ago. They're made by Fabergé and they have been in his family. I want you to have them. They'll look sensational with that dress. Try them on. No, they're not made for pierced ears. Let me show you. Yes, just like that, see that little screw on the back. Let's have a look, oh, yes, perfect." Her voice broke and she smiled as she watched her granddaughter swing her head to let the movement catch the blue dazzle of the diamonds.

Nina had never seen these earrings before and as far as she could judge, they must be quite valuable especially as they were still in its original Fabergé *etui*.

Sophie was cooing with delight, watching herself in Magda's mirror.

"Gramma, I don't believe it. They're beautiful, just stunning. Thank you, thank you." She threw herself onto Magda's bed and hugged her and the empty box fell onto the floor. Nina picked it up. She touched the black velvet inside and admired the silk that lined the lid where the name Fabergé and St. Petersburg were printed in gold letters. St. Petersburg? Nina wondered if her seldom-spoken-of father had bought them or inherited them. She had not seen them before and she did not have the courage to ask her mother. Magda had always told her that the few jewels she had brought to Paris had been sold during those first years in Paris.

"Gramma, tell me about my grandfather. You never talk about him. All I know is his name. Zoltan, wasn't it?" Sophie was asking the question that Nina had asked all during her childhood only to be rebuffed with a short, "Not much to talk about. Your father is not part of our family any more." Nina waited to hear the same words again, but Magda leant back against her white pillows and smiled.

"Your grandfather, darling Sophie, was a wonderful man. He gave me these earrings on my twenty first birthday, they had belonged to his mother. Oh, you would have loved him, he was so handsome, so strong. And he, he would have loved you."

"Well, he certainly didn't love me. He never came to see us or write to us" interjected Nina with a querulous tone to her voice.

Magda ignored her daughter and pushed Sophie's hair away from her face as to get a better look at the earrings.

"Yes, he would have loved you."

Nina took the photographs with Magda's old Kodak and as she watched her daughter through the viewfinder she was astounded that this vision was her Sophie, not any more a denim-clad teenager but a young, elegant woman with Magda's innate style.

Nina felt empty, as if she had somehow lost her daughter.

~

Magda deteriorated as soon as Sophie left. It was almost as if her presence had been vital for her survival. George arrived on Saturday, the day after Sophie's departure. His firm had suffered from his absence and his mind was on the next auction at Sotheby's, at which he hoped to sell a couple of Russian oil paintings.

"Did you know about Magda's Fabergé diamond earrings?" Nina could not wait to ask George. "She said they were a gift from my father. I've never seen them before."

He looked surprised.

"Fabergé? Are you sure? Your father was not exactly a pauper but I doubt if he had that kind of money, or someone in his family, for that matter. He had a pre-war title, but there was no money there, land, masses of land, yes, but that was before the Russians came and grabbed it all."

"It's so odd. She told Sophie that my father was handsome and strong. She's always told me he was not part of the family and you've said to me that he was very ordinary."

"Women. Don't ask me to explain how they view men. You all seem to have different criteria. And I suppose for that I should be grateful. As far as your father goes, I don't want to say anything against him. I hardly knew him, but he didn't make a great impression on me. But I am surprised about those earrings, especially as I know how Magda had a very meagre time during those first years in Paris and had to take any job she could in order to pay the rent. She sold off everything she had, apart from the icon she gave you, but obviously these earrings were special to her and she saved them for you, or Sophie, as it turned out."

They shared a silent drink of whisky before Nina retired to bed. She tossed restlessly hoping she would not have any more dreams about Tessa and Jacques.

George woke her up. It was still dark. He put his arms around her.

"I've phoned Dr. Bernard. Now don't get too upset, but Magda has gone. She must have died in her sleep. I came into see if she was alright. I woke up about ten minutes ago, don't know what time it was and just felt I had to see her.

It was if she'd called me. I took her hand and it was warm but I knew she was gone. I think she wanted to die alone, always private. Until the end."

George took Nina's arm and almost dragged her from the bed. His soft dressing gown smelled of lemon and Nina hid her face in its folds. She felt him shaking with sobs and hearing him Nina could not control her own tears.

"Here, my petal. This won't do. Dr. Bernard's coming soon." He handed her a damp handkerchief.

Nina followed George into her mother's bedroom. The bedside light was on and through the drawn curtains a weak sliver of light squeezed through. Magda's eyes were closed. Had George done that or had Magda died in her sleep? She could not decide if Magda looked peaceful or not, she just did not look like her mother any more. Nina did not move but she heard George leaving and quietly closing the door.

What was she meant to do? How can you say farewell to a person who is already dead. Should she whisper I love you or thank you? Thoughts were whirling around Nina's head.

She sat down on the bed and stretched out her hand to touch Magda's, but she could not make herself do it.

"Oh, Maman, all I can wish for you is peace, peace at last." Nina stood up and turned her back to the bed. "How I wish I could cry for you, but I cry for my lost childhood, for the loss of a mother I never really knew, for the mother I can see you *could* have been if you only had loved me like you love Sophie."

In the days that followed George took over. He dealt with the undertakers, organised a small memorial service in the church around the corner and afterwards took Nina, Paul,

Sophie, some neighbours and Edward, who had suddenly announced that he wanted to be present, to a small Hungarian restaurant in the Marais quarters. He drank far too much wine and later sobbed on Sophie's shoulders.

"There will never be a woman like her again. Your grandmother was unique. I loved her all my life." His tears fell on the tablecloth and Sophie tried hard to comfort him.

Edward was clearly embarrassed by this emotional outburst and offered to pay for the taxi back to the hotel, where they were all staying.

Next day Edward travelled back to England with the children and left George and Nina to clear out the flat. When pulling out the drawer of her bedside table she found a large envelope. "For Nina. To be opened on my death".

She sat down on the bed, now stripped of its bedclothes, holding the heavy envelope in her hands. "I'll deal with that later," thought Nina and put it in her overnight bag.

CHAPTER EIGHT

Nikolai Chalpin

Dear Nina,

Nina waited until she got back home to Wyckham Wood before opening the heavy envelope. There was no date on the typewritten letter, but a photograph fell out as she unfolded the stationery. It was of a young man, rather handsome and in a sober suit of an old-fashioned cut. His hair was dark and wavy and the chin was determined, yet the smile was unforced and seemed to light up his large eyes. This was not Zoltan Gostonyi, her father, who had had a thin and angular face. Magda had, after some pressure, showed her a wedding photograph. Magda in a simple pale suit with a feathered hat and Zoltan in a uniform. None of them looked particularly happy. She recalled that she had been fascinated by the flowers, which had been made of silk. Magda had told her that it impossible to get real roses during the austere fifties. They had got married at the mayor's office in Nagykanizsa, not far from Magda's parents' home near Lake Balaton. That was all Magda had told her, "soon afterwards we broke up, it was a mistake, a terrible mistake and then the uprising 1956 and off I went to Paris with you in a basket."

Nina turned the photograph and written in French were the words Always in my dreams signed with the initial N.

This is not an easy letter to write and I hope you will forgive me, when you have had time to think it all over. You might have wondered why I never wanted to discuss my life in Hungary, why I always insisted that our life started, when we arrived in Paris in 1956, when you were only a few months old.

I left my parents, who hated me for what I had done and I left a country I could not live in any longer.

One of the many things I never told you was that I had a sister. Eva. She was five years older than me and a real beauty. She was the apple of my father's eye, his first child, clever and witty as well as pretty. She was fifteen in 1944 when the Russians crossed the borders to liberate us from the Nazis. I remember as if yesterday how we had to hide our valuables in the farm buildings, when we heard they were coming. I thought it was like a game and Eva and I helped by wrapping our pictures in old sacks, we had used to store wheat in. My father worried most about his books and the paintings.

It took a couple of months before the Russians arrived in our region. We had heard of looting and other atrocities, but my father insisted that the Russians could not be as barbaric as the Nazis.

Then they came. It was early November, three months after they had entered Hungary. One night five Russian soldiers stopped at our house. I will not tell you what happened except to say that Eva was raped by all of them. My father had hidden us both in the upstairs linen cupboard, but when they attacked my mother, Eva rushed out to help her. I stayed behind, in that linen closet and I could hear their screams. Father was knocked unconscious, I thought he was dead and I just prayed and prayed, hardly daring to breathe.

The soldiers left that night. They found Papa's bottles and some food and later we found that they had taken our last horse to pull our sled, laden with their loot. A year later, Eva died. I do not know if it was because of her injuries or because she just did not want to live any more. My parents never really recovered. I always feel guilty that Eva and my mother had to face it all and I was saved. I think I worried more about Petruschka, she was our last horse and I adored her.

Once the war was over and the Russians were in command, our estate was taken from us, land that had been in the family for generations. It *hurt Papa to see how our old farm workers ruined the soil, which they now were put in charge of. We were left with an acre and Mama grew vegetables, some we were allowed to keep for ourselves, the rest was sold to the commune, the kolchos.*

At least we were alive, but my parents could not stop talking about Eva. They hated the Russians with a self-burning intensity. Not that they ever dared to show their contempt, they knew only too well that any criticism could lead to imprisonment and even death.

Somehow we managed to have a life. I was sent to the conservatoire in Budapest, because my school found that I had a talent. Piano lessons from the age of four had paid off. It was in Budapest I met Nikolai Chalpin. He was one of the many advisors attached to Soviet-led Hungarian government.

Nikolai loved music and we met at a concert. He was bright, handsome, in his mid-thirties and I was in my late teens and very innocent Well, what can I say? I fell in love and very soon I became his lover. I knew he was married, that he had children he adored in St. Petersburg—or Leningrad as it was then. That did not stop me, maybe I was overwhelmed by his generosity. After years of nothing, and I really mean nothing, I was given luxuries un-thought of: food coupons, nylons and best of all a record player. For my 21st birthday he gave me a wonderful pair of diamond earrings, which I never dared to show to anyone.

Nina put down the letter. She saw in front of her eyes Sophie in a black and white silk dress, swinging her blond hair and showing off the diamond earrings her grandmother had given to her. But she had told Sophie they were a gift from . . . .

We had three happy years together, then I became pregnant. I had to tell my mother. She insisted on an abortion. When my parents found out that the father of the child was a Russian it almost killed them. "We will not have a Russian in our family" said my father and although a fervent Roman Catholic he agreed with my mother that an abortion was the only solution.—I never told them Nikolai was already married.

I refused point blank to have an abortion. I think my father thought it was on religious grounds. So he arranged a deal with our neighbour's son, Zoltan Gosztonyi. He would marry me, give the child a name and in return he would get paid. So we married when I was three months pregnant and this was in early 1956. It was a pure business arrangement. I continued to see Nikolai, but then in October, when you were three months old Nikolai told me that there was some unrest among the students in Budapest. They had torn down a statue of Stalin and they were planning more riots Nikolai wanted me to take you to Paris. He would make sure that I got the necessary papers to get out of the country. As soon as things had calmed down he would come and see me in Paris and we would then decide where you and I would settle.

Well, you know about the uprising and how over two thousand Hungarians were killed in the riots and many executed in the aftermath. More than two hundred thousand fled the country and had to more or less crawl across the border. We were lucky. I had Russian stamped papers.

Nikolai never came. I never heard from him again. I tried to find out, year after year. You were his pride, his little cherry blossom, and in your face I see him. When you were born he gave you the icon I later gave you when you married Edward. I saved the earrings for Sophie.

Should I have told you? How could I? By the time you grew up you thought of Zoltan as your father.

I have not told anyone about this. I always hoped that Nikolai would turn up one day and then he could explain.

I hope I have not been a bad mother. I was determined to have you and it is a decision I have never regretted. I do, though, regret the lies and the deception. I did it to protect my parents and then, well, by then the lies had turned to some distorted form of reality. You were real enough but the lies created a wall between us. Without you knowing it I always waited for your father to come and find us in Paris. I never heard from him and it clouded my love for you. Please forgive me for these lies.

Your loving mother

Magda

Nina dropped the letter on to her lap. She felt sick, as if she had swallowed something acid. Her breath was laboured. Water, she needed water and then she would be able to think. In the kitchen she found a glass and she let the water run to cool it down. Instead of filling the glass, she cupped her hands and let the chilly water brim over her fingers before splashing her hot face. Her tears mingled with the cold water and she fell to her knees in front of the sink.

"Oh, Magda, why didn't you tell me? Why? I would have understood. All I wanted was a father. One that I could miss and long for just like you did with Nikolai." The name sounded odd, but it was the name of her father. And somewhere in Russia she had half-brothers and sisters. And Zoltan, the man she had spent her youth thinking of as her father was nothing, a nobody, who had given her a surname in exchange for money. Her own children had Russian blood, did they need to know? Should she tell them or let Magda's secret be buried with her? Nina's head was aching. She splashed more cold water on her face, dried her tears on a kitchen towel and turned off the tap. She'll think about all this tomorrow, not today.

~

135

CHAPTER NINE

Peter McLennan

Women. No, I don't understand them. Mrs Riverton is just as crazy as her daughter – and all I tried to do was to help out. Shit happens, but this was just too bloody much.

"Mummy, I'm on the train from Newcastle and I'll be home by nine. Do you mind?" Nina heard immediately that something was wrong. At first she thought it was the death of Magda that had finally hit Sophie. Her daughter had taken it so well albeit her mourning had been eased by finding that Magda had set aside a surprisingly large amount of money for Sophie in her will to spend "on something useless and fun". Nina had also been given a sum, much smaller, with no instructions attached to it.

"I need to come home", said Sophie on a crackling line and Nina knew it was not Magda's death that was on her daughter's mind. "It's all such a bloody mess. Oh, I can't talk about it now, not until I see you. About nine then, ok?" The line went dead and with the humming tone Nina sensed her nerves knotting. It had been too much lately. Coming back from Paris she had finally had time to think about the contents of Magda's letter. First she had felt cheated; her whole childhood had been a lie. It was days later she was finally taking some comfort in the fact that Magda had actually wanted to have her and that she had resisted her parents by refusing an abortion. Nina was not the result of some fumbling, love-empty episode with Zoltan Gosztonyi, no, it was clear that Magda had really loved Nikolai. And she had waited for him like some Chekovian heroine for years. What Nina remembered as

Magda's various affairs had been nothing but diversions while waiting for Nikolai. No wonder there was always an emotional distance between her mother and her lovers. But why had Magda not confided in Nina, once she had grown out of her narrow-minded teen age years?

Her thoughts returned to Sophie. Her joy of soon seeing her was mixed with worries. But first she must get everything ready and there was dinner to prepare. Nina had forgotten the pleasure of feeding someone else, the joy of cooking. On her own she ate whatever she could find in the fridge or larder. Occasionally she would throw a chop in a frying pan and dress a salad, but she thought there was something almost obscene in laying the table for one and serving meals out of dishes rather than the saucepan. Nina examined the offerings in the fridge, not much. It would have to be a pasta with that jar of pesto hiding behind the half full milk bottle, but she would have time to whip up a lemon drizzle cake, Sophie's favourite.

By nine the table was laid and a bottle of red had already been opened by Nina, who was humming while putting the golden, still hot cake on a plate. When the doorbell rang Nina ran to the door.

"Darling, how lovely to see you." Nina hugged her daughter close to her floury apron.

"But how come you can leave Newcastle just like that? What about your week-end job in the record shop?"

"I'll never go back there, never" said Sophie.

Nina looked at her ashen daughter, who did not return her mother's welcoming smile. Sophie's eyes looked across Nina's shoulder and seemed to focus on the mirror over the hall table. Sophie's silent stare unsettled Nina, who with hollow cheerfulness pulled Sophie into the kitchen from the hall and after having kicked her soft sports bag aside. Here

Sophie fell to the floor and hugged the half-sleeping Larry, who rose on rheumatic legs from his basket.

"Larrikins, sweetie, how I missed you." Sophie burrowed her nose into his soft fur.

"Now what do you say to some pasta and a big glass of Rioja? And I've got a still warm lemon drizzle cake for our after dinner coffee." Nina smiled at herself.

"Oh, Mum," she managed to drag out the word with contempt. "How come you think you can always sort out any family problem with a bloody cake?"

Nina bit her tongue and turned her back to Sophie. She busied herself at the stove and then poured a glass of wine for Sophie.

"Please, Mummy, for god's sake, sit down. Please." There was a note of urgency in her voice that made Nina stop with Sophie's glass still in her hand. She pulled up a kitchen chair and sat down.

"Darling, now tell me, what's wrong?"

"It's Peter. He's left me. It's hell." She stopped to blow her nose into a scrunched up tissue.

"I don't know what to do. What have I got to live for now? He's the only man for me, I knew that the minute I met him." The words fell out of Sophie in nervous bursts.

"Oh, my darling. But why has he left you? I thought you two got on so well. Has he given a reason? Is there someone else or just a tiff? These things happen at the beginning of a relationship," said Nina in a soothing half-whisper.

"He went back to his wife."

"His what?"

Nina's arms fell onto her lap as if they had become paralysed and she just managed to save the still un-proffered glass. Sophie did not look her mother in the eyes and squirmed on her chair.

"You heard what I said. His bloody wife!"

"Did you know he was married?" Nina asked as soon as she trusted her own voice.

"Of course I did, but he doesn't love her. He told me so again and again. And now she's having a bloody baby. Forced him to it, and do you know why?" By now Sophie's voice had risen to a high-pitched cry.

"Just so that he couldn't leave her. Disgusting isn't it? And he's a decent man, he's says he'll have to do his duty and then maybe we can get back together later. He's just too good for her."

Nina swallowed air.

"Oh, Sophie, I can't believe this. Whatever made you have an affair with a married man?"

"Mummy, this is not an affair. We love each other." Sophie wrenched her hand out of Nina's grip. "He's a man, a real man, the first one I've really loved. Not some silly little boy. I just can't let him go."

"God! You call him a real man? Making love to his wife while having an affair with a much younger girl, you call that grown-up? I call that immoral, cheating two women." Nina's voice rose.

Sophie finally looked at her mother and there was pure, untamed anger in her eyes.

"Just like dad, that's what you mean, isn't it?" The words hit Nina like sharpened arrows. The two women stared at each other, both unwilling to be the first to turn away.

At the stove the water started hissing under a clattering lid and broke the silence. Nina got up and turned down the gas. With her back turned to Sophie she collected herself.

"First of all you must give proper notice. Have you done that? Then we'll look for a summer job, either in Maidstone or Bromley. You still have Gramma's money to live on and it doesn't cost you anything to live here, so money is not the object and I'd love your company."

Sophie did not seem to listen, she twiddled her unfurled tissue, pushing it in and out through her silver ring.

"The baby's due in October and, I suppose he has to stay with her until the baby is a couple of months, what do you think? Then I can go back to Newcastle. Definitely not before that. I don't want to be there until he's ready to leave her and settle down with me."

"So what happens to your studies? That's what you should really worry about, not when you can get together with that man again. Grow up, darling, do you really think he'll come back to you, with a new baby around?"

"Are you saying that just because daddy won't come back to you? This is totally different. Daddy fell in love with someone else. Peter loves me."

Nina closed her eyes. This was not a discussion she wanted, not now. Only yesterday she had had Tessa on the phone, excited about her new Provencal home but even more excited about Jacques Debrel. Nina had not heard a word from him since she left for Paris in spite of her many messages left with his stern secretary. She had tried hard to excise the memories of his hands on her hip, his smile early in the morning. And she did not even dare to think of him and Tessa together. She could almost smell the bile rising in her throat.

"Let's talk about this tomorrow. You must be tired after your journey. Let's just eat the pasta while it's still hot and then gorge ourselves on cake. What do you say?"

"No cake for me. I'm not hungry. I'm going to phone Peter."

After two forkfuls Sophie put the cutlery down on her half-eaten pasta and left the table. Nina grabbed the wine bottle and poured herself another glass. Tomorrow they would speak.

Next day the sun was already playing hide and seek behind some cauliflower clouds, when Nina woke up. The garden was cheering her up with its bright colours. Nina brought her coffee out to the patio. In the kitchen the table was laid for Sophie, who was not yet awake. Nina had slept badly. In the early hours she had tried to separate her anger towards Peter from her own disappointment in Edward, — and Tor and Jacques for that matter. Whar was itJen had called men? Junk male, that was it.

It was ten by the time Sophie came down the stairs. Her eyes were red-rimmed and her blond hair in a tangle.

"I finally got hold of Peter. He had turned his mobile off last night. He said he couldn't speak to me. He was with her, of course. I tried to talk to him but he just turned off the phone. Didn't say he was going to phone me later or anything. What do you think, mummy?"

Nina swept her daughter into her arms and Sophie cried like a small child, snivelling and snorting.

"Everything's going to be all right, just you wait and see."
Both of them knew that it was a lie yet both felt strangely
comforted by it.

Peter did not return Sophie's calls and three days later, after
yet another meal with red wine and tears, Nina told her
daughter about Magda's letter. She went to her bedroom
to fetch it and handed it over, almost reluctantly but still
relieved to share the contents with Sophie.

Sophie read it and was silent for a long time, read it again
and then she looked at her mother. Her face was blank, then
she smiled.

"I'm so glad that Gramma had a real love in her life. And
that it is her lover who's your father and my grandfather.
So what if he was a Russian? He must have loved her, too.
I wish we could have talked about it. All we have is this
photograph."

Sophie looked intently at the black and white photo as if
trying to find some clue to her own identity in his features.

"Do you know what I'd like to do? I'd like to use some
of that money we got from Gramma and go to Budapest
and see if we can find out anything about him, this Nikolai
Chalpin. What do you say?"

Nina hugged her daughter and for the first time since
Provence a sense of belonging warmed her chilly veins.

Next evening the phone rang after the nine o'clock news had
finished. Sophie had gone to see one of her school friends
and Nina had just turned on the taps for her evening bath.

"Can I speak to Sophie please." An irritated voice broke
through the background noise of people chatting and
laughing.

"I'm afraid Sophie is out tonight. This is her mother speaking. Can I take a message?"

"Could you just tell her Peter phoned and I'll try later. Maybe tomorrow night."

Nina straightened her back.

"I'd rather you didn't. I think you've done enough damage to my daughter. It's high time you concentrate on your own family. I want you, no, I insist, that you leave Sophie alone."

"I don't know what you're talking about, Mrs . . ."

"Riverton" she interjected sharply.

"You've got no idea about your daughter. You've got this totally wrong. As you might know she's been working in my shop. We had a few drinks, after work like, that's all. Then she invited me to some ball or other at the Uni. I came with her, only because she went on and on about it and how she had no one to go with. I suppose I felt sad for her and she does a bloody good job in my shop. I felt I should go. As it happens we had a fun evening, maybe we drank a bit too much, but that's all it was and since then she's been phoning me at all hours and not only at the store but also at home.

"That couldn't have pleased your wife."

"I told Sophie from the beginning that I was married. We have a fairly open marriage, but now my wife is pregnant with our first child and this constant phoning is getting her down."

"You've been having an affair, is that not correct?" Nina's voice was icy.

"Affair? That's a bit rich. And besides I don't think that's any of your business, Mrs.

"Riverton !"

"Well, there you are. Just tell her I phoned and I will do as you say. I will **not** get in touch, but tell her to stop pestering me."

Nina never mentioned the call. And Sophie never asked.

Sophie managed to get a summer job through her father. One of his clients needed a girl to answer the telephone and emails, while his secretary was away on her holiday. Before starting her job Sophie and Nina had decided to spend a long week-end in Budapest to see if they could find out anything about Nina's father. The first thing they did was to call George, but he was equally surprised at the contents of Magda's letter and he had never heard of Nikolai Chalpin.

"Are you sure? Well, it does make sense. I never understood why she married Zoltan. Actually, I'm quite pleased, always thought he was a bit of a bore. Look, let me ask around and I'll come back to you."

Two days later George phoned and said that he had talked to someone who had known Magda's landlady in Budapest, when she was at the conservatoire. The landlady was dead since years back, but her youngest daughter was still alive, "and I have spoken to her and she is willing to see you in Budapest. Her English is quite good. I also suggest that you speak to Mr. Kovacs, who is a researcher and archivist at the university." He gave all the details to Nina, who wondered if she had the right to investigate her mother's private life.

"Of course you're not intruding," said Sophie. "She wouldn't have told you about Nikolai if she thought so, would she?"

Nina had only been to Hungary once before. Magda had always refused to return and it was with Edward Nina had gone an early spring some years ago. The children stayed with Edward's parents and Nina saw the trip as a second honeymoon. Budapest was a romantic city, but the room they'd been given at Hotel Gellert was noisy and the bed so narrow that Nina preferred to sleep at the sofa. They ran through the museums, did a daytrip on the Danube and bought painted baskets and a mirror for the bedroom. The food had been too rich and the wine too sweet and Edward was quite relieved to leave a country, where he could not even read the street signs. He felt emasculated having to rely on his wife. Against her hope Nina did not experience a returning to her roots. The country was as uncomfortably exotic to her as to Edward, except that she could make herself understood. In a way it would have been easier if they both had been strangers.

After trawling through guide books with Sophie Nina had booked a double room at a small hotel near Fisherman's Wharf in Buda. Thanks to her speaking Hungarian the room rate fell by almost half and she was offered a room with a view of the Danube. Sophie organised the air tickets, happy to be involved in the planning.

They set off Wyckham Wood early on an early August morning, almost to the day a year since Edward had left home. This was an anniversary Nina could do without. Together with Sophie she had planned a programme. On Friday morning they would see Mrs Lipótváros, the landlady's daughter. On Friday afternoon they had been given an appointment with Mr Kovacs, who agreed to see them at his research office in Andrassy Street. Saturday Nina wanted to take Sophie sightseeing and then go for a slap-up meal in the evening. "And we'll still have time for some shopping, mum, won't we? A chum told me that CDs are cheap." Nina realised that Sophie had lost her discount when she stopped working for Peter. "As much time as you like, darling."

It was late afternoon when they landed at Ferihegy airport, southeast of Budapest. For more forints they had bargained for they took a taxi to Fisherman's Wharf. The evening sun was setting over the river and after having unpacked in their small room, Nina and her daughter walked out into the August dusk. Nothing looked the way Nina remembered from her trip some fifteen years earlier. The place was busy with tourists and the buildings Nina remembered as pock-marked by bullets were now freshly painted in cheerful pastels. Chic little bistros and pizzerias replaced the beer halls which had served garlic scented sausages and swollen goose livers.

"Somewhere around here your father and I found a small restaurant that served bear stew. Can you imagine the uproar that would cause in England? It was dark and dense and very delicious. I suppose they're not allowed to serve that any longer." Sophie wrinkled her nose, she had spent some of her teenage years as a vegetarian and still regarded hunting animals in order to eat them as a wanton cruelty.

They never found the restaurant, maybe it had run out of bears, and instead they picked an Italian-style trattoria in the castle district near the Matthias Church. Nina was excited; this was the first time Sophie and she had been travelling together just the two of them. No Edward to set out a detailed programme for each day, no Paul, who complained about early starts. They could do what they wanted and they were determined to enjoy their new-won freedom. Sitting on a wooden decking outside the restaurant, they were watching the people passing by. Young men threw furtive glances at Sophie, who smiled back. Nina had never seen her prettier, it was as if Peter had never existed. Nina's own thoughts of Jacques were still clouded by bitterness, she was not jealous just irritated with herself for having been taken in by his charm.

After dinner they strolled around the cobbled streets and Sophie noticed a poster for a concert. The next day an orchestra would play Mozart's Requiem in the Matthias Church. "Let's go," said Sophie excitedly, "I'll buy the tickets. This'll be my way of remembering Gramma and saying thank you to you as well. I know it is one of your favourites."

Nina hugged her daughter and wished that her mother could have seen them here, in the city where she had lived and loved.

Mrs Lipótváros lived not far from the hotel. It was a small side street, away from the busy tourist area. The house, when they finally found it, smelled of cabbage and the paint along the staircase was falling off in shards exposing the grey plaster. The door to the flat must once have been painted a pale blue, now there were streaks of ingrained dirt darkening the wood. A handwritten card with the name of Lipótváros written in biro was stuck above the letterbox. Nina rang the bell.

The woman, who opened the door had a cap of soft grey curls, her dark eyes were surrounded by fine wrinkles, while the cheeks were plump and smooth. "Come in," she said and held out her hand. "You must be Nina, Magda's daughter." Nina liked her immediately, she could not say why, but there was an openness, which washed away any awkwardness.

The smell of fresh coffee also helped and as they were led into the flat Nina noticed that here everything was neat and tidy. On the low table in front of the sofa was a plate laden with sugary cakes and next to it an album.

"I do remember your mother very well. I was eight years younger than her and I thought she was the most beautiful young woman I'd ever seen. I wanted so much to be like her. She played the piano like an angel and we all adored her. She must have been eighteen when she moved in with us. I had only brothers so I was delighted to have a girl joining our family. My two brothers, although much younger than Magda, both had a crush on her and would do anything for a smile from her. I'm so sorry to hear that she's died. We never heard a word from her after she left Budapest. We knew she had married and that surprised all of us, as we knew she hadn't married her beau. But then we didn't know she had a child either."

"Did you ever meet her . . . beau?"

"Only a few times, when he took her home after a concert. He was Russian, you know and we didn't really want to associate with them. But I did like him. Once they got caught in a storm on the way home and my mother felt pity for him and asked him in to get dry. She gave him some tea and I remember that we stood behind the door looking at this Russian. Magda and he were clearly in love, I can still see them laughing as they pulled off their wet coats. Just at that moment Papa came home and as a good host offered Magda's friend a shot of vodka. A Medicinal Papa called it. I suppose he wanted to show his gratitude to my parents in some way and when he saw the piano, my father taught at the Conservatoire, he asked if he could play some Russian music for us. He sat down and my brothers and I crept out from behind the door when he started playing. He was a brilliant pianist and my father insisted on hearing more. Magda was glowing with pride and at the end they did a piece for four hands, something Russian I think. It was a lovely evening, but we never saw him in our home again and we never asked Magda about him. The less you knew the better. We had heard that he worked as some sort of advisor for the government. You didn't want to be too close to those sorts. But here, let me show you." She leant forward and lifted the leather bound book from the table. "This is my parents' photo album and I found several photos of Magda. She stayed three years with us, well, until 1955." Mrs Lipótváros had inserted empty envelopes in the album to quickly find the relevant photos. Nina's breathing quickened and she softly caressed Sophie's hand.

Nina recognised her mother immediately. The dark-haired young girl was laughing towards the camera. She was dressed in a traditionally embroidered blouse and a wide skirt.

"This must have been taken the year she moved in with us, so she was about eighteen. You can see my younger brother watching her in the background. No wonder he was smitten, just look at that smile."

Sophie took the album from Nina's hands. "How pretty Gramma was." Nina looked closer and disregarding the hair colour, she suddenly saw her daughter in that photo.

"And here is Magda with some of her friends. This was taken at her name's day celebrations, must have been 1955. We had a small party for her here in the flat." Nina looked closely. There were six youngsters sitting at a table and behind them was an older woman, probably the landlady herself. Yes, there was George, erect and slim, with a small posy of flowers in his hand. On the table were more flowers and several tall bottles of wine.

"We have one from her twenty first birthday celebration, too. Look, here it is."

Nina leant forward. Magda was in the centre of a larger group of young people, and could that handsome girl in the corner be Mrs Lipótváros? She looked again and suddenly Nina noticed that Magda was wearing a glittering pair of earrings, those she had given to Sophie for her ball. She pointed them out to Sophie.

"Yes, I remember those earrings. They were a gift from her Russian friend. He had told Magda that they were real diamonds, we wouldn't know, would we? But they were pretty, whatever they were."

"Would it be possible to borrow this photograph and have a copy made? Magda gave those earrings to Sophie and I never ever saw her wearing them, but they must have meant a great deal to her. She looked radiant in them. Sorry . . ." Nina found her handkerchief and blew her nose loudly. Now it was Sophie's turn to stroke her hand.

"We're forgetting the coffee and cakes. Let me put a fresh pot on and you must try my almond strudels. Please. Now, tell me all about Magda and Paris. Are you her only child and I also want to know about you and your family?"

After two hours and two pots of coffee it was as if they had known each other for years. Memories of Magda came flooding back and Sophie was able to see her grandmother in a new light, as a young, irresponsible but happy girl. Neither Sophie nor Nina had ever heard her mother play the piano. "Maybe it reminded her too much of her time here in Budapest? She never spoke of her youth, never wanted to come back, not even after the Russians had left. It was as if she preferred to remember **her** Budapest."

When Nina and Sophie left, they had exchanged addresses and in her handbag was the photo of Magda with the Russian earrings.

They found the house in Andrassy Street, where the archivist was working. It was a fine, wide esplanade, which must once have been the centre of the city's more elegant area. The corner building was hidden behind scaffolding and Nina and Sophie wondered if they had the right address.

"We have an appointment to see Mr Kovacs. My name is Nina Riverton from England." Her Hungarian had an old-fashioned twang to it, but the girl behind the desk seemed not to mind and said he was expecting them. Nina and Sophie waited by the desk until they heard heavy footsteps behind them.

"Mrs Riverton, I presume?" He pronounced her name in perfect English. "And this must be your daughter?" Nina stretched out her hand and smiled. He was in his early forties, balding but his eyes were still young and he bent over and air-kissed her hand. He turned to Sophie, who was not quite sure what to do with her hand, so she just slightly bowed her head.

"I'm Sophie. Pleased to meet you. You speak very good English!"

"Well, I did spend two years at Cambridge, studying Russian history" he said. "I must have picked it up then together with a never-ending love-affair with warm beer."

He guided them up the stairs to an office with several steel desks and walls covered with files.

"Now I have had a look at this name that I was given by George Solyom. Nikolai Chalpin, wasn't it? And I have found something, which I think might be of interest. Come and sit down."

He led them to two simple typist chairs, which he had pushed up to his desk. On the desk were several files covered in beige cardboard with different numbers.

"Now. Let's begin from the beginning. Nikolai Chalpin came to Budapest in 1952 as an advisor to the Hungarian government. He dealt with questions of housing and was considered something of a rising star. He must have been clever to get to that level at such a young age, either that or he had some important contacts. He came from Leningrad, where his father had been high up in the mayor's office. Chalpin had been to Moscow University after the war. He was, of course, too young to take part in the war, but his father died in the siege and his mother, well, I can't find anything about her. According to his university papers, he studied architecture but also was a member of the

University Philharmonic Orchestra, played the piano, I believe. While at university he also helped out at the town planning department and they seem to have been impressed with him. I can't find out why he was sent to Budapest in 1952. Our archives are not complete. Too many of our files have been destroyed." Mr Kovacs smiled and shook his shoulders.

"He was married to a doctor in Leningrad and had three children, but she did not accompany him to Budapest. There is no document to prove that she even came here to visit him. I'm sure it was one of those things, neither of them had time to get a proper divorce. I gather your mother . . ."

"Yes, she was his lover for three years and I am, well, he was, is, my father. I only found out after my mother died some weeks ago."

"Mrs Riverton, I'm sorry to have to tell you that your father is also dead. He died in 1956 in the aftermath of the uprising. He was killed instantly, shot by a Russian soldier by mistake. Or, at least it's on file as being a mistake. Things were not always what they seemed in those days." His smile never reached his eyes.

"Your mother would not have been informed. His wife, still in legal terms, was next of kin. I see here that his body was returned to Leningrad in November 1956. But we did find his last will and testament in the files. I don't know why this was registered here in Budapest, still, it was. And I managed to get a copy. As you can see there is a sum set aside for your mother and you, he mentions you by name, so it must have been written after you were born. It's dated September 1956."

"Yes, I was two months old then."

"It says here that they tried to get hold of Magda Gozstonyi and her daughter Kristina but that they had left the country. Is that correct?"

"Yes, we left just before the uprising, at the end of October. I gather that my father, it still feels odd to think of him as my father, arranged for my mother and me to have exit visas. We left for Paris and I think the plan was for them to meet there once the uprising was over."

"Well, let me stress that the sum he wanted to give you was not enormous. You have not missed much from a financial point of view. I suppose whatever he had went to his wife. But I'm sure you are pleased to know that he thought of you and your mother. I have no record of his children, but I might be able to find out if you want to know more."

"No, only he was part of my life. His wife and children are not. And besides, they will probably not want to meet a half-sister at this time in their lives. I am so glad to hear that he didn't just desert my mother. She never stopped waiting for him. Quite a story, isn't it?"

Sophie, who had been sitting quietly, looked at the files and almost whispered.

"I think it's so romantic."

"Yes, it really is, "Mr Kovacs replied. "I don't think anyone would wait a life time for a lover in these days. I'm so glad that I've been able to help."

Nina and Sophie said goodbye, but he rose from the desk and asked if they would like to see the rest of the building.

"It's going to be turned into a museum. This is the house where the Hungarian Nazis and later the Communists had their headquarters. Both parties used the basement for interrogation and executions. It has really been a house of terror, but now, finally, we hope to one day open this to the general public so that they can see this house and remember those who died here. We must never forget our wretched history. Never."

He smiled. "We are in great need of funds for this project. If you feel that we've been of any help to you, you'll find a box for donations by the front desk."

Nina and Sophie both opened their bags and in silence they dropped some brightly coloured but worn notes in the wooden box.

Chapter Ten

Edward Riverton

In a strange way Magda's death brought Nina and me closer. These damned lawyers try their best to separate you, but some ties are too strong to sever. I know that Magda never saw me as the ideal son-in-law and it is true that we didn't get on very well. She was totally and utterly egotistical. Never a good mother and I think Nina had rather a tough childhood and I think Nina needs me now and she's still my wife.

And now when Sophie has moved back home, yes. I still call it home, odd that, and I hope I'll have a chance of mending fences with my daughter. And also to come to some sort of terms with Nina. She has changed, seems younger and more content suddenly.

After returning home from Budapest Sophie started her summer job and life returned to almost normal for Nina. She was being a mother again and enjoyed having dinner on the table for Sophie when she returned home and she found a certain pleasure in complaining about the dirty clothes dropped on the bathroom floor and grimy coffee mugs left all over the house. "I seem to enjoy this streak of masochism," Nina thought as she happily gathered the clothes from the floor.

Paul was still on his gap year and planned to return for his first university year in September and by then Nina's life would be almost back to normal. Except without Edward. The divorce was slowly grinding its way through heaps of papers and the decree nisi arrived after Nina's return from Budapest. Edward and Nina had, without the help of their adversarial lawyers, reached some kind of agreement, which meant that Nina would stay in the house until the children left home. After that the house would be sold and Nina would move to a smaller place and the money raised would be put into a pension fund for her. Pension, a word that immediately conjured up grey hair, soft slippers and Saga cruises.

Sophie still refused to meet her father on her own. The two of them had always had a special bond and she saw herself as the wronged party just as strongly as Nina did. The name of Sasha Ledger was never mentioned in Wyckham Wood. Nina knew through Joshua Green that Edward still lived in her flat up in London, but Nina would only ever contact him at his office. His secretary always sounded embarrassed when Nina phoned, she had almost been part of the family and had spent many Sunday lunches with them. Nina had always suspected that Miss Greenhalgh had harboured a crush on Edward; her eyes would never leave his face when he spoke. At times even Edward found it slightly disconcerting with this unfettered admiration. Things had changed after he had left home and Miss Greenhalgh now had a chill in her voice, when mentioning Edward's name. She felt forsaken, too.

When Sophie returned to her mother Edward must have seen an opportunity to make a move on his recalcitrant daughter. He telephoned Nina and invited himself to dinner with the excuse that there were still papers to go through and they also needed to discuss the insurance of the house, which on paper, at least, still belonged to them both. "And I'd love to talk to Sophie about her allowance for next term. If need be, I'm willing to increase it. Tell her that!" Nina admired his tactics while at the same time she hoped her daughter would see through his ruse and stay away.

They settled on a date at the end of the week and Nina went into planning mode. This was the first time that Edward would come to the house for a meal since he moved out and she wanted it to be perfect and not like one of their "married" dinners, it had to be different to show that she was now in charge. When Sophie came home that evening Nina told her that Edward wanted to increase her allowance, but that he needed to discuss it with her in order to reach a satisfactory sum to both of them.

"If I were you, I'd make up a budget with all your outgoings, that'll impress Dad. And it'll make him more amenable to a proper rise." Why was she collaborating in Edward's ruse? She knew it was because she needed Sophie there as a support.

"Do I have to see him?" Sophie wailed. "I can do the budget and then you can discuss it with him."

"No, Sophie. If I can see him, so can you. And eventually you have to talk to him. You hardly spoke to him in Paris at Gramma's funeral and he was terribly upset. Paul has lunched with Daddy several times and I know they talk over the phone quite regularly and . . ."

"Yes, I know, and it's because Paul needs more money. It's a simple as that. Who do you think supports Paul, while he's swanning around Latin America? Dad, of course. And he also needs an allowance for his first year at Newcastle."

"Well, Daddy could play this game, too, and insist that now, when you've got your inheritance from Gramma, you can contribute to your own education."

"But Gramma said it was for me to spend on something fun and university isn't fun."

In the end Sophie reluctantly gave in and said she would be present at the dinner. Nina saw Sophie's change of heart as a success then realized, with a pang, that it was a victory for Edward, not her. She was still doing his bidding.

~

The early September evening was still warm; laughter travelled from neighbours' gardens and lifted Nina's spirits as she put a Provencal tablecloth and some flowers matching the sun-drenched colours of the cloth. In a cooler she put the bottle of Rosé, she had learnt to appreciate with Jacques, hoping that sipping it would remind her that she had a past with a lover, or at least, had for a couple of nights. She was not the deserted wife, praying for her erring husband's return, not any longer.

In the oven was one of Edward's favourite dishes, a stuffed leg of lamb. They would have drinks and olives in the garden and then the meal would be served in the kitchen. Nina had contemplated the dining room, but for just the three of them, that seemed a bit too formal. She had taken equal care with planning her outfit as with the menu. The red sundress Sophie had inspired her to buy was a bit too summery and would not look the same with a cardigan thrown over her cold shoulders. Instead she had selected a skirt in blue cotton with swirls of white and with it a white long-sleeved T-shirt, casual but still slightly dressy.

Sophie changed from her rather smart office attire and appeared in torn jeans and a T-shirt with a name on it, a pop-band Nina guessed. The shirt had obviously been thrown into the wash with something dark as it had an all over greyish tint that made the name illegible.

"Why did you change, darling?"

"I've been in bloody uniform all day, skirt and blouse and TIGHTS, ghastly. I think I've the right to relax when I get home."

"But you know your father is coming for dinner?"

"Yeah, so what?"

Easy, easy, Nina thought to herself. She did not want to have Sophie in a sulk by the time Edward arrived, no, she wanted to show him a family that coped perfectly well without him. She swallowed her response and went back to laying the kitchen table.

As the time got nearer to eight, Nina became more tense. She looked at the roast again and again, changed the cutlery and brought out the silver, then realised it was from his family and he would probably ask for its return, so out with the stainless steel again. Should she have the cut glass decanter for the red wine, or would that look out of place in the kitchen?

Was she smelling of lamb? Nina took two steps at a time upstairs and in the bathroom sprayed some more of Edward's favourite scent on her neck and on her wrists. She regretted it immediately. She should have used some of that new citrussy cologne she had bought at the Charles de Gaulle airport. That scent was non-committal unlike the seductive Chanel, which had never suited her.

The bell rang and Nina's hands felt clammy as she opened the door. Edward's face could hardly be seen behind a large bunch of pink roses.

"And here is a one of freesias for Sophie", he said with the stiff smile of a gate-crasher.

Nina was grateful for the two bouquets, wrapped in matching tissue paper and tied with expensive silk ribbons. This was not an impulse buy from the petrol station down the road. The flowers gave her an excuse to leave Edward in the garden as she went in search for two vases.

"And help yourself to a glass of wine, and pour me one, too," she called from the utility room. "Sophie is joining you in a second, she's on the phone." Nina waved and indicated with her hands that Sophie should join her father. "NOW!" she mouthed to her daughter, who pretended not to see her mother's gesturing.

She put the roses on the sideboard and handed the smaller vase with freesias to Sophie.

"From your father and they're from that very fancy florist in Sloane Street," said Nina as her daughter finally came off the phone.

"Bet they're the price of at least two CD's."

Together they walked out to join Edward on the patio. He had already uncorked the wine and poured three glasses. He had not touched his.

"Darling Sophie, I can't tell you how wonderful it is to see you. You've lost weight."

"Do you think so?" There was a slight coyness in her response. "Thanks, and thanks for the freesias. You know, they were Gramma's favourite flowers?"

"That's why I bought them." They smiled at each other and for a moment they had both forgotten that it had been months since they actually had spoken to each other. Nina lifted her glass and looked at her daughter and wondered if he was right. She could not see that Sophie had lost any weight.

"We're glad you could come and join us for dinner. We've a lot to discuss, so I suggest you two talk about Sophie's allowance, while I potter in the kitchen. We can eat in about twenty minutes. Is that ok?"

Neither of them looked up. Sophie pulled a sheet of paper out of her voluminous bag and put it on the table.

"I've prepared a budget, Dad. You'll see exactly what I need for rent and food. Then there's books and well, just living . . ."

"Well, done darling. Now let me have a look." Their heads were close together as Sophie went through her figures. Nina knew they would not miss her as she left the garden. She took a deep gulp of the icy rosé and spread the smoked salmon on some blinis and topped them with horseradish cream. This was a dish that Sophie and she had been given at a small restaurant in Buda. At least she could talk to Edward about their trip.

Suddenly she heard laughter from the garden.

"You don't mean that, dad. After all this time. How could she? And what are *you* going to do without her?"

"I'll survive. And the next one will be the oldest and ugliest girl I can find."

For a split second Nina's heart stopped. Her ears turned towards the garden.

"Well, Miss Greenhalgh has been with me for eighteen years and maybe she thought it was time for a change."

They both laughed again and Nina's heart resumed its beat.

"I've forgotten how lovely this kitchen is on a summer's night with the French doors open. And I must say, Nina, the garden is looking great. The roses have never looked better. Stupid of me, I should have brought you something else, but I know you've always loved them." He glanced at the vase on the sideboard.

Edward complimented her on the smoked salmon, which gave Sophie an excuse to tell her father about their trip. He listened attentively as Sophie told him of Nikolai Chalpin, Nina's real father and how they had found out about his life, and death, in Budapest. Edward suddenly stood up and laid his hands on Nina's shoulders.

"Nina, dear Nina, you always felt neglected by your mother. I tried so hard to make that up to you. Now, maybe, you understand Magda better and why she was so reticent about her life before Paris. Poor Magda, poor Nina."

He leant forward and kissed her in a brotherly fashion on the forehead. Instinctively Nina wanted to bring his head down and kiss him properly. She turned her head down and closed her eyes, afraid that he had seen that moment of attraction.

"Now for the main course, roast lamb, stuffed with mushrooms as you like it."

Nina lifted the lamb on to the sideboard and turned to get the carving knife. She brought out the steel to sharpen it and suddenly Edward stood up and took the knife from her hand. They stared at each other.

"Let me carve. A bit of outer, isn't that what you want, Nina?"

Nina gently took the knife from him.

"No, I'll carve", said Nina resolutely. "You're our guest."

Edward sat down and his shoulders sank. He did not cheer up until the summer pudding was served, another favourite. Edward had once told her that Sasha did not cook, she would only microwave ready cooked meals. "And they're not that bad," he had said without too much enthusiasm, "but then she is a fulltime lawyer."

When the coffee was ready Nina carried the cafetiére into the living room. Sophie slumped down in the sofa next to her father.

"I wish you could've come with us to Budapest, Dad. It was great."

"I wish I could have, too. I remember only as if yesterday, how old were you Sophie, when we went to Budapest? Five? Your mother and I wanted to have a bit of a second honeymoon and we stayed at this old-fashioned hotel, can't remember the name."

"Gellert." Nina smiled at the memory.

"and they'd given us a single room and that was the last room they had. One tiny single bed and I had to sleep on a rather lumpy sofa."

"No, Edward," Nina said with a laugh, "*I* slept on that sofa, well, I didn't sleep all that much, actually, but you did. So it didn't turn out to be too much of a second honeymoon, did it?"

"Don't we have some photographs in our album from that trip. I remember I had a new camera. Wouldn't you like to see them, Sophie?"

Nina stood up and went next door. She rummaged around the shelves in the study and finally he found the right album. Budapest, yes. It had been thirteen years ago.

She spread it out on the coffee table and there were the photographs of the Elisabeth Bridge, the Castle on the top of the Buda ridge, the Houses of Parliament and there a photo of them together taken by another tourist when they had travelled by boat along the Danube down to Sztendre. Nina looked at they younger version of herself, smiling at the camera with Edward's arm around in a manner indicating ownership rather than passion.

"Nina do you remember? That was that Sunday. We couldn't read the timetable so we missed the boat back, but a funny little man with an enormous moustache, he was a brewer, took us back to Budapest in his car. You were dead scared, because we could literally see the ground move under our feet, so thin was the floor in the car. To thank him, more for our survival than the lift, we invited him for dinner at the hotel. He'd never been there before but found to his delight that his beer was sold there. You do remember, don't you? And he insisted that we try some of his brew and strong it was, too. He helped us navigate through the menu and we had a fantastic meal and it all came to a fiver or less than that even. Yes, we did have a good time, Nina, didn't we? "Nina smiled, heat rushing to her cheeks.

"Budapest was special, and now, knowing about your mother's time there with your father, it must be even more special." He rose again from the sofa and walked over to her chair.

"Come on, Sophie, let's give your mum a hug." Sophie stood up and for a minute or two all three embraced each other without saying a word. As if given a signal they moved away from each other, embarrassed by this tactile encounter.

"Mints" Nina held out the silver salver and remembered not Budapest but the night when Edward had told her about Sasha. The warmth from the unexpected hug evaporated. She shuddered.

Edward returned to the album and looked at photographs with Sophie, their heads again so close. Nina thought of the twenty years she had lived with and for this man and now he seemed to be a stranger, someone with whom she shared certain memories but nothing else.

After a while Sophie stood up and gave her father a hug.

"Thanks for the cheque, dad. It was nice to see you, but I've an early start tomorrow and need an early night. But it was really nice." She pecked Nina on the cheek and thanked her for dinner. And without looking back at either of them she danced out of the room and up the stairs. Two minutes later they heard the water cascading in the shower.

"Thank you for inviting me tonight. As you know Sophie has been quite awkward since I left. I've had no trouble with Paul, but Sophie has not returned my calls, not wanted to see me for lunch in town and although she doesn't return my letters, as she did in the beginning, she still doesn't write back. It's been tough. I've missed her, no, all of you all so much."

Edward patted the cushion of the sofa that Sophie had just left.

"Come and sit here, Nina. Let's talk."

Nina moved from her chair and sat down as far away as possible from Edward, leaning over her elbow on the armrest.

CHAPTER ELEVEN

Edward Riverton again

In a way I feel as if I've been on a holiday. I am a different person when I'm with Sasha. She's interested in what I do, my thoughts and she cares, yet, there's something missing. I've always hated change and nothing could be more of a change than leaving your wife and children after twenty years. I actually miss the boredom, the predictability of my former life. The dinners with old friends and neighbours, Sunday lunches with my mother down in the country, a duty which was easier to cope with when I was accompanied by Nina and the children. My mother is not quite sure how to deal with the new situation. She's polite to Sasha and then I can see how she feels disloyal to Nina and she closes up like a mussel. We see my mother in London or in a pub near her home, she has yet to invite us to the cottage and I know she still has photos of Nina and the children on display, even a silver-framed photo from our wedding.

Nina was tired but she could see that Edward wanted to talk. The thrill of seeing Edward for the first time back in the house had been oddly dispiriting and had left her feeling wrung dry. He pointed out that she had changed a few pictures around, but did not bring up the question of who should get what out of the household chattels. Whatever they had, they had bought together except for a few things that they had been given by Edward's parents, when they had moved to a smaller house. Their Victorian chest of drawers had ended up in the guest room and the two tallboys were on the landing still reeking of Mrs Riverton's mothballs.

The grandfather clock in the hall she would miss, not for its looks or value, but for the comforting tick-tock, which always forced Nina's own heart to slow down. She looked around the room, their living room, and everywhere were pieces of furniture or ornaments, which had become part of their lives. They were like archaeological finds, able to tell future historians the story of their marriage. The mantle-piece clock they found in a small shop in Brighton and which they thought was such a treasure. It later turned out to be reproduction and not worth a tenth of what they had paid, but they still thought of it as a treasure. The fruit still-life in its ornate golden frame, that Nina had fallen in love with at an exhibition. Edward had gone back later and bought it as a surprise for her birthday. Every object had a story to tell, even the house itself.

Nina remembered when she first saw the house. For months she had been scouring the property pages of the local paper for a house nearer the children's school, but nothing suitable ever came up. Then one blustery autumn day she drove down Wardell Drive and saw two men affixing a For Sale sign on the iron gate of a redbrick Victorian house. She stopped the car and wrote down the number of the estate agent on the back of her hand.

This was the kind of house she had wanted, one with character. The roof was slate and edged with a border that must once have been painted white, now it was a flaky grey. Wooden curlicues like dirty lace framed the windows and a half rotten ornamental pole rose proudly from the peak of the upper bay roof. It was a solid building that tried hard to resist both age and neglect. The sash windows were curtain-less and the whole house had an air of desertion. Next to the faded front door grew a tall cypress. The teardrop shaped tree made the house look even sadder and made Nina think of the small cemetery near Magda's flat in Paris. The drive was tessellated but most of the old tiles were broken and along the drive rusty heads of hydrangea drooped in weedy flowerbeds. For Nina it was love at first sight. She looked around and on both sides the houses had been done up. There were boxy estate cars in the front drives.

Magda will hate this house, Nina had thought. So suburban, so English. But Edward had agreed, not because he liked it all that much, but in his eyes it was a house of possibilities, which meant it would go up in value. They left their flat in London and moved only weeks later. Nina lived nine months with builders, so long that she could not imagine what it was like not to have a thin film of dust everywhere, even on her tongue. Her love affair with the house grew and every time she returned to put the key in the lock she felt that there was a special welcome for her. Edward had never been involved with the house the way she was, Nina almost ached of longing after a holiday away. She needed to be close to her things, be in her own private space, touch her books and rest her eyes on pictures she loved.

They had bought the sofa they sat on when Edward had been given his first salary cheque as a partner. A comfortable two-seater now covered in russet linen, a change from its original psychedelic flower pattern. Just as their tastes had changed, so had their home. It had become more and more like the house where Edward grew up. Muted colours, dark mahogany, small occasional tables dotted with polished silverware, potted plants in French cache-pots. Whatever happened to their minimalist life-style, the Picasso reproductions Nina had brought from France, their Scandinavian furniture?

"Do you remember that pattern, those blobs of orange flowers, when the sofa was new? How could we ever have fallen for that?" Nina asked Edward with a smile.

"How could I forget? But you thought it was the cat's whiskers. Very trendy, you told me. I also remember that it cost over two hundred pounds, which was more than a month's salary then. My mother thought it vulgar and she was right, of course. It was not long before we had it recovered."

Nina had forgotten her mother-in-law's face, when she had proudly shown off their expensive purchase.

"Very brave of you, Nina, to go for something so bold," had been her tight-lipped comment. And as Edward said, his mother had been right, it was far too bright, but, vulgar, no. Nina lost her courage after that and went for safe and traditional. The Picasso prints bought in Bordeaux during her university days were now stored in the attic. The plain teak furniture was long gone, exchanged for Victorian auction finds.

"You wanted to talk." Nina poured some tepid coffee into Edward's cup. He cleared his throat.

"I don't really know how to say this, Nina. It's been a hellish experience leaving home—and my family. I miss you all so much. I had no idea how close we really were. I even miss the dog! And don't think that I haven't seen the misery I've caused. Sophie doesn't trust me any more, Paul only gets in touch, when he's run out of money and you, well, I seem to speak more often to your rotweiler of a lawyer than with you. And even my mother seems to think that I have behaved appallingly. As you know, we haven't got our degree absolute yet, so we can still stop it all." He looked at Nina.

These were the words that Nina had dreamed of hearing for months after Edward had left her. Now they brought her no joy, only more question marks.

"What do you mean? Are you saying that it's finished between you and . . . Sasha? It's over? You want to come back home? Is that it?"

"Sort of, yes."

"Sort of? What do you mean?" Nina heard her own voice with an unexpected sharp edge to it. "Is it over with Sasha or not?"

"Well, it will be, if I come back home again."

Nina rose and walked away from the sofa. She did not dare to show her face to Edward as she was hot with rage. Her hands were clammy and she wiped them as if her skirt was an apron.

"Are you telling me that you will only leave her if I take you back? Is that what you're saying?" Her voice was shrill.

Edward looked intently at the creases of his well-pressed trousers and after thinking for some seconds, without lifting his head, whispered. "No, no, you make it all sound far too dramatic."

"No, that's what you mean, isn't it? If you come back, then you'll leave her?"

"Yes," he answered, now finally looking at Nina. "Yes, of course, darling."

"And does Sasha know about this plan of yours?"

"Let's leave Sasha out of this. We're talking about our future, of us being together as a family again."

Nina walked back to the sofa and sat down. She took his hand in hers and said with the same voice she used when talking to the unruly children at the gallery.

"Edward, this has come as a bit of a surprise for me. I can't really take it in just now. I suggest you go home, wherever that may be, and then we talk later in the week."

"Is that a No then?"

"Give me time to think. Please." She lent forward and kissed his forehead. Then stood up and carried the coffee tray back to the kitchen. Edward followed.

"I'm glad you liked the roses. I wanted to buy red ones. Oh, darling Nina . . ."

"Not now, Edward. We'll talk later in the week." She gently manoeuvred him towards the front door. As it closed she leant her face against the cool glass pane.

"Bloody Edward" she whispered before turning the light off in the hall.

She was shaking. As usual it calmed her nerves to stack the dirty dishes in the machine, wipe clean the surfaces. She poured some hot water in the sink to wash the glasses by hand. "Crystal, never in the dishwasher, it ruins the flavour of the wine" she could still hear the advice Edward had given her years ago. Without even thinking about it, she pulled out the tray and put the wine-stained glasses in the dishwasher.

She felt strangely elated by her gesture of defiance and even more so, when she poured herself a glass of Edward's fine brandy, drunk only on special occasions. She sat down at the kitchen table, put on some Mozart and stared out at the unlit garden. As her eyes got used to the darkness, she noticed the outlines of the bushes, the fruit—heavy apple tree and the sculpted hedge. It looked mystical and romantic at this time of night.

Her thoughts tumbled in her brain. She tried to conjure up the scene of Edward's proposal, if that's what it was. There had been no passion in his plea, it was more like a man who wanted to come back to his old barber after trying a more fashionable one. He had looked old. His hair, his suit and even his face were grey. Was this man the one she had mourned and cried for until she ran out of tears? Nina swallowed the last of the expensive brandy and was not sure if it was the drink or the evening's events that made her head spin.

"Darling, darling. I have wonderful news. Are you listening?" Tessa's dark tobacco-tinged voice made Nina sit down on the chaise longue. She knew that Tessa always took her time with good news, bad news she usually kept to herself.

~

"Jacques and I are getting engaged. You remember Jacques? Don't you?"

Nina's felt as if a fist had hit her chest.

"But you're not divorced yet."

"Is that your way of saying Congratulations? I thought you'd be pleased, especially as we see you as our fairy godmother. You brought us together. We were hoping you'd be my matron of honour. No, we're not planning a fancy wedding, just a small intimate one, here in St. Remy and then dinner afterwards at Chez Julien. Just before Christmas, we hope. It all depends on how quick the lawyers can work. Thank God, my dear ex is as eager as I am to get out of this marriage. And Jacques is already divorced. So what do you say?"

"Tessa, of course I am delighted for you. It was just a bit unexpected, to say the least. You hardly know each other."

"You sound exactly like my mother."

"No, Tessa, I'm really pleased for you, for both of you and of course I'll be your matron if that is what you really want. By the way, I had Edward here for dinner yesterday and he wants to come back home."

"That's fantastic news, I'm so glad. So when is he moving back?"

"I don't know. I don't even know if that's what I want. It's all so confusing . . ."

"But you've missed him, haven't you?"

"Yes, but do I still miss him? Or is it being married that I miss? I haven't said yes yet. I've asked for some time to think about it."

"Maybe you're doing the right thing, but if I were you I'd get him back sooner than later, before that other woman gets her claws in too deep."

They decided to meet for a drink the following week, when Tessa was coming home for a week.

"And give my congratulations to Jacques. He's a very lucky man."

As Nina said it she tried not to think of his hands caressing Tessa's inner thighs.

As she put the phone down Sophie came into the living-room.

"Mum, did I hear that Dad is coming back, that he's leaving that woman?"

Sophie's face, both expectant and worried, reflected Nina's own feelings.

"I don't know yet. There's still a lot to think of. And I need time."

Chapter Twelve

Sasha Ledger

*I never thought of myself as The Other Woman. I did not lure
Eddie from his wife and I certainly did not put any pressure on
him to leave her. He was unhappy, that was clear for all to see and
I make him happy.*

*I've never met Nina, but through Eddie I have quite a picture of
her. Houseproud, suburban and, sadly, she's let herself go a bit.
Some women don't deserve their men, it's as simple as that. She's
never shown any interest in Eddie's work, even though he is a
brilliant deal maker.*

*His mother adores him and is proud of him, she never was.
And I think she has turned the children against him and that's
inexcusable. Pure spite. Women of her kind do get bitchy, they
don't behave like the English, do they? Hungarian I think Eddie
said, well, there you are.*

"So what are you going to do with Dad?" Sophie asked the
following morning. She was up early and had washed her
hair, now hanging in wet strings down her back.

"I really don't know. I think we should discuss it together.
And maybe even talk to Paul and see what he thinks."

"Mum, we can't make up your mind for you. You have to
do that. And whatever you decide we'll be behind you. I'm
sure Paul thinks the same." Sophie twisted her damp hair
around her finger. She looked as if she was embarrassed that
her mother had turned to her for advice, Nina thought.

Nina had not given Edward a time by which she would give her answer, somehow she wanted to keep him on tenterhooks, a mean-spirited revenge for the long nights she had waited for him. Of course, she would say yes, there was no doubt.

She enjoyed these sweet days. Nina had finally some power over Edward — and even more so over Sasha, this shadow of a woman that she had learnt to hate as symbol of her broken marriage. Did Sasha ever think of her? No, Nina did not think so, but soon enough she would.

Nina did not think much about Edward, it was as if he was almost incidental. Would she be happy to have him back in her bed? She had to admit hat Jacques had given her more pleasure, but then their affair had the feverish flush of newness and exploration. Edward was known territory. She knew every crevice of his lean body, his smell and the softness of his hairless chest, his padded feet with the sunken arches. She thought of him cutting the hair in his ears, a Saturday morning ritual that always irritated her as she had to scoop the offending hairs out of the basin. His irritating tidiness, how he always folded his trousers onto the trouser press, even when they were about to make love.

It was as if the year away from Edward had changed him, not her and she was not sure she was in love with the new Edward. It was the marriage she wanted back, not him. But her marriage was with Edward, and once he was back all her doubts were bound to clear like mist on a summer's morning.

Before the week was over Edward phoned. He thanked her for the dinner, as if he were a polite guest and then suggested Saturday dinner at La Bottega in the village, their favourite restaurant, where they had celebrated so many anniversaries and birthdays.

"I'll pick you up at 7.45. Can't wait to see you and we can discuss further the matter we touched on last time." He made it sound like a business proposition.

When Saturday arrived she took a long scented bath and this time she frothed in Chanel-scented bubbles Edward had given to her for their last Christmas together. The expensive lingerie given to her by Tessa came out of its box and she wanted to show Edward the blue dress she had bought for her dinner with Tor. The memory of that disastrous night was almost gone from her mind, but she still liked the dress, and it had, after all, worked. She had invested, no splashed out on, a new pair of high heels, something she seldom wore and her hair had been recently trimmed and the grey streak covered by tint. Not too bad, thought Nina as she paraded gingerly in her heels in front of the mirror.

Exactly at quarter to eight Edward rang the door bell. Sophie was away for the week-end with a girlfriend in Essex and Nina had already changed the sheets on the double bed. She would ask Edward back for a cup of coffee, and then, maybe, if she felt like it, invite him upstairs. She walked slowly to the door, as not to show how nervous she was.

"I've booked for eight, so we'd better set off now as not to be late," Edward said without coming into the hall. He pointed to the open door of his car parked in the street, not next to her car in the drive as he used to. She went to get her coat and closed the front door. It was a soft evening with just a hint of autumnal cool in the air. The leaves had just started turning and soon the front drive would be covered in gold. The hydrangeas had turned from vibrant pink into a resigned rusty red and the lavender had lost its blue heads and their long-legged stems drooped towards the ground.

She stepped into Edward's car, a company perk, and leant her head back on the leather-covered headrest. She had forgotten the pleasure of a smooth ride. Her own Japanese car was more of a shopping trolley. Her hand stroked the smooth leather and her eyes wandered to the pocket in the door. A map, some brochures hastily put there and, Nina looked again, a pair of pale blue leather gloves. Sasha's. She noticed the Dior logo on the cuff and immediately priced them in her mind. Nina lost her gloves on a regular basis and always bought the cheapest she could find. And Sasha seems to have misplaced hers as well, she thought, but being a well-paid lawyer maybe she can afford the loss.

They did not exchange a word during the ten minute ride down to the centre of Wyckham Wood. Edward parked the car on the verge just outside the oak-beamed restaurant with its thatched roof, not very Italian and Roberto, probably as Italian as the building, rushed out rubbing his hands in exaggerated delight.

"Nina, Nina, what a pleasure to see you. I told Eduardo, when he phoned to book, that it has been far too long since we've seen you here. Come on in, welcome."

He managed to kiss her at the same time as he patted Edward on the back and relieved her of her coat He pushed them into the small dining room, where his wife smiled and pointed to a table in the corner. It was the only table with a white table cloth, the other oak tables had linen place mats and on the table was a red rose in a crystal vase, a bottle in an ice bucket and two lit candles.

"Eduardo said it was a special evening, so here we are, we made it a little bit special for you, here in a corner." He winked theatrically as he opened the bottle of champagne.

"Why not push the boat out a bit?" Edward said with a rather sheepish smile. "It is a celebration after all."

Nina froze. It was all too quick, too pat. She wanted to drag it out, enjoy the excitement.

Roberto and his wife fussed around them all through dinner and there was no time to bring up the real subject of how to stop the divorce. After a molten chocolate soufflé, Roberto finally left them alone, and they both stirred their coffee vigorously to break the silence.

"Well, as I said, I have missed you all very much and would like to come home. I think it would be best for all of us to do it as quickly as possible."

"I have to ask. Is it the family you have missed or is it me?"

"Both of course." There was an irritated tinge in his voice.

"And it's all over with Sasha?" It was half question, half statement.

"Well, it will be, once I tell her I'm moving back in with you."

"What do you mean, you're still together? Does she know about your plans?"

"I *will* tell her, but not until you give me the go ahead."

"So you're going back to her after tonight and what do you tell her? That I'm just another dinner with a client, like you used to tell me when you've been out with her?" Her voice rose and Roberto came over and proffered some brandy. "Not now", Nina said with more irritation than she had meant. Edward looked both morose and angry.

"Listen," said Nina, once Roberto had turned his back, "I don't even want to discuss us getting back together as long as you're living with her. Move out, and then we can talk. Now I think it's time to pay the bill, don't you?" She hated the edge in her own voice, but her plans for a romantic evening had melted quicker than the ice in the bucket.

Even Roberto realised that things were not right and his ebullience was muted as Edward finally paid, — with the company credit card, Nina noted.

"I'll phone you later." Edward did not even get out of the car once they were back in Wardell Drive and before she had managed to unlock the Yale and the mortice he had driven off.

Nina was too tired to be upset. She took off her blue dress, her fine silken underwear and stood naked in front of the mirror again.

"I'm all right. I AM all right"

That night she slept naked between the clean sheets.

Two days later there was a message on her telephone answering machine. It was from Edward, who informed her that he was off to his annual shindig in Washington and would be back in ten days' time, when he hoped they could set up another meeting.

Nina felt more like an appointments secretary than an object of courtship.

She did not count the days and had quite forgotten about the offer of a meeting when she received a letter from Edward. She was surprised to see his sloping handwriting on an envelope and thought it must be some legal papers he had forwarded. She brought the envelope to the kitchen and sat down with her morning cup.

"Dearest Nina,

You might remember that we discussed me moving back in at Wardell Drive again, when last we met. I was slightly surprised at your reaction, but now realise that it was for the best.

On my return from Washington Sasha told me that she was pregnant and I therefore want to marry her as soon as possible. May I therefore ask you to hurry your lawyer up as I have instructed mine to set the wheels in motion.

I will be grateful if you'll let me inform the children. The baby is due in six months time and we hope to marry before Christmas.

In no way does this reflect on my feelings for you. I will always remember our years with gratitude and wish you all the best.

Yours ever,

Edward

PS. We might have to discuss the question of the house contents sooner than planned. Sasha and I have made an offer on a house in Pimlico."

Nina read it and read it again. The words did not make sense to her. And without even noticing it, she started crying. She knew she did not want Edward, but she did not want Sasha to have him either and the thought of a semi-sibling of her own children made her feel nauseous. This, in Nina's eyes, was the ultimate betrayal.

When Sophie came home that night from work, Nina was desperate to tell her, but in spite of everything she felt she owed it to Edward to let him tell Sophie and Paul. Although, she did admit to herself, that Sophie was bound to react the same way as she had; with a mixture of disbelief and horror. Still, Nina remained silent.

Edward told Sophie the following week, also by letter, and she screamed and swore until she was hoarse. Her father's desertion after having offered to come back home was a greater crime than leaving in the first place. That night she crept into Nina's bed and they lay huddled together and only fell asleep when the first grey light peeped in through the heavy curtains.

During the long night the name of Sasha Ledger was never mentioned. She was only referred to as That Woman.

CHAPTER THIRTEEN

Mrs Edward Riverton

*Edward's wife was trouble until the bitter end. She tried to slow
down the process of the divorce but we would have none of that.
We used a very good lawyer, who finally got things moving. The
one Edward had to start with, he was useless, some old friend
of his. His ex-wife, I'm relieved I can say that now, quibbled
about every stick of furniture and in the end I told Edward – For
god's sake, it's not worth the fight for some Victorian mahogany.
Surely, he could see that I wanted to have things WE had chosen
in our new home.*

The divorce finally came through at the end of October
and soon afterwards Sophie received a formal invitation to
the wedding of Sasha Ledger and Edward Riverton at the
Chelsea and Kensington Registry office to be followed by a
luncheon at The Savoy.

Sophie tore her invitation up into small pieces. "I'd rather
go swimming with sharks than turn up to see that fat
woman marry my father." Edward had tried to jolly Sophie
along to a theatre evening with Sasha, but Sophie had
turned it down at the last moment. "I'm not into musicals
and anyway seeing *Chicago* about women murdering their
errant husbands might just be a bit too inspiring," she told
her shocked father. It was only the threat of a cut in her
allowance that made her re-think her recalcitrance, and
when it was followed by an offer of a cheque to buy a
nice outfit for the wedding Sophie changed her mind. "I
suppose I have to meet her eventually," Sophie said and
glued the invitation together again. Paul accepted by email
from Ecuador when his father had promised to pay for the

air ticket. Mrs Riverton, Edward's mother, telephoned Nina to tell her that she was wearing her blue outfit, last worn at Ascot ten years earlier. "I do not approve of the pregnancy and this hurried re-marriage. Edward's father would turn in his grave, well, his urn, but I think I should be there. Besides, the girl's nice enough and I am rather excited about another grandchild, well, I didn't expect that, did I at my age?" Nina thought she might as well has said "as you're obviously too old."

Nina had spent one evening with Edward since their unsuccessful evening at La Bottega. He had turned up with a list of the things he expected to have delivered to his new home in Pimlico. Nina had to admit he was generous and just wanted things that came from his parents' home — and the computer, which Nina never used anyway. "You can stay here until you feel ready to leave. Or the children have left home. I'll do my best to help you financially, but with our son soon to be born . . ."

"So you know it's a son?" Nina interrupted.

"Yes, it's wonderful isn't it? We're thrilled." He stopped himself and looked down on the list. "Well, it wasn't planned. You must believe me. It's not exactly the right time for Sasha. She's just been made a partner in her law firm. She never thought she wanted a family, but now she's quite excited and a boy, well, that's special."

"You're not expecting congratulations? Are you?"

"Sorry, I shouldn't really have mentioned it. I haven't told Sophie it's a boy yet. I find she's not all that interested. Paul knows. He looks forward to a brother, at least that's what he says."

"It seems to be a busy season for weddings. Tessa, you remember her, she is getting married in December down in St. Remy to a French estate agent, who."

"An estate agent? Oh, no, surely Tessa could do better than that."

"Actually, he is a charming man. I brought the two of them together and Tessa's asked me to be her matron of honour."

"Matron, that sounds a bit spinsterish. But I suppose you're past the maid of honour stage."

"Thanks," Nina said with a laugh. "But I AM a spinster now again, aren't I?"

"No, my darling, you are a woman with a past and, no doubt, with an exciting future ahead of you, while I'll be spending my nights nursing mewling babes."

For a short moment they looked at each other and both were aware that their years together could not be erased as easily as the lawyers had promised.

Paul came home a week before the wedding. Nina had always had a very special relationship with her son. They had never been close, but they had an emotional attachment, which none of them could explain in words. Like Edward, Paul was quiet and introverted. During his childhood he had never been shown any signs of temper, he just wanted to be left alone with his books and paints. He had always preferred his own company, while his sister needed stimulation and company. From an early age he had showed artistic talent and Nina and Paul often spent time together in galleries and museums in town. They never discussed the paintings they saw, just enjoyed the experience in silence. Paul gave her art books for her birthday, often artists she had never heard of. She loved forcing herself to look at paintings through his eyes.

When he was sent off to Edward's old boarding school Nina experienced an almost physical loss and it was made worse, because she knew he was unhappy. Not that he ever complained, but she noticed it in him, like a light being switched off. He did badly at school, a letdown for Edward, but in his last year he won a travelling award of a thousand pounds for his art portfolio. When Nina suggested a water colour course in France, he rejected the idea outright. He wanted to tour South America and he wanted to go on his own, he was, after all, over eighteen.

Paul was tall, a head taller than Nina, and never seemed to put on weight. His sand—coloured hair was straight and always fell into his hazel eyes. He had few friends and there had never been a girlfriend as far as Nina knew. He was a loner, just like Edward, when she had first met him.

After Magda's funeral he had set off from Waterloo to Brussels, where he had found an airline that cold take him to Ecuador for almost nothing. Nina had tried to look cheerful as she waved him off. He had eaten a big lunch with his father, who had given him an envelope stuffed with travellers' cheques, which made Nina's proffered pound notes seem paltry in comparison.

During the first few months through his reversed phone calls Nina could almost hear how he grew up. His voice deepened and he seemed to enjoy working in the settlement office of a banana importer. He had found a room in a family and admitted he liked being away and that Quito had great charm with its proud but dilapidated architecture. His phone calls were short and not very informative, there was always more static interference than news, but Nina relaxed just hearing his voice.

She hardly recognised the young man she picked up at the airport. He had grown a beard, well, more of a fuzz than a beard, and his skin now had a darker sheen. His body had filled out and even his walk was different. Over his shoulder was a multi-coloured woven bag, which he threw on the ground in order to kiss his mother.

"Great to see you Mum. Is Dad here, too?"

"No, darling, he'll take you out to dinner tomorrow, so that you can chat and also for you to meet his . . . well, Sasha. His girl-friend."

The word jarred.

"Great Mum. Now, how are you, let me look at you." And he swept her into his arms again. He smelled differently.

In the car she turned to her son. She suddenly felt awkward. He had seen a country she had never visited, he had got himself a job and now he could cope with a language she did not know. He returned her quizzical look and both smiled in silence. Nina wondered if she had changed, too.

"I want to hear all about Quito, the job and the family you stay with, how you're getting on. Can you cope on your wages and how's your Spanish coming on? Are there any senoritas you like? And why the beard?"

"Hey, Mum. Stop the interrogation. I've only been back twenty minutes. We've got plenty of time to talk during the next week." He patted her arm resting against the steering wheel. The rest of the drive down to Wyckham Wood was quiet apart from a purring whoosh from Paul's earphones. Nina thought she could hear Latin American rhythms.

At home Sophie hugged her brother and in no time the two had settled in the sofa, chatting away, while Nina prepared dinner. Although she was happy to hear her two children laughing, as if Paul's months away and Sophie's broken love affair had not changed anything, Nina desperately wanted to creep into their laughter rather than be an outsider. With a jolt she realised that soon they would be gone, having lives and homes of their own and Nina would be nothing but a provider of a guilty conscience if they did not visit her often enough. "Poor Mum, on her own", they would say to each other. Edward, on the other hand, would not be alone and he would provide them with both cheques and siblings.

"Darlings, dinner's ready".

Over Paul's favourite lasagne Nina fell into their laughter and her heavy thoughts lifted like steam from a kettle. Little by little Paul told them about his job, "I supply the invoices to the wholesalers, who buy our bananas. No, it's not boring. I get to talk to people all over the world." The people he stayed with was "super" and looked after him as if he were family, and, yes, hadn't he mentioned that they had two sons and three daughters? After some gentle ribbing Paul confessed that he was interested in the youngest, Maria. She was seventeen, but very mature for her years. It was the first time Paul had ever mentioned a girl and Nina and Sophie teased him until Paul tired of their questions and asked about Peter McLennan.

"I don't want that name ever mentioned in my presence. He's a shit, a real jumbo shit." To Nina's relief Sophie smiled as she said it.

It was odd seeing the children dressing up in their best clothes and knowing she would stay behind. Sophie had bought a silk dress in petrol blue and a feathery contraption, which was neither hat nor hair pin, in matching blue. Paul looked rather handsome in a dark grey suit with a blue tie. They had been told to dress up and Edward had even phoned Nina to make sure that they would be spruced up.

"Sasha's parents, are very particular, so tell, no ask, Paul to shave off that ghastly fuzz of his and I'd rather Sophie didn't have bright blue nail varnish. You understand, don't you?" It turned out that Sasha's father was some mighty mandarin in the Ministry of Justice and he had not appeared too delighted when he heard that his only daughter was to marry a divorced man. "So it's important that the kids look OK and behave." Nina did manage to persuade Sophie to use pale pink on her nails, but Paul was adamant that his beard was to stay, but he pruned it.

Nina took them to the station, she had refused to drive up to London. Instead she had invited Jen for lunch at the wine bar. "How do you spend the time when your ex gets married?" she had asked Jen, who immediately replied "with your best friend and a bottle of Chablis." The hours dragged and Nina hardly listened to Jen, who was seriously worried about the speed with which Tessa had decided to remarry.

"I want to hear all about this estate agent chap." So while Edward was repeating his vows to a new wife, his old wife extolled the virtues of her ex-lover about to marry one of her closest friends. She did not, though, tell Jen that Jacques had been her lover, but she did admit that Edward had suggested coming back. "Thank God you said no, can you imagine what you'd be going through now, if he'd left you again?"

Nina shook her head. That was a thought that had not occurred to her.

The children came back close to seven o'clock. Nina had not picked them up at the station, not after all that wine with Jen. They looked happy, whether it was due to champagne or the occasion was not a question Nina wanted a reply to. Still, she was fed all the details, "the bride was enormous and in baby blue, obviously to match all the baby clothes she'll be buying soon and her parents were very formal, boring actually, but some of Sacha's colleagues were quite nice," admitted Sophie and Paul suggested that the bright young lawyer with the Porsche, who had given them a lift to Victoria, "obviously fancied Sophie something rotten".

After the Savoy luncheon the couple had set off for France in a hired Rolls-Royce, "baby-blue, that, too," and the guests had exchanged polite farewells and thank yous to Sir Alan and Lady Ledger, who seemed relieved according to Sophie that the whole thing was over.

Nina Rivington, Mrs Edward Rivington, once they had been one and the same woman, now Nina had to share not only her husband but also her surname with a woman she had never met.

CHAPTER FOURTEEN

Madame Jacques Debrel

Sine the day I first met Nina at the Gallery I've liked her. She married the wrong man, but then don't we all make some marital mistakes? She's loyal, she listens and she has a gentle sense of humour. If only she had a bit more self-confidence. She's so talented in many different ways; she can cook, she can paint and she speaks several languages, while I can just about defrost a dinner and make myself understood in English.

She has wonderful children, no, I don't think I would've been a good mother, too selfish, but she put her all into motherhood. I've always loved Sophie, she's such a sparkling girl. And I do envy her that special relationship. Is Nina my best friend? Well, at my age it's a bit silly to use such phrases, you have different friends for different needs, but she's the one I asked to be my Matron of Honour.

Since Tessa found her house, and through it her man, she had stayed in Provence. She reluctantly gave up her unpaid job at the Gallery. Now she spent her time together with Jacques choosing interior decorators — and in Provence they seemed as plentiful, and as expensive, as in Mayfair. They looked at furniture for the house, the garden and the loggia by the pool. There were curtains to be made, a new kitchen installed and colours to be chosen. When Jacques was busy with clients Tessa discussed the December wedding with events organisers, disco suppliers, caterers and marquee rental firms.

"Jacques leaves it all to me," sighed Tessa, when she finally had time for a phone call. As Tessa's French was more English than anything else, she had to turn to the more expensive firms from Cannes and Nice. What had been planned to be a small wedding for just a few select friends followed by lunch at Chez Julien had escalated into a planned feast for hundreds. "They even suggested that Jacques and I should arrive at the house after the ceremony in a lace-covered air balloon. I told them I get vertigo on a kitchen chair and no way will I land having puked in my bouquet."

Nina regretted that she had promised to act as matron of honour. Big parties frightened her and she was not quite sure what her role would be. As the wedding came closer, Nina made up her mind to stay at home. She did not want to be there to see her friend marrying her ex-lover. There was no jealousy, just a hint of envy knowing that Tessa had succeeded where she had failed.

Nina felt lonely. Edward had more or less disappeared out of her life. Paul phoned once a week but his calls got shorter and shorter and Sophie was back in Newcastle having the fun she was meant to have. Her episode with Peter McLellan was totally forgotten; new names were mentioned at a regular basis. To combat the sense of desertion, and to fill her empty wallet, Nina busied herself with occasional translation work, her two mornings a week at the Picture Gallery and then there were the daily walks with Larry, whose rheumatic hips slowed them both down to a gentle amble. When Nina thought she was turning into a hermit, she would telephone Jen and they would take in a movie or a concert, but they never had the easy, carefree friendship which Nina had enjoyed with Tessa, pre-Jacques.

As the date for the wedding slid nearer her resolution to cancel her matronly duties melted. She could not make herself say no to Tessa, who was now in a state of flux, surrounded by French-twittering aides, who did nothing but ask for decisions all day long.

"I don't know what I'd do without you. You're the only one I can speak to. Jacques seems to have got the wobbles and spends more and more time at his office and that dragon of a secretary keeps saying he's out with a client every time I need to talk to him. Can't you come a few days earlier, just to calm my nerves. I was never like this with any of my other weddings. Do you think it's because of the language? Jacques insists that part of the ceremony must be in French, I suppose that will make him feel married. I have to actually say some of the wows in French and I haven't got a clue what I'm going to promise I hope it's not to obey him? No, that won't do."

Finally Tessa laughed but there was an echo of hollowness, that Nina found disturbing.

Four weeks before the wedding Nina received a note from Tessa, scrawled in her large hand.

"Enjoy! This is my wedding present to you and my way of saying thank you,"

Attached to the note was a copy of a letter to a Miss Jonessy, personal buyer at a big department store in London, in which Tessa asked her to help Mrs Nina Riverton to find the perfect outfit for a wedding and to make sure that all of it was debited to the account of Mrs Tessa Kingsley-Havers. Nina was touched that Tessa had figured out that she could not afford both the trip and an outfit. She was even more moved by the elegant way Tessa had solved her problem. But how could she now turn her friend down?

Jen, who was also coming to the wedding, had never had a personal buyer either and together they made an appointment with Miss Jonessy. Nina appeared at the department store early, half an hour before she was due to meet Jen at the Prima Beauty counter. She circled around the glass desk, laden with scented creams and potions watched over by girls in pearly white coats and immaculate skins.

"Can I help you?" whispered one of the immaculates. "We have a special make-up offer on for women with," there was a slight pause, "mature skin. We will show you to make the most of," another pause, "your assets and how to minimize your . . . . drawbacks."

Nina wilted like a flower on a hot summer's day and before she knew it she was sitting in a contraption, not unlike a dentist's chair. From behind a white curtain appeared a girl, even more perfect with chiselled cheeks and eyebrows knitted to perfection.

"Ah," she said with the glee plumbers use, when they see a burst pipe. "We have a challenge here, don't we?" Her smile was as artificial as her eyelashes.

"Now, what kind of foundation do you use?"

"None," answered Nina and shrank in her uncomfortable chair.

"None?! Well, that's like slapping paint on a cement wall without primer."

The girl brought down a camera from a shelf and then took a photograph of Nina's cheek.

Two seconds later the Nina's skin was shown on a small computer-like screen.

"Look, look here." She pointed her long, blood-red fingernail at the screen and her voice rose an octave. Women loitering by the counter dropped their pots of crème and all looked at the screen as if mesmerised.

"It's like a lunar landscape, craters everywhere."

The beautician tutted and gave another of her chilling smiles.

"Now I want you all to look." Half a dozen heads turned back from the screen. With vigorous strokes the beautician applied a foundation to Nina's face, then with more gentle patting another creamy lotion and finally she dusted her down with some powder.

"Look at this," she exclaimed with the pride of a Nobel prize winner to be. "We've found the answer to craters. Not a single one to be seen." Nina had to admit that the skin looked smooth on the screen.

"And what else can we do to improve this face? Let's see."

Nina gave up and closed her eyes, while the girl brushed, stroke, smoothed and pummelled her face.

"Open your eyes, Look down, now up, no, up I said." A wand with midnight blue came closer to her eyes and Nina automatically closed her eyelid shut.

"Up, up I said!" Shivering Nina did was she was told. Lipstick was brushed on, outlined and then smeared with gloss."

"Now that's what I call something. You've turned into a real beauty." There was a damp applause from the girls behind the counter and to her horror Nina noticed that the women, who had watched her transformation, also clapped their gloved hands.

"Anyone else for a makeover?" The bystanders smiled shyly at Nina and disappeared quickly.

"Now this is what you need to use as part of your daily routine, sunblock and daycream, our foundation, I think Princess Beige would suit you best, then cheek blush in russet, eye colour, the powder is always best for mature eyes, in dusky plum and then blue mascara with our very special lash-build and Princess Pink for your lips. This one stops any feathering, so common a problem for mature women."

Her long finger nails plucked at the keys of a small computer and she pulled out list and with it the total price for Nina's recommended daily routine. It came to more than two hundred pounds and Nina paled behind her freshly applied colours. The girl looked at her, still tapping keys with her long nails. The silence was achingly long.

"I'll think I'll have the lipstick. Princess Pink, yes, that's it. I'll come back another day for the rest."

At that very moment Jen appeared by her side. She looked at Nina and then burst out in a cheerful laugh.

"Nina, dear, you look like a Roman whore. Whatever have you done?"

Nina smiled with relief and with her short nailed finger pointed to the beautician.

"I haven't done a thing. It's been done *to* me. And actually," she looked at the startled girl, "I don't think Princess Pink is my colour after all."

The two women were still laughing as they left the Prima Beauty counter. In the ladies' cloakroom Nina managed to wipe off most of the beige a la mode, but she could not get rid of the blue eyelashes.

Miss Jonessy was not at all as frightening as the immaculate beautician. Her smile seemed genuine and she tried very hard to please both Jen and Nina. While they were sipping a glass of champagne, which seemed part of the service, she rushed around collecting what she thought suitable for a French wedding, or rather an English wedding in France. There were dresses in silk, feathery fronds for the hair, elegant shoes in palest colours, which would collapse after one dance, bags to clutch with room only for the dinkiest lipstick and a hankie. Soft shawls in shades of pastel for the evening chill. Jen immediately found a silver grey coat and dress, which fitted her perfectly. Nina could not make up her mind between a pale eau de nil silk dress with a short jacket or a blue coatdress in thick satin. In the end she picked the blue outfit, knowing that she already had blue shoes. Seeing the price tag of the dress, she did not want to abuse Tessa's generosity. Jen was not bothered about price-tags, she flicked her credit card with the unflinching ease of a well-paid lawyer.

Nina did travel down two days before the wedding as Tessa had asked her to. She picked up a car at Marseilles airport and drove the now familiar road to St. Remy. The air was chilly and damp, not like when she had been with Jacques during those hazy summer days. There was almost a smell of snow in the air and Tessa was glad she brought her warm coat. The light, though, still had that special lustre as if dusted with silver. As she got closer to Tessa's new house the sky darkened with the speed of a falling blind. When she arrived at the closed gate, she wondered how she would react to seeing Jacques again. And would he feel nervous about seeing her?

The gate purred open and she parked the car next to Jacques' blue estate car. Parked there were also a small red Renault, which Nina recognised but could not place and Tessa's silver Audi. The garden was just shapes in the darkness as only the path was lit up by lights. Suddenly the door opened and in a channel of light Madame Galine stretched out her arms.

"Bongjour Madame Riverton,"she said in her Provencal twang. She clasped Nina's hands and led her into the hall. It had all changed. There were comfortable sofas everywhere, covered with colourful throws, lights flowed from rustic lamps in wrought iron and a large, low glass table dominated the living room. Nina heard the clippety-clops of Tessa's high heels.

"Darling, how wonderful to see you. You do remember Jacques, don't you."

He was standing just behind Tessa and suddenly Nina felt her knees give, but just for a second. She had forgotten how handsome he was. He stretched out his hand, then pulled her to his chest, there was that same musky aftershave she had liked so much.

"Our special Matron of Honour, welcome to our home. What do you think? Tessa has done a fantastic job. But you must be tired after your long journey. We have some champagne on ice, as you are our first guest. Tomorrow my brother and his family will come and they are all staying in the house. For the rest of the guests we have arranged hotel rooms. It's easy at this time of the year." He smiled politely, but his other hand never left Tessa's shoulder.

"And I've got Mrs Galine to come in and help us four days a week. She does all the shopping and most of the cooking, but I'm learning, aren't I, mon amour?" Tessa was coquettish, there was a childlike quality to her voice, which had not been there before.

After unpacking and changing into trousers and a warm sweater, Nina came downstairs. Jacques and Tessa were embracing each other on one of the white sofas. Nina knew they had heard her coming down the stone stairs, she understood this was Jacques' way of sending a message to her and she got it loud and clear.

Madame Galine had produced a tray of appetizers and the champagne was the finest, but the atmosphere was strained. Nina talked about their friends and served up, as her contribution, some gossip from Wyckham Wood. Tessa appeared not interested; she only had eyes and ears for Jacques. She was curling herself like a kitten around his folded knees and all too often she would smile at him and shake her blond hair. Jacques seemed to take this admiration with a mixture of delight and embarrassment, and Nina did not think she was the cause of the embarrassment. It was Tessa and her girlish twitters that got to him.

They ate the dinner that Madame Galine had spent so much time and effort to produce but to them it was just a prop, something for them to tackle in order to hide the silence. Nina made her excuses before coffee, blamed her tiredness on the journey and went early to bed. The last thing she heard was Tessa's giggles accompanying the heavier tread of Jacques on the stairs. Every step made Nina's stomach turn.

Next morning Nina hoped for a breakfast alone and tiptoed down to the kitchen to find not only Madame Galine but also Jacques. He looked shower-fresh and Nina could smell his aftershave.

"Did you sleep well?" he asked in English and then, shaking his shoulders, he repeated it in French.

Nina answered in French, glad to be in her own language, their language.

"Tessa is enjoying her mornings in bed, she needs much more sleep than I do. I'll bring her a cup of coffee later. Sit down, Nina. Coffee?"

Madame Galine busied herself at the six burner stove and handed Nina a fresh pot.

"I remember you like it strong" she said with a smile. "Now I'm off. It's market day in St. Remy and I'll have a big dinner here tonight."

As soon as Madame Galine had left the room, Jacques leant forward and almost whispered.

"I heard about your mother, Nina. I am so sorry. I did try to phone you in Paris, but somehow I never reached you, and then with Tessa, well, I just didn't know what to say."

Nina nodded, there was not much she could say either.

"You haven't told Tessa about our little fling, have you? I think that would be unnecessary, don't you agree?"

"I value my friendship with Tessa more than our *little fling* as you call it."

Jacques did not seem to hear the ice in her voice.

"I'm so glad and we really are so pleased that you will be present at the actual wedding. Tessa hasn't really got any family and I think she sees you as more than a friend, a sister even."

The coffee tasted bitter suddenly. Nina went to the fridge to see it she could find some milk. There was none. Milk was a habit she had acquired since she moved to England. She used to gulp down fresh milk in her first years, golden top Jersey with a wonderful plug of thick cream at the neck. Now it was all semi-skimmed with a blue tinge instead of rich yellow. But in those days she had missed the crème fraiche and fromage frais for her sauces, which she could find now in any supermarket, even the Indian grocer in Wyckham Wood sold it. But the rich milk was gone.

"I want you to know," Jacques continued, still with her back to him, "that I did not see it as a fling, it was an affair that never had the chance to develop. You left, remember?"

"Well, what could I've done? Leave my dying mother alone?"

Jacques stirred his cooling coffee vigorously.

"That's not what I mean. Of course not. I see it as a holiday romance, which I will remember with pleasure."

"I'd rather not remember or even think about it," Nina retorted. "You're getting married to my closest friend and I hope that we two can be friends as well. In order for that to happen we must both forget what happened during the summer."

Nina thought she heard him sigh. Of relief probably.

"I think I'll take the car into St. Remy as well. There're a few things I need to get. Is there anything I can get for the house? And tell Tessa that I'll lunch in town and will be back in the afternoon."

Jacques nodded and he reminded her of Larry and his droopy look when he was told off. She smiled at the thought of Jacques turning into an old dog, although he smelled better.

The day was icy but clear. The air was like a soothing balm on her hot forehead. She had no idea of what she wanted to do, she got into the car and drove down the drive edged with the pale grey bushes of lavender. There was hardly any traffic. She loved these straight French roads, the plane trees, the ugly stone — houses, which had not been bought by rich foreigners. Nina wanted to do a painting of the multi-coloured laundry flapping on lines, the rusting parts of deserted cars, the vegetable patches. She knew that behind the road there were the fancy houses, where the laundry would be dried in Hotpoints and expensive cars parked in garages or under picturesque trellises covered in vines.

She parked at a side-street far away from the square and its market that spread all through the inner city. She admired glistening, black aubergines, bright red tomatoes and wondered where they came from so late in the season. Pencil-thin green beans with thread-like tails, and there were those plump wax-coloured beans she had tried to find in England. She had to paint again. Her stints at the gallery with the schoolchildren were just an excuse not to take up painting properly. From her bag she brought out her pocket camera and took a few shots of the vegetable display after having asked permission. The red-faced farmer and his bored wife shrugged their shoulders as reply.

The town was different in winter time. Nina enjoyed her walk along the narrow side streets. Gone were all the displays of bright coloured pottery and quilted tablecloths. The residents seemed to prefer china in off-white or antique grey, she noted. She found it drab. Edward had always complained about the boot of the car being cluttered up with bright yellow pottery wrapped in newspapers. She had always behaved as a tourist in her own country. Nina remembered trailing the markets in France, while Edward was waiting with a coffee nearby after having secured a day-old Daily Telegraph. And not only pottery, there would be baskets, wrought iron, embroidered linen, still unused in her linen cupboard as it was so difficult to iron and no one used starch anymore.

Edward was more in her thoughts now, when he was married to another woman than he had ever been. It was as if his marriage had been the final cut; there was no way back. It was these short, sharp realisations that it was all over that jolted her, when she least expected it. No regrets, just sadness that they would not share their old age, the joy of becoming grandparents. She missed the comfort of marriage, now she was a foreigner again, an outsider.

After a quick Croque Monsieur she walked back to the car. It was too early to go back to the house. Instead she drove back to Bonlieu, where she had spent some time with Jacques. She needed to purge herself of those memories and standing by the old fortress above the church she burst into tears. It made her feel better and she drove to the post office and put through a call to Sophie. "I just wanted to hear your voice, darling. Of course I'm all right. Yes, it'll be a big wedding and his family arrives tonight and tomorrow's the big day."

Sophie's clear voice and lack of interest in Tessa's wedding made her feel better. She drove back and arrived at the same time as Jacques' family. Happy voices, hugs and congratulations filled the air and Madame Galine was again doing the rounds with canapés and champagne. Jacques' brother Bernard was a maths teacher now working in Bordeaux and Nina felt at ease with him immediately. Bernard's shy wife did not say much, but fussed about her two daughters, who had been assigned the roles of flower girls. Bernard was going to be best man.

"My English is very bad and that makes it difficult for me to talk to Tessa, but you've known her for years. I gather she has been married before, just like Jacques."

For a moment Nina thought she should mention that this was going to be Tessa's fourth wedding, but she held back.

In spite of a delicious meal cooked by the indefatigable Madame Galine, plenty of wine and after-dinner brandies, the atmosphere never warmed. Tessa was nervous, Jacques wanted his brother to admire his choice of wife and Bernard's wife Caroline uttered exactly two words during the whole dinner and those were "Quiet please" to her two daughters. Nina worked hard to get the conversation flowing, but having to translate Tessa's stiff dinner conversation did not help. Everyone used the next day as an excuse for an early night.

Tessa was up early. Her hairdresser arrived at eight and while Tesssa was having her hair done she practised those phrases in French that would turn her from Mrs

Kingley-Havers to Madame Debrel. Jacques left to collect the flowers for his bride and the buttonholes. Bernard chatted happily with Madame Galine, who also had been invited to the service. Caroline was drinking endless cups of coffee, ate nothing, but made sure that her daughters filled up on the offered fruit juice and flaky croissants. Outside the caterers were setting up their kitchen in a smaller marquee and men in overalls were rushing around shouting and carrying endless stainless steel trays.

At eleven the bridal couple and guests were ready to set off in three chauffeured cars. Tessa and Nina in one, Jacques and his brother in the next one and Madame Galine with Caroline and her daughters in the last. The convoy drove slowly off and reminded Nina of a funeral cortege.

During the journey Tessa held the paper with the vows and silently whispered the phrases over and over again.

The registry office was in the mairie of the neighbouring town. Already men were out on the square playing boules under the plane trees. The café had opened up and glasses of golden beer were waiting for the players. When Tessa stepped out of the car the men looked at her and whistled appreciatively. Nina had never seen her looking lovelier. Her silk suit matched her golden hair and on her head was not a hat, more of a crunched up net topped by a matching silk rose.

The registrar welcomed the congregation and brought them all into his office. There was no music. After a few welcoming words, the registrar started. Nina clutched Tessa's bridal bouquet and pretended not to hear Tessa's mangled French phrases. The two young girls stifled their giggles: Caroline sniffled in her hankie and the bride looked just blank, as if she were not present. Only Jacques beamed. His smile lit up the glum office. Ten minutes, a couple of signatures and the deed was done. The first post-nuptial kiss seemed to go on for ever.

"Felicitations" shouted the boules players as they emerged into the daylight. Madame Galine sprinkled some rose petals on the couple before she was driven back to the house. The rest squeezed into two cars taking off for Chez Julien. Nina hoped Julien would remember her, but at the same time she did not want Tessa to know that she had been there with Jacques, as Tessa had referred to it as "our place".

Julien met them at the door and champagne was handed to them all, even the pre-teen daughters were given glasses. His smile was genuine and he hugged Tessa with such fervour that he crumpled her flowers. "Someone has finally made him an honest man and it could not have been anyone but a woman as beautiful as you." At last Tessa smiled and Nina's shoulders fell in her blue satin. Of course *she* had not been beautiful enough. Nina took a deep draught of her champagne.

The atmosphere lightened up during the lunch. Julien had organised a festive meal with lobster followed by duck and a raspberry tarte as dessert, all accompanied by the finest wines from his cellar. He gave a bottle of 80-year old brandy to Jacques and presented the new Madame Debrel with a crystal decanter before giving an impromptu speech in which he declared his undying love for Tessa and eternal friendship with everyone else — "and what a pleasure to make the acquaintance of my dear Nina" and as he said it he winked conspiratorially at her. The drink was getting to him.

It was after four by the time they set off. The guests were arriving at eight, which gave everyone time for a short siesta. That was the plan, but there was so much din coming from the marquee; sound engineers testing the equipment, temperamental chefs shouting at their underlings and furniture being hauled from lorries parked outside the gate. Madame Galine felt invaded by these storm troopers and sulked in the kitchen.

Nina could not sleep. She undressed and slipped into her bed but it was too noisy to relax. She opened the curtains and looked at the chaos in the garden. Would all this be ready by eight? Tessa and Jacques had disappeared to their room and Nina wondered if this was the first moment of marital sex. She remembered her own wedding night. At a three star hotel in London. Magda had come over and then there was George and a few of her friends, but the Rivertons had used the wedding as an excuse to invite distant relatives, friends, business contacts and neighbours. A few of Edward's school and university friends were there but most of the guests were total strangers to her.

Nina had drunk far too much champagne. She hated to be the centre of attention, these were people she did not know. Edward had not yet acquired his professional carapace and was equally shy and together they toasted and toasted, lifting their glasses to known and unknown well-wishers. By the time the reception was over they almost crawled back to their suite and Nina fell asleep before she had removed her lacy underwear, that her mother had insisted she wear. It was six in the morning when she woke Edward up and afterwards they phoned for room service and ordered champagne. Both were disappointed that married sex was no different from the unmarried sort.

There were over a hundred guests in the marquee. The caterers had set up a buffet along the short wall and there were round tables seating ten. Nina stuck to Bernard and Caroline as she knew no one except Jen, who immediately had found a Belgian lawyer, who had bought his house through Jacques. Tessa still looked dazed, but her husband proudly introduced his bride to all the guests. Nina suspected that he had used this event as a way of thanking clients, suppliers and VIPs in the area. He was now living in a house that all could admire, as he led them on guided tours in small groups. He sounded like an estate agent trying to sell his own house.

Nina drank champagne to cool down. The disco was blaring pop music from the early eighties and the guests were bopping around the floor laid down for dancing. Lights were flashing off and on and Nina suddenly felt very tired. She deserted Bernard, who seemed perfectly happy to chat with a tax inspector, who had helped many of Jacques' clients. Drooping with tiredness Nina undressed and without warning she was sick. Fizzy vomit spurted on to her bed and she rushed to the bathroom. For half an hour she lay on the cool floor, shivering and dreaming of sleep.

Chapter Fifteen

Paul Riverton

I never really thought much of Mum. Somehow she was always there. Isn't that what mothers are meant to be. But now, when I'm away from her I do think about her and I find that I miss her. She's had a tough time, I can't understand Dad leaving but then I don't want to get involved. They're both my parents. My sister Sophie is livid with Dad, but I'm sure he had his reasons. And I'm not sure I want to know them.

Mum is a real at-home mother. Sometimes I envied school-friends who had really sexy and attractive mothers, but then I found out that they were not all what they seemed. I know I could always trust my mother and now with a continent between us I realise that she means a lot to me.

With shame Nina remembered waking up before dawn after the wedding and how she had scrubbed the soiled bedcover with her nailbrush and lavender soap. She had put her nausea down to too much champagne but deep down she knew it was the result of her nerves being stretched too far. Trying so hard to look as if she had enjoyed herself, she had danced with friends and colleagues of Jacques and even smiled at his glum secretary, who looked irritated that her employer had finally been captured, and by a glamorous foreigner at that.

Nina was relieved to be home again. Jen had decided to stay on for a few days. It turned out that the Belgian lawyer was on his annual holiday and he invited Jen to stay with him. He would love to guide her around Roussillon, where he had bought a house.

"Never been to bed with a Belgian before. Isn't there a joke that no one can name a famous Belgian?" Her Belgian, as it turned out, was quite famous, albeit in Belgium only. He was a respected high court judge—and a widower. Better still, according to Jen, he seemed quite smitten by his new English friend.

"Maybe you should look for a man who's more your own age, and one without a wife. Just for a change." To Nina's surprise Jen agreed. Tessa's wedding had obviously shaken her, too.

Work was a relief. Nina loved her classes at the gallery. The children made her laugh and the colleagues made up for the absence of her friends. As a single woman the invitations to dinners had slowly and almost imperceptibly dried up. And not only that, the nest was empty and although she was glad to be able to get a bath when she wanted and not to have to step over heaps of discarded clothing, she felt the solitude not as a solace as it had been when she had the house full but more of a penance. She filled her evenings by playing solitaire, battling with crosswords she could never quite solve and with music.

Her plans for her second Christmas without Edward were up in the air. Paul had already told his mother that he was not coming home, couldn't afford it he said. Nina had immediately offered to pay for the flight, but Paul had made up his mind. "Can't leave the firm in the lurch, promised I'd work over Christmas, and besides, Mum, it'll be interesting to see how they celebrate it in Ecuador." He had provided too many excuses for Nina, who wondered what the real reason was.

Sophie realised that as the only young Riverton in the country she had to spread her goodwill of the season. Edward was spending the holiday with Mrs Riverton Senior and he wanted Sophie to be there. Sasha was exhausted by the pregnancy and needed help from Sophie to manage Christmas with her new husband and mother-in-law. Is she still **my** mother-in-law, Nina asked herself, or did the decree absolute put an end to that relationship as well?

The answer to her first question arrived some weeks later. Not by phone but by letter. Nina was not used to getting letters from Paul, not since he was forced to write his weekly missive by the house-master at his boarding school. At first she hardly recognised Paul's cramped handwriting but knew it had to be from him, as she did not know anyone else in Ecuador. Out of the thin envelope fluttered pages of uneven writing. A knot tightened in Nina.

Dear Mum,

I didn't know how to tell you about all of this over the phone, so I took the afternoon off and I'm now in the library to get some peace in order to write this letter to you. I've got wonderful news, well, wonderful for me but I'm not quite sure what you'll think.

Maria Eugenia and I got married last week. She is the daughter of Senor Delmonico, where I've been staying since I arrived and he is the manager at the Fyffes banana depot. She is the loveliest girl ever and I'm so happy. The reason why all this happened so quickly is that, well, I'm sure you can guess. Yes, Maria is pregnant and the baby is due in April next year. It's all I want and I couldn't be happier.

The family has been very kind to me and I do feel I am one of them. They have welcomed me with open arms and since our marriage we've been given two rooms of our own in the flat. Maria is at University but will make a break in her studies to have the baby and then we hope she can start her studies again as soon as possible. Her mother Dolores, you'll like her, has promised to look after the baby, while Maria studies. I earn enough to look after us both as we are staying rent free.

The wedding was a low key affair at a local registry office and there was a small gathering afterwards with just family and a few of Maria's friends. We will have a real celebration as soon as the baby is born and then we hope you, Sophie and maybe even Dad can come over and meet

Maria and her family. The parents don't speak a word of English, though, but Maria and her sisters are learning.

I thought they would hate me for making Maria pregnant, but once they got over the shock, they've been nothing but helpful.

I can't say what this has meant to me. Don't take this wrong, but I've never felt part of our family. I was on the outside looking in. I hated school, never felt at ease when I had my breaks and always envied Sophie, who was allowed to stay at home. You and Dad were both kind and even-handed parents and I can't say that I had an unhappy childhood, but I was lonely, not good at fitting in. Here I've been part of a large and bustling family. We eat together, cook together and play together. We seldom watch TV and the Delmonicos are not interested in books, but they love games and music. My piano lessons are finally paying off. Almost the first day they took me down to the community centre and signed me up to sing with their local choir and I now sing several evenings a week at church with Maria and her sisters, that is, when I'm not watching football with her brothers. There's always something to do and we do it together.

I get on well at work and I have been offered some more interesting projects in the export division. There's also a hint of a promotion as soon as my Spanish improves and it does, daily.

I am sending an additional letter with some photographs from the wedding. Once you see them and how lovely Maria is you'll understand everything. As you might have guessed by now I won't be home for X-mas, but I'll phone you next week and we can plan a date for you to come here. I've not told Dad the news yet. He seems so busy with work and Sasha and the baby she's expecting. I find it hard to grasp that my half-sibling will be an uncle to my own baby. Maybe you can tell him. And Sophie and Grannie.

I love you Mum, you've always been a good mum, no, a great mum. So please be happy for me.

Lots of love

Paul

PS Maria sends her love, too

Nina had to read the letter three times. It did not make sense to her. Suddenly she had a daughter-in-law who she had never met, she was to be a grand-mother and Paul had not said a single word about coming back to England, only mentioned Maria continuing her studies once the baby was born. Her first thought was to phone Edward but then she stopped as soon as she had dialled two digits. She needed time to think, to swallow the news and digest it before she could relay the contents of the letter to Edward, "busy with work and Sasha". Nina had been so occupied with her own feelings of desertion and anger that she had not fully been aware of how the divorce had hit the children. Sophie's almost paranoid stalking of Peter McLellan and now Paul's rush into a marriage, where the family seemed as important as the love he felt for the girl.

Nina decided not to talk to Edward until she had received the wedding photos. Somehow she hoped that seeing Maria's face would provide some answers.

A thick brown envelope covered in brightly coloured stamps arrived a week later. Nina tore it open with itchy fingers. Ten photos fell out. The first one was of Maria, she supposed, standing next to Paul who was dressed up in a suit she had never seen before. His smile was heart-achingly happy and the girl, petite and slim-hipped, was dressed in a pale blue dress with long sleeves and a neat white collar and she looked far too young to be a university student. Nina tried to see if a bump was showing. Nothing. Her long, dark hair was tied in a ponytail with some white flowers, her only ornament apart from a slim ring on her left hand and a large crucifix on a plain chain. The eyes were wide apart, which gave her a startled look as if marriage had come to her as a happy surprise. She smiled not at the camera, her eyes were turned towards Paul.

There were two more photos of the bridal couple and Nina had to admit that Maria was not only pretty but had character in her young face. There was one photo of Maria standing with three girls and on the back Paul had pencilled *Maria and her three sisters, Carmen, Bianca and Mercedes.* Then there was one with Paul and Maria's brothers and one of the parents surrounding bride and groom. The mother looked serious with her school-marm chignon of silver-white hair. She had a draped flowery dress over her wide hips. The father in a smart suit smiled at his young daughter. He was erect, not much taller than his wife but still with a dark crop of hair without a dash of grey. Nina suspected hair-dye. The next two photos must have been taken at the reception afterwards. Nina could see a table in the background laden with dishes and in the forefront people sitting with glasses filled with red wine. It looked as if the father was giving a speech or suggesting a toast as all had their glasses lifted. The last one she picked up was of Maria and Paul sitting at a street café feeding fat pigeons with breadcrumbs, both laughing. Was this taken before the wedding? Nina suddenly realised she did not even know when Paul had got married. She turned the first one over and in pencil Paul had written *Our wedding November 14.* Nina picked up her handbag and found her diary. November 14, a Tuesday and all she had written for that date was gallery at 9.00-12.00 then dentist at 4.40. What was the time difference? Was Nina having her teeth done as her only son got married?

Now there was no excuse not to phone Edward. She dialled his number and after exchanging the kind of pleasantries you do with someone you only half-know in order to mask any embarrassment, Nina told Edward she had to see him. No, she did not want to discuss it over the phone. They decided to meet for lunch the next day.

"We were young and it worked for us. Well, it did for some twenty years and that's not a bad record these days," Edward said as he slowly poured some wine in her empty glass. Nina had gulped down the wine, while tearfully telling him about the wedding and showing the by now well-fingered photographs. Edward had taken it more calmly than she had expected. He did not seem to care that his son might settle down on the other side of the globe. But then he will soon have another son, an heir and a spare, unlike me. Nina glared at her ex-husband.

Nor did he comfort her tears when she told him that she saw his letter as an accusation of them not being good parents. "He seems happier with the Delmonicos" Nina sobbed and wiped her eyes on the napkin.

"Why must you always find the negative? Paul fell in love and that affects his relationship with her family. Surely you should know that coming to another country, another culture also makes everything more exciting."

Nina was not convinced but she could not tell Edward of those fearful Sunday lunches she had to endure with his parents. Mrs Riverton had corrected her English at every opportunity. "We don't say horse-riding, my dear." "It might be serviette in French, in English it is a napkin, please try to remember." Edward's father the gentle Mr. Riverton, never corrected her but always treated her as a person slightly handicapped by not being born English. "I suggest you read some English novels. Jane Austen, an English author you might have heard of, writes most brilliantly and will give you an understanding of how we think." If Edward thought those interminably long lunches were exciting it just showed how little he had understood her and the feeling of being an outsider, which she had carried with her for years.

"Paul was always a loner," Edward said, now with gentleness in his voice, as if he had read her thoughts. "You were and have always been a perfect mother and look, here," he pointed to the end of Paul's letter," he stresses how much he loves you, while I get very much second billing." His laughter was hollow. Nina stretched out her hand and touched his. "We were good parents and we will continue to be good parents whatever happens."

Edward was not able to plan a trip to Ecuador. "I can't ask Sasha to fly across the world while pregnant and once our son is born it'll not be very practical, will it?" Instead Edward was willing to buy airline tickets for the family to come over, "well, not all the brothers and sisters, but the parents and Paul and his wife, what's her name, yes, Maria. We can then organise a celebration, maybe in April, when Sophie is twenty-one, and make a real party of it."

Edward seemed excited about the idea and even promised to inform his mother of yet another family arrival, her first great-grandchild.

"Mama will be excited, although I know she'll feel a bit worried about Paul marrying into a Catholic family."

Nina's lack of religion had been seen by Mrs Riverton as another of her character flaws, but her mother-in-law had been delighted every time she had joined them for their habitual Sunday outing to the village church. It almost had made up for the French accent. When the children were born both had been baptised in that sweet village church and no one had ever asked Nina if she wanted them to be brought up as Catholics.

Edward promised to write to Paul and suggest a later celebration in London, "they have excellent facilities at my Club" and that he was willing to pay for four tickets. He settled the restaurant bill just as Nina started to relax. "Must dash back, so much to do at the office towards the end of the financial year. It was lovely to see you and promise to be in touch if you hear any more news." He stood up and held out his hand.

"Do you mind if I stay and finish my coffee," Nina asked and half-rose from the table. It had been a lunch with a stranger and she needed time to think — and for one more drink.

Chapter Sixteen

Sophie Riverton

My Dad has really changed since he married that woman. He seems happier and somehow it now looks as if Mum finally has accepted that Dad is gone. I find it hard, really hard and I just wish that all this had never happened. I want it all to be back to normal. I can see why Paul is not exactly rushing back home.

Nina was tired. It felt like the marrow had been sucked out of her bones. It was Christmas she was worried about. Her colleagues at the Gallery asked about her plans out of consideration rather than curiosity and Nina just answered, "Christmas? Oh, just the usual; rushing around like mad, cooking like a lunatic and spending more than I can afford." The truth was that it was going to be the first Christmas Nina had ever spent on her own. Tessa had asked if she wanted to come down to Provence "to share our first Christmas" but Nina knew that they did not really want her there, the words "our first" made that clear. And Jen had decided to spend Christmas in Brussels in the company of her newfound Belgian judge, Paul was staying in Ecuador with his "new" family and Sophie was spending Christmas Day with Edward. She tried not to feel jealous at the thought of Sasha having both her ex-husband and her daughter. That left no one she could spend Christmas Day with. She tried to tell herself that it was only one day out of three hundred and sixty-five, so really it did not matter. Yet, every commercial, every ad presented happy families gathering around laden trees opening presents with electric toothbrushes or famous scents. Glowing mothers, never aged more than twenty-five, lifting golden turkeys out of their immaculate ovens to the acclaim of smiling children and handsome husbands. Suddenly she hated the sound of jingle bells.

She regretted all those years she had complained about the hassle, the queues, the cooking and now wondered what she should prepare for one. A ham sandwich?

Two weeks before Christmas Sophie came down from Newcastle. Nina hugged her like never before. She wanted Sophie to confirm that she was a good mother, she needed to hear that Sophie had never thought herself as outside the family like Paul. To her relief Sophie just laughed and said, yes, as a matter of fact, she *had* felt left out, but that was because Paul was the one, who had been sent to boarding school, "and that in spite of my school reports being far better than his."

Nina overcompensated. She tempted Sophie with all her favourite dishes and eventually she achieved the longed for victory. Sophie would spend Christmas Eve, a day as important to Nina as Christmas Day, with her and then Nina would drive Sophie down to Beverly Downs, where Edward and Sasha were spending Christmas with Mrs Riverton. She would drop her at the bottom of the drive. Nina did not want to come in for a sherry while Sasha welcomed her step-daughter, no doubt sitting in the straight-backed chair by the fireside, Nina had preferred when she was pregnant. Nor did she want to return, still remembering the turkey-and pine-scented cottage, to go home to her own echoing silence in Wyckham Wood.

Sophie made sure that all the Christmas decorations were taken down from the attic and put in their usual places. Every year the children had bought an ornament each for the tree at the village fete and each year the tree had to be bought a size larger to house all the baubles and bells. Nina pointed out that it was silly to go to all that trouble for just two but Sophie insisted.

"I'll only be with Grannie and Dad for some hours, the rest I'll be here with you. And I want a proper Christmas at **our** home with that French yule log, that you always do and we must have champagne on Christmas Eve. And remember I'll be back on Boxing Day as soon as the trains are running again and then we'll have a lazy day with cold turkey sandwiches and our new books to read."

"I'm not cooking a turkey just for two," Nina said with mock indignity knowing full well she would, only to please Sophie.

Sophie's determination that Nina's first Christmas on her own should be as normal as possible touched Nina and she started planning; a ten pound turkey, decorations, plum-pudding, hyacinths for the dining room, a small Christmas tree, holly wreath for the door and electric white lights for the large juniper tree by the front door. It would be like every year.

So when people asked nearer Christmas Nina did sigh, this time with conviction. "Christmas? Oh, cooking like a lunatic and spending too much." Money was scarce and the turkey weighed in at a measly six pounds, the tree was small enough to stand on the side table and Sophie dressed it with a few of her favourite ornaments. Hyacinths were bought at the supermarket and the holly wreath was a last-minute bargain from the petrol station. But there were ginger biscuits made with fresh spices and a rich chocolate yule log and so what if the champagne was a vin mousseux?

Nina bought fewer presents. Would she really have to buy the traditional Floris bath salts for her now ex-mother—in-law? She would leave that duty to Sasha. To Paul and Maria she had sent a cheque, more than she could afford, wanting them to buy something they needed. "A proper wedding present will come when you are over here for the celebration of your wedding and Sophie's twenty-first." For Sophie a leather handbag in dark purple she eyed greedily and for

Jen she bought a cookery book—her Belgian judge was a keen cook and Jen wanted to impress him, something she had never shown an inclination to do with any other lover. For Tessa and Jacques she had found some antique linen towels, easy to pack and send.

And then there was George. He usually bought her some expensive scent, probably picked up absent-mindedly at some airport and in return she would hand him a heavy almond cake, baked after a Hungarian recipe he had once given her. Since Magda's funeral she had not heard much from George. He mourned Magda more than Nina had expected. For many years he had spent one of the Christmas days with the Rivertons, often with Magda present, but this year Nina had not asked him. The two of them sitting alone in the dining room with some Tokaj talking about Magda, no, it was not how Nina wanted her Christmas. And besides he had not phoned her for weeks.

Christmas Eve turned out to be a happy evening. Paul phoned from Quito and Nina spoke to Maria, a clear voice with an unexpected softness as if she caressed her consonants. She struggled with her English but they understood each other and both talked about the "bébé". Paul crackled with happiness and in the background Nina could hear laughter and singing. "We're singing at midnight mass tonight and then up early for matins tomorrow, very busy time for the choir, but we enjoy it." She exchanged a few words in her home-made Spanish to Maria's parents and then the line was cut off. She tried to get reconnected but was told "all lines to Ecuador are busy at this time. Please try later."

Sophie had had time to scream Merry Christmas to her brother before the cut-off and to promise him that they would talk more next day, when she would be phoning from Grannie's. After the call Nina and Sophie opened the vin mousseux, which tasted just as good as champagne, and they drank a toast for the safe arrival of Nina's first grandchild and Sophie's niece or nephew. None of them mentioned the coming birth of Sophie's half-brother.

It was still dark when the peep of her alarm clock tore into her swollen sleep. Nina turned over and regretted the last drops of wine they had finished at midnight. They needed an early start for the drive to Beverly Downs. The bed was warm and she could hear the rain patting gently on the windowpane. Her hand stretched out, as it so often did, to the empty side of the bed. "Bugger you, Edward, bugger you." She laughed to herself, this was not exactly the spirit of Christmas and she threw off the duvet. To make up for her cursing Edward she would prepare a breakfast tray for Sophie with those freshly baked ginger biscuits. The same biscuits she had baked every year for Christmas.

Still dreaming of the past she pottered but the sound of the singing kettle pulled her back to the present. There was Sophie upstairs, her beloved, fun and loving daughter. Life would go on. She bit into one of the biscuits and the flavour of cinnamon and cardamom lifted her spirits.

Sophie handed over her present, an orange box wrapped in brown ribbons. Wrapped up in finest tissue was a wonderful silk scarf she had bought in Paris for some of the money Magda had given her for the dress. It was an Hérmès, like those Magda had stacked in her drawers and Nina now had in hers but could not bear to use. They were Magda's signature. "I thought you should have one of your very own and in colours that suit you" Sophie said as she watched her mother try it on. The moss green was lightened by swirls of golden horse-bits and tackle. Nina smiled at Sophie's reflection in the mirror. With tears in her eyes she hugged her daughter. "You couldn't have given me a finer present. It even makes my old nightie look elegant." Sophie must have planned it months ago. Just the thought of it made Nina guts dance.

After a giggly breakfast that neither of them wanted to finish, they got dressed warmly and set off for Beverly Downs. There were few cars on the roads and somehow the atmosphere was different. People smiled as they crossed the road. The shops on the parade were all closed, even Mr. Patel had taken the day off. As they left the village and finally turned on to the M20 they felt as they were in a movie set. There were no lorries, no heavy pan-technicons, just a few private cars often with excitable children in the backseat. Sophie sang along to the pop channel and Nina enjoyed the silly lyrics and tried to join in.

In less than an hour they reached the green, where Mrs Riverton had her cottage. A large Christmas tree was covered in bright lights and underneath parcels were stacked. A small sign proclaimed that the tree and decorations were sponsored by the local estate agent, "Jones & Young for your dream home". Now even the community spirit was up for sale, Nina thought, but then remembered that the Gallery had sponsored the tree on the Common. She turned into the drive, out of old habit, then stopped as she saw the cottage, surrounded by its well-cut hedges. Light shone from each window downstairs and the kitchen window was misty with steam.

"I'll drop you here, if you don't mind. I'd rather not go in and say hello. Wish them all happy Christmas from me." Nina leant forward and kissed her daughter.

"Are you sure, Mum?", Sophie asked, but she had already opened the door to put her left foot on the ground. She gathered her bags with presents and rushed towards the cottage with a quick wave. Nina stared at the door after it had closed and tried to imagine Edward hugging his daughter, their daughter.

She changed the radio channel on the way home. Without Sophie the pop seemed inane.

The house looked inanimate as she arrived back. The windows were dead eyes and she regretted that she had not left any lights on. Larry was still asleep in his basket, even he seemed to have lost his lust for life—he hardly stirred as Nina jangled his lead for walkies. They met no one on the Common. The wind swept up some dried leaves, the only sound she could hear apart from her own footsteps. She walked past the Gallery, through the new estate, up towards Wyckham Hill. She wanted to walk until her legs ached, hoping that she would sleep away the afternoon.

It was after three when she finally arrived back at the house. A car was parked outside.

"Lucky that I had a bottle of Tokaj with me to keep warm. Where have you been, petal?" George pulled himself out of the car, heaving a large bag, a rather tatty Fortnum & Mason carrier. "Happy Christmas, sweetheart. I need a basin full of hot, strong coffee. I've been here for at least an hour."

Never had Nina been so happy to see George. She fell into his cold, woolly arms and drew in his citrus smell, now combined with the sweetness of the wine. "Happy Christmas to you, too. But what are you doing here? Why didn't you let me know?"

"It was meant to be a bit of a surprise. Sophie and I planned it. She didn't want you to be on your own—and you, my foul friend, had not invited me this year! So here I am and I even have a present for you, but first things first. Coffee!!"

Nina unlocked the door and pulled an excited Larry away from George's long coat. Suddenly the empty house was full of light, sounds and scents. The turkey, that Sophie had insisted on, had slow-cooked in the oven since their early morning departure and the red cabbage with onions and wine vinegar made the kitchen smell welcoming. While Nina prepared the potatoes and beans they sipped champagne, a surprise from the Fortnum &Mason bag, and gossiped. George had been to Paris and he had visited the cemetery, where Magda's ashes were placed behind a small plaque only giving her name and date of death.

"Magda would never have forgiven us if we had mentioned her date of birth" George said with a melancholy smile.

"Only if we had deducted a few years," Nina added and they both laughed.

After the meal Nina served coffee in the kitchen. The warmth and the aromas from the oven made it much cosier than the living room. She gathered up the Christmas tree from the small table and carried it into the kitchen, where she placed it on the dresser. She had wrapped up a bottle of wine and hastily tied a red ribbon around the neck.

"Happy Christmas, George, and thank you for coming. I can't tell you how happy I am to see you."

George suddenly looked like a small boy, his eyes glittered as he bent down to bring up the pale green carrier bag.

"Do you remember that you once came to me with Magda's icon in a Sainsbury bag. I thought that was most inappropriate. Now . . ."

"Yes, I remember. You told me it deserved at least a Fortnum &Mason bag."

"So, here is my Christmas gift to you, in a bag I hope you'll find appropriate."

He handed the bag over and inside there was a parcel, shoddily wrapped in brown paper. She unravelled the paper and inside was layer after layer of newspaper and finally inside was some taped-up bubble-wrap. By the time Nina reached the bubbles she could see the blue, that startlingly blue she knew so well. It was Magda's icon.

"But, George, I don't understand this. You sold it! And here it is."

"I bought it back from the Russian oil millionaire. I realised what it meant to Magda and I sensed that she really wanted you to keep it. Especially now, as we found out that the icon was given to her from Nicolai, your father."

Nina could not hold back her tears. She held the icon tight to her chest.

"I don't know how to thank you. This is the best Christmas present I've ever had."

She kissed George on both cheeks and he wiped her tears off his face.

"Come on, petal, here's my hankie. Now for some Tokaj and I sincerely hope you've baked me an almond cake."

And she had. Sophie had insisted on it and now she knew why.

CHAPTER SEVENTEEN

Nicholas Riverton

"Have you seen it? It's in the Times, page forty three." Jen's voice was excited in spite of the early morning. The pale spring light had not yet had the courage to peep through Nina's curtains. She threw a glance at her icon and smiled.

"Seen what?" she asked.

"Edward and Sasha are announcing the birth of their son. Let me read it, you're obviously too lazy to go downstairs to get the paper."

"I take The Independent, now that I finally am."

"Here goes," Jen cleared her throat and read with a la-di-da voice.

"Riverton, Edward and Alexandra, née Ledger, proudly announce the arrival of their beautiful son Nicholas Edward Hannibal, born on April 3rd at Portland Hospital, weight 8,2 lbs. Much longed for half-brother of Sophie and Paul."

"Does it really say that, I mean, longed for by Sophie and Paul? Bloody Edward. Do they even know that he has arrived? I suspect Paul has not been told and when I spoke to Sophie yesterday, she didn't mention the birth of any longed-for half-sibling."

"Maybe Edward felt that the readers of The Times should be the first to know. And besides, what's this with pounds, aren't we all metric now? Or have babies been excused metrification?"

Nina was grateful that Jen tried to cheer her up. Although she had known about it since Edward had told her more than six months ago the baby's actual arrival shook her and she shivered in her woolly nightie.

"And what kind of name is Hannibal? For God's sake, have they've gone mad?"

"Edward hero-worships Hannibal, he's read all the books ever printed about him. Don't ask me why."

"Well, I personally think Napoleon's quite sexy, but that doesn't mean that I would christen a poor mite of mine Napoleon."

"Nicholas, isn't that odd? You know that's the name of my real father. Nicolai. I don't think I've told Edward his name. I like it. Nicholas Riverton, yes, it has a certain ring to it."

"You're not going all gooey now, are you?" Jen's voice had a sharp edge to it. "I'm not suggesting that we wet Hannibal's head but I do recommend a dinner at Adelphi at the earliest opportunity."

Nina jumped out of her warm bed and finally found her diary in a coat pocket. They fixed a date.

Later Nina telephoned Sophie. Her hands shook as she dialled the number to Newcastle.

"Darling, have you heard? You've got a little half-brother called Nicholas Edward Hannibal." She stressed the last name, stretching the vowels.

"Yes, I know. Daddy phoned me from the hospital. I think he must have been at the gas, he sounded completely freaked out. He was there for the birth. Dad, who usually faints at the first drop of blood. I didn't tell you, Mum, because I just didn't know how to. Are you OK with it?"

"Yes, I'm fine, but it says in the announcement that Nicholas is a much longed for half-brother to Sophie and Paul. What a thing to say. Where did he get that from?"

"Well, Dad asked if we minded. It makes no difference to me, but Dad said something about us all being family and I suppose he's right in a way."

Nina felt doubly betrayed. This was a family she was excluded from. Her anger was now flushing through her cold veins. Come to think of it, Edward had certainly not helped *her* during the delivery of the children. He had rushed out to buy flowers when the actual birth approached and as soon as a midwife or nurse came into the room, he quickly disappeared through the door. Yet, with Sophie in his arms, he had looked so very proud, as if he had delivered the pink bundle on his own. When Paul was born, Edward had been in New York on a business trip and maybe that was a reason why he never developed that special relationship with his son as he had with Sophie.

Edward had been distant with both children. He had never pushed a pram, "woman's work" and he had left her to deal with nappies, mumps and school projects. If the children were naughty, and Sophie often was, Nina only had to threaten with "I'm telling Dad" and they would behave. He had an in-born gravitas and the children listened, with Nina they had always pushed the boundaries as far as they dared.

Later in the week, when speaking to Paul, she found out that Paul had also had a phone call from the hospital.

"I can't really get to grips with the idea that Dad's baby will be an uncle soon. Maria's getting quite big and, Mum,

I can actually feel little feet kicking, when she's lying down. We're discussing names, it must be something that works in both languages. If it's a girl, we're thinking of . . . . no, I'd better not talk about it yet."

Paul's voice seemed different from that of the young man she had waved goodbye to only some months ago. He had a life she knew nothing about. Nina could not picture her shy son putting his hand on a pregnant tummy. It was not only a geographical distance, emotionally Nina felt jet-lagged. She was soon to be a grand-mother but like after a long flight she was not quite sure how she had reached that destination.

One afternoon, almost as if to punish herself, she brought out the albums she had filled with photos of the first years of Sophie and Paul. There were pictures of Sophie's first bath, her in a gingham-covered Moses basket, Sophie having her nappy changed, Edward holding his daughter while they were sitting outside a pub, hundreds of photos in bleached colours. It was a life Nina could remember, but it was not hers. That woman, slimmer with naturally dark brown hair, was someone she knew but had nothing to do with today's plump and grey-streaked Nina. There were fewer photos of Paul and after some years the albums had stopped and there were only old wine boxes with photos thrown in, some with people she could not even identify. Happy snaps from pic-nics on rocky beaches and holidays in Scotland, where the sun seemed to shine all the time. Forgotten were the grey misty days when they tried to amuse the children with Monopoly and card games. Then she had thought that her tight-knit family could never unravel. Now there were new shoots sprouting on the old family tree and odd new branches.

With a sigh she put the boxes away. Behind the boxes she found a large envelope. She opened it. In it were a dozen letters Edward had written before they were married. She had forgotten that she had saved them. There was no red ribbon around these, Edward's letters did not deserve that. They were almost formal in their tone. Had he saved hers? She had written to him almost daily when she spent time with Magda before the wedding. All her love had poured onto pale blue paper with her favourite fountain pen, a school-leaving gift from George.

She took the letters without reading them and carried them to the fireplace. With a match she lit the pile and watched as the thin papers danced in the flashing flames. Why save old love-letters, when the love was no longer there, she thought and warmed her hands on cold love.

She was frozen to her core. Nina could not remember such a cold spring. The lawn was covered in freshly laundered frost and each bough of the apple tree was laden with buds, tightly furled to keep their heat. She put out more nuts for the birds and each morning they delighted her with their wings gratefully flapping. The foxes left delicate footprints in the lacy frost as they arrived for their morning meal of vegetable peelings and bacon rinds.

Paul talked about the hot weather in Ecuador and Nina thought about a break away in the sun, but the money was not there. Her translation work had almost dried up and she was grateful for the money her now paid work at the Gallery brought in. Then one morning, over the coffee machine, Jane Hartwell, the tough director's PA, said there was talk about making her position three-quarter-time, would she be interested?

"If so, I'll tell Dr. Jordan and you can apply. It'll have to be announced and advertised, but I happen to know that Dr Jordan is very impressed with the job that you do."

Jane smiled conspiratorially.

"I'd love it, no more than that, I'd be for ever grateful."

Jane, feeling important after Nina's outburst of gratitude, came by Nina's lecture room just before lunchtime and handed her the application form.

"Good luck," she whispered and made an almost regal wave to the school-children.

Nina filled in the form and handed it in next day. Interviews would be held at the end of the month. She tried to find out from Jane if there were many applicants, but she refused to say anything. "Wouldn't be right, now would it?"

Three weeks later, via the post, Nina was told to turn up for an interview at the Gallery. For over six years she had been a part-time lecturer cum artist in residence at the Gallery. For the first couple of years only for some hours a week at no pay, but then after two years the gallery wanted her on a part-time contract for a two mornings a week and they offered her a post paying the same hourly rate as the Gallery cleaning staff. Nina had not complained; she was just happy to be offered the job in spite of only getting what her lawyer had referred to as "pin money".

For years she had turned up at the Gallery in trousers with a colourful smock, trying hard to look artistically bohemian: that would not do for a proper interview. She often saw the director sailing past in the corridors and he was always immaculately tailored and with a silk handkerchief in his breast pocket. He had never acknowledged her presence with more than a nod. The Gallery was lucky enough to have a cadre of middle-aged women with middle-class aspirations "to do something useful". They dealt with ticketing and staffed the shop, which sold overpriced copies of the Gallery's most famous paintings and gift items, which everyone liked to buy but no one wanted to receive.

Nina trawled through the wardrobe. She needed to look serious and worth a proper salary, but still not too business-like to frighten the director. She had never been

JUNK MALE | 229

interviewed for a job before and was not quite sure what was expected. She had better talk to Jen, she constantly interviewed people for her law firm and also helped her clients to select the right person for top positions.

"Navy blue is too safe and just too boring," Jen said next day as Nina laid out her three choices of outfits for the interview.

"You're not applying for the job as an abbess. The red is OK, but I don't think the colour does you justice. My choice is this green skirt with the moss green top and off-white jacket. It's both chic and shows a good colour sense. And I love the scarf, is that an Hermés?"

"It was my Christmas present from Sophie. She bought it in Paris."

"You're a lucky woman, to have a daughter who spoils you. You realise that, don't you?" Jen's eyebrows arched.

"Yes, I do. I really do." As she said it, she meant it. Their phone calls, their confidences were real gifts. There were times when Nina had envied Jen her latest car or the designer-labels, but Jen would never be given an expensive silk scarf by a daughter. Maybe Jen envied her? That was a thought that had never occurred to her before.

"Now, don't tell the director what you want and how good you are. Let him set the tone. He already knows you are good, otherwise he wouldn't have asked you, albeit indirectly, to apply. So keep that positive thought in your mind. He needs you just as much as you need the job. Ask him what **he** thinks you can contribute. Ask about how he sees the future for the educational department and its role for the image and branding of the gallery. I have a feeling he likes the sound of his own voice. Listen to what he says and agree as much as you can without being toady and then ask a few questions, so that he can feel intelligent when answering them. Look him straight in the eyes and don't fidget whatever you do. Everyone hates a fidget."

"Do I ask how much I get, or should I tell him what I want?"

"Let him tell you and promise me, Nina, that you see that first figure as the starting point for negotiations. Have you found out what the other gallery lecturers get? If you can't get hold of that, speak to other museums and galleries and try to wheedle out how much they pay. State-run galleries must be open about their pay-rates. Still, it's not only about pay. Make sure that you find out if there are any other fringe benefits like health insurance, pension scheme or simple things like a discount in the shop or free exhibition-tickets for the family."

"I don't want to be seen as too greedy . . ."

"You have rights, remember that. No more of that forelock tugging. You've always been too accommodating with Edward — and sometimes with your children as well. Now you're on your own and you must learn to stand up for yourself." The tone was sharp but her smile softened the reproach.

Edward did not often telephone. She was surprised and even more so when she felt a sharp churning of her guts just hearing his voice.

"I don't know if the children have told you about Nicholas? No, he's fine, but I thought I should tell you myself. We're going to have him baptised. It doesn't really mean anything to me, or to Sasha, but it does to Mama. So we're doing it for her sake and, actually, I think Sasha's parents are quite pleased, too. Speaking of Mama, she sends her love to you and I think it would be a good idea for you to give her a ring, maybe meet in town for lunch? She's always been fond of you."

"Well, why doesn't she phone me?"

"Now, now, Nina. No high horses. It doesn't suit you. Now, about the baptism. I want Paul to be present but he doesn't want to leave that wife of his, what's her name again? Maria, yes, they're all called that, aren't they? Could you have a word with him, please and underline how important it is that he is present when his brother is baptised."

"His *half*-brother, Edward."

"What's the matter with you. You're all prickly. Sophie is the same. I've spoken to her and she talks about exams and says she hasn't really got time to come down to London. It will look very odd if they don't turn up. How do I explain that to Sasha and her parents?"

"That's not really my problem, is it?" Nina saw the children's stance as support for her and she was warmed by their reaction.

"Well, you are their mother and you'd better talk to them. The christening takes place Sunday in four weeks' time. I will send them proper invitations." There was a slight hesitation and Nina heard only the gentle burr on the line. "Do you think the children would come if I invited you?"

"Thank you Edward, but this has nothing to do with me and I suggest you deal with Sophie and Paul directly."

"All right, all right. I don't know what's wrong with you. You sound very sulky and bitter."

"You only get in touch when you want something from me. You never ask how I manage or how I feel."

"How *do* you feel, Nina?"

"Never mind, Edward. I will speak to the children."

And she did. Just as she had always done whatever Edward asked her to. The ties were not yet unbound. When both said "no" she was relieved.

Chapter Eighteen

Christina Riverton

The interview turned out to be a pleasant chat with Dr. Jordan over a cup of cappuccino from the café next door. Dr Jordan even offered almond croissants as he told her that he appreciated the work she had done with the children from the local schools.

"Some head honcho in our local council has obviously been impressed and we're very lucky to have been offered a grant in order to extend the educational department. That means we can offer a part-time position for the first time and I'm so pleased you are interested."

Nina bit her lip and remembered Jen's advice.

"Before we talk about my interest I would be grateful if you'd like to tell me how you see the development of the department and its importance for the Gallery as a whole." Nina looked at Dr Jordan and smiled.

"I'm glad you asked me about that. He nodded and rubbed his sugar-dusted fingers.

"I see our educational programme as vital to the role of the Gallery in the community. It is also a function of the Gallery close to the heart of our benefactor, Sir Maurice Green, who donated his fine collection and the funds to build the gallery. As you know he made his fortune out of West Indian rum and I expect he wanted be remembered for his beneficence rather than a sickly alcoholic drink distilled by black slaves. He had no children of his own and was keen that the collection should be made available to the young people of the area. I have always been of the opinion that the children who come here today will be the sponsors of the Gallery tomorrow. Through our educational programme we'll also come in closer contact with the teachers and the local educational establishment and that's why the Lottery Fund gives us brownie points. Now, what I have in mind is extending the programmes to the older students, the teenagers who think art is elephant dung and graffiti. We must inspire them and the person in charge must devise a programme of lectures, events and seminars that will attract that age group. What do you think?"

"That is a brilliant idea, Dr Jordan. I think you're absolutely right. There's a niche in the market." Nina did not know where she got that phrase from, but it seemed to please Dr. Jordan, who smiled benignly and offered her another croissant. She declined but admired the way he brushed the fine crumbs off his dry lips without getting his fingers sticky.

After that it was "call me Derek, please, and I trust I can call you Nina." Even the feared discussion about money went off without a hitch. Nina rejected the first offer and he said the budget would not allow what she asked for. Within four shaky minutes they both accepted a figure between the two, which was almost double the rate Nina was paid as an hourly employee. And she would be getting paid holidays, sickness benefits and even that discount in the shop Jen had insisted on. Her worst money worries were over and that meant she could stay in her house.

She started her new job in early February and although she found the bureaucracy a nightmare, something she had not been aware of in her earlier position, she loved her new tasks. And she found that she was good at her job; inspiring the part-timers, setting up rotas for the classes, dealing with young academics and selling the new idea to the schools.

Even the budget fascinated her; it was like a crossword. After the first four weeks Dr. Jordan called her in.

"Nina, I've had a word with Gregory Finn at Wyckham High and he's very pleased with the programme you've devised for the sixth formers. They're signing on and with them aboard it'll be easy to enrol the other local schools. I've even had a letter from Hampton Gallery, who must have heard about your plans and they want to send the head of their educational department over to see what we're doing. That's really a feather in our cap."

His confidence in her made her own grow. Nina did not even mind the dawn walks with Larry on wet February mornings before setting off to work and Larry seemed to have accepted his change of lifestyle with equanimity. It might have been a part-time position on paper, but Nina spent her afternoons off working on ideas, writing letters and telephoning schools and universities. And in the evenings she struggled with her French and Hungarian translations for a tractor company. Nina had no time to feel lonely, no time to be depressed.

Her calls each week with Paul were getting shorter. All he could talk about was the imminent arrival of the baby. Maria Eugenia had grown enormous and suffered from heat rash, bloating, palpitations and insomnia. Paul was clearly worried about his wife but Nina could not worry about someone she had never met nor knew and this made their conversations awkward. Although she longed to hear his voice, she often felt disappointed afterwards and somehow wished she had not phoned.

The baby was due in April and Nina had already packed a box with baby clothes, it had been such a treat to shop such small, dainty little socks, mittens and bonnets. There was a blanket in white, a rattle covered in knitted material (sold at the Gallery shop and at that fought for discount!), romper suits in yellow and white as she did not know if it was going to be a boy or a girl. She had also added a soft bed jacket for Maria as Nina remembered those chilly night-feeds, while Edward snoozed next to her.

Nina was fixing the lead on Larry, whose tail was wagging in anticipation, when Paul rang early one morning.

"It's a girl, it's a girl. She is only 2.8 kg but she's beautiful, absolutely gorgeous. Maria is fine and so is the baby. Mum, it is just fantastic. I'll send you photos. And Mum, we're going to call her Cristina Maria, well that's after you of course. Your first grandchild."

Nina burst into tears. It was not the arrival of the baby, but that her son and this girl, who she did not even know, had never met, had wanted to call their first born after her. That afternoon Nina spent half a month's salary on the flimsiest baby dresses in pink at Harrods. She found a silver rattle, no discount here, and bought that as a christening present. The girl behind the counter smiled, indulging her as she talked about her newborn grandchild.

When Paul phoned again, they were home with the baby and the whole family came to the phone to say in halting English how beautiful Cristina was, that she slept during the night and hardly ever cried. As good as Paul had been, when he was a baby, Nina thought, but she did not mention it as The Delmonicos were so proud of their new addition to the family.

One week Nina heard a small gurgle from the baby when Paul phoned and it touched her more than any other sound she had ever heard. The child was constantly on her mind and she stared for hours at the photos Paul had sent. Cristina looked like most babies, she had dark thick hair and kissable folds of baby-fat. She was photographed in one of the pink Harrods dresses that Nina had sent and in a flash she felt a connection, there was something she recognised as from her, Cristina's grandmother.

She tried not to show the photos to Jen or at work, but if she had a chance and someone asked, out would come a buff envelope with a handful of snaps. She made copies and sent them to Sophie in Newcastle, who showed a negligible interest in her niece. She was far more taken by the young lawyer she had met at her father's wedding and who had sprinted up to Newcastle several times in his Porsche, that first caught her eye. Now they were planning a trip to Paris during the Easter break, "I want to show Chris Gramma's Paris," Sophie declared. Nina's children were having a life of their own — and she was both proud and sad.

~

Summer came and Nina spent two weeks down with Tessa in Provence. The house had been done over by yet another interior decorator, who had added muted tapestry cushions which were scattered on the white sofas, tassels big as fists on the raw silk curtains hanging from medieval iron poles. Madame Galine had become their permanent housekeeper and she had moved in to a small *mas* next door, which Jacques had snapped up before it came onto the market.

The embarrassment Nina had felt while staying with them at the time of the wedding had disappeared and she found it odd to think that Jacques had once been her lover. He seemed so perfect for Tessa, who still had that newly-wed shine in her eyes. Tessa complained that Jacques worked too hard, though.

"I see far too little of him, but as I'm now a co-proprietor of his *agence mobilier* I suppose I should be grateful."

"Is that wise, to mix work and marriage?"

"Well, what else should I put Jack's money into? It rather pleases me that my ex-husband supports my present husband. Jacques's ex-wife was his sleeping partner and that's a phrase and thought that didn't appeal to me, so

I bought her out. Therefore, my ex not only supports my present husband but also *his* ex. It is a kind of logic that amuses me."

As Jacques worked long hours Tessa and Nina spent their days either lounging by the pool side or driving around the region in Tessa's silver Audi, another gift from Jack. By the time they came back Madame Galine had a meal ready for the three of them and Nina sometimes felt a twist of envy, which sharpened her enjoyment like an olive in a Martini.

After two weeks Nina was sad to leave but relieved that her relationship with Tessa had not been affected by the odd guilt she felt for having slept with Jacques — odd, Nina thought, because if any one should have felt any guilt it was Jacques. Nina still treasured her memories of those sunny days. She seldom thought of sex, it was almost a relief not to have that urge, instead she could concentrate on budgets and baby-news. She had learned to sleep in the middle of the bed and she enjoyed the space, there was room on the double duvet for books, art magazines and, on special occasions, a bar of dark chocolate.

Sophie spent her summer working in London, staying with her lawyer boyfriend Chris. Lodging was the expression she used and that assured Nina that Sophie planned to go back to Newcastle for her last year. "Of course, we sleep together, yes, and I **am** careful." Nina had met Chris a few times and he reminded her of Edward when he was young. Neat, polite and restrained, but he seemed able to deal with Sophie, who had regained her bossy gustiness.

~

"Now listen to me before you reject the idea." Edward let his irritation travel down the phone line, like a distant hiss. "Sophie wants a 21st, and don't you think we ought to celebrate Paul's wedding? The Delmonicos did. And then there is the birth of Cristina — and of Nicholas. We have so much to celebrate as a family and I am willing not only to pay for a party but also for Paul and his little family to come over here. Yes, I know you're busy at the Gallery, that's something to celebrate as well, but Sasha has time on her hands and she's very good at organising. We've had a look at the private room at Bologna Vecchia, our local Italian. They could organise a gathering for sixty people. Buffet-style. This restaurant just happens to have one Michelin star. And then the youngsters can dance afterwards, you know, to a disco. I have talked to Sophie and she loves the idea. She can ask twenty guests, Paul the same and then twenty of our friends and family. No doubt, you want to ask George, and your friends Jen and Tessa and that estate agent of hers."

"I wish you had discussed this with me before you made any plans, I'd . . ."

"Why should I? I'm going to pay for it after all."

"Have you discussed this with Paul as well — and have you fixed a date?"

"As a matter of fact, yes. He is coming back to me with a date, as soon as he has discussed it with his boss. I have a feeling he's desperate to show off his baby — and to see his little brother Coco, that's what we call Nicholas." There was a short pause. "And to see you and me, too, of course."

Nina had very little to add and the following week, when talking to Paul, she could hear how excited he was. "Dad has even offered to pay our flights." A date was fixed without consulting Nina. And soon afterwards she received an engraved invitation.

In elegant copperplate it stated that Edward and Alexandra Riverton were hosting a celebration of the 21 st birthday of Sophie Riverton, the wedding of Paul and Maria Eugenia Riverton and the baptism of Nicholas Riverton.

With it came six blank invitations and a note on a bright pink Post-it."Please use these for your family and friends. Edward has already dealt with his side of the family. Welcome, kindest regards, Sasha R." The "R" grated.

Jen said she would love to come, but Tessa and Jacques were busy with friends coming over from England. George would not miss a party for anything and as for family, she had no family except Edward's. Unlike her daughter she could not muster much enthusiasm for this celebration and in order to compete with Edward's generosity, she spent far too much on a single string of pearls as a present for Sophie. In order to pay for it, Nina had sold her engagement ring. She knew she would never wear it again anyway.

Nina counted the days, not to the party but to Paul's arrival from Quito. She organised the guestroom, which had a double bed and put a borrowed cot in his old room. The week before their arrival she laundered the curtains, made up a nursing table for Cristina and laid in a larder full of Paul's favourite food. They would stay with her for one week and then after the party go on to Mrs Riverton, where they would spend a week-end with Edward and "his side of the family" as Sasha had put it and from there go to Heathrow for the flight back. A day Nina feared more than the party.

On the day of their arrival she drove up to London and finally managed to find a parking space for the Honda in one of the short-term car parks. The smell of urine and old cigarette butts sickened her and for a moment she thought she would have to lean against the car and throw up. An Indian family, stuffing their boot with plastic bags and paper cartoons girdled by brown sticky tape, threw her suspicious glances before turning their backs on her. It took her ages to find the machine with the parking tickets. Her nerves were tightening and her stomach heaved again. She must relax, she told herself and then she noticed that the plane was soon due to land.

The plane was late, several hours late. Then suddenly, as if the time had concertinad into nothing, she saw Paul coming through the double doors, a petite girl by his side, and he steered a pushchair on which was laden two heavy suitcases. But where was the baby? Then Nina saw it. In a shawl-like contraption tied around his chest a small dark head was visible. Cristina. Nina's heart started beating so fast, she almost fainted.

"Here, Paul, here," she screamed at the top of her voice, so loud that the taxi driver next to her lost his scribbled name sign. Paul turned his head and his face lit up as he saw his mother, he leant forward to Maria and pointed to Nina. Maria's eyes followed his finger and until she met the eyes of her mother-in-law and she smiled nervously. Nina thought the girl looked tired, there were dark circles under her eyes and she was very thin, almost skeletal.

Cristina did not stir, not even when Nina hugged her son close to her. She put her arms around Maria, but she did not know what to say. She mumbled a welcome and then turned to Paul.

Questions about the baby, the flight, the Delmonicos and talk about the party kept the awkwardness at bay. Nina talked too much and too loudly all the way back to Wyckham Wood, through heavy traffic with belching smoke and fumes. She looked through the back view mirror and noticed that Maria had fallen asleep, her head resting on Paul's shoulder.

"Maria is so beautiful, but she doesn't look well. Are you sure she's resting enough after the baby? Does she breastfeed Cristina?"

"Shush, Mum. She hasn't got enough milk and she's very upset about that. She lost quite a lot of blood during the delivery but she's putting on weight now and she's fine, but, please, don't say anything about breastfeeding."

His hand gently caressed Maria's dark hair and suddenly Cristina woke up. Her little head peaked up from the baby-sling and Paul kissed his daughter's head. Nina looked at them and they reminded her of a Nativity scene. Paul bent down and next time Nina looked back he was bottle feeding Cristina. Maria had not even stirred.

Nina had put flowers everywhere to make Maria feel at home. The smell was almost overpowering as she opened the front door.

"Coffee? And are you hungry, tired? It's been a long flight." The young family was sent upstairs to unpack while Nina prepared the coffee. She brought a tray into the living room and on the side table were presents wrapped in silver and pink.

Maria looked fresher and had put on some pink lipstick.

"We have a gift from my family," she said and handed over a large parcel.

"Before we open our presents please let me hold little Cristina."

Nina leant forward and almost snatched the baby from Maria's arms. Two deep blue eyes looked into hers, they were like marbles, clear and unsullied. She remembered how Magda had once told her, when she was a little girl, that every lie left a small cloud behind the eyes. These sapphire-blue eyes had yet to lie.

A tiny finger gripped her thumb and those eyes kept watching her steadily. Nina sat absolutely still, not daring to move. The voices of Paul and Maria disappeared, there were just Nina and the baby present, surrounded by a gossamer membrane. Peace and stillness flowed into Nina, like a transfusion, and she wanted to keep the moment for ever.

"Did you mention coffee, Mum?"

Nina looked up and her cheeks were wet.

The days went quickly and new routines were established of which the baby was the centre. Cristina was indeed a quiet and good baby, but only if things happened at her pace. Paul worshipped his daughter and was not embarrassed to show it. He bathed his daughter and soaped her tiny rose-coloured body with a gentleness that touched Nina. Maria seemed far less interested in her daughter and spent much of her day sleeping and resting. Nina had taken some days off and with Larry on his lead and Cristina in her buggy Paul and Nina would go for long walks across the Common and into the Wyckham Wood Forest, a tautology that always amused Nina, "only because you're foreign," Paul pointed out.

Sophie arrived and the house turned into a happy circus. Blaring pop music, baby noises and laughter. Maria and Sophie seemed to get on and Sophie's presence perked Maria up. Nina babysat so that Sophie, Paul and Maria could travel up to London for some sightseeing and lunch with Edward and Sasha. Being alone with Cristina was a real treat and Nina cooed and chatted, never letting the baby out of her sight. In the evening she bathed her and kissed her little chubby legs, which made Cristina laugh. Nina could not remember when last she had been this happy

The Bologna Vecchia had a doorman dressed in a bright red uniform at the door. He looked at Nina and her children, dragging a buggy and baby-seat, as if they were travelling gypsies. Inside the welcome was equally frosty until Edward rushed towards them and kissed them all, even Nina.

"Come on, Sasha is upstairs and in a bit of a state. The DJ has blown a fuse, no literally a fuse, and the room is in darkness and the table cloths are not he colour she was promised. Please Nina, see if you can help."

He had obviously forgot that his present wife and ex-wife had not properly met before. Paul must have thought about it as he took the baby and with long strides led them upstairs. Nina followed slowly behind Sophie and Maria, while Edward tried to get some help from a hapless waiter downstairs.

Sasha, dressed in baby-blue, was not the elegant, slim girl Nina remembered having seen those awful nights she spent in the car outside Edward's flat. Her weight must have ballooned during pregnancy. Her hair, as Nina remembered as silken blond, had lost its shine and was cut short. It immediately made Nina feel better. Sasha was clearly irritated and held a lit candle in her hand. The flame flickered but it was enough for Nina to see that Sasha's cheeks were red with indignation.

"Michelin star, indeed! Can't even find their bloody fuses. And the guests will arrive in less than an hour. And Edward is completely useless, leaves it all to me."

The cheeks took on an even deeper colour. At that very moment Edward turned up with an electrician — and a glass of champagne for Sasha.

"It's going to be all right, darling, absolutely all right. Now, darling, take a deep breath and then a sip of this glorious champagne — it's on the house". Nina stood next to Sasha, mouth open. She had never seen Edward so defensive and subservient.

Nina helped to place the name cards on the tables, arrange the flowers in the buffet area and soon the lights came back on and music was pouring from the now functioning loudspeakers. As if in a well-rehearsed ballet, waiters kept turning up, pleating napkins into fans, giving the silver a last polish and turning the glasses towards the light to make sure they were spotless. Dishes with nuts and almonds were placed on small side tables and by the time the first guest arrived, and it was Margaret Riverton, Edward's mother, soon followed by Jen, dressed in silver grey jersey. She hardly left Nina's side during the whole party and cheered her up no end by referring to Sasha as "that blancmange."

The evening was a success and Nina had to admit that Sasha had planned it beautifully. Before the buffet was served, the marriage of Paul and Maria was celebrated with champagne toasts. Paul, her shy son, surprised everyone by giving a touching speech to his bride, who proudly showed off little Cristina. After the main course, and Edward had been very generous, it was time to toast the babies, Nicholas and Cristina, who both were given fingertips dipped in champagne to suck.

Suddenly all the lights went out and Nina expected another outbreak from an exasperated Sasha, but instead in came a cake as big as a table with twenty one candles. The Italian waiters sang Happy Birthday, out of tune, and everyone joined in. Now it was Sophie's turn to be celebrated.

"The reason why we picked an Italian restaurant for these festivities is simple. Sasha and I love Italy and as a present to our beloved Sophie we hand over this."

Sophie smiled expectantly as she received a large box wrapped in silk ribbons the colours of the Italian flag. She tore off the ribbons and found a card.

"A week for two in Venice, at Hotel Fenice! Oh, Daddy, that's just great." She hugged her father and threw a happy glance at Chris. "And I know who I'll take," she cried.

George stood up and gave a small speech to his god-daughter and mentioned Magda. "You were the light in her life. And if you have half her courage you will never be short of real friends." Nina looked at her radiant daughter and noticed that she was wearing Magda's earrings. Love travels down the generations whatever hiccoughs there may be on the way, Nina thought. She rose and walked towards Edward.

"I would just like to thank you for a most wonderful party, so generous. It's been wonderful for me to see our children together again and with Maria and little Cristina, our granddaughter."

Edward pulled her into his arms.

"Thank you, darling Nina, thank you. That means a lot to me, too. Now, what about a dance for old time's sake?"

~

CHAPTER NINETEEN

Nina Riverton

Life is still full of surprises. I never knew that I could enjoy work as much as I do. We're a fine team and I must say that Dr Jordan, Derek, is a most inspiring head of the Gallery. He's very knowledgeable, but at the same time very private. I know nothing about him, although the rest of us gossip about him for this very reason. He used to work for the National Gallery as a curator and before that he taught history of art at Cambridge. Top drawer all the way, but he's not at all snobbish and terrible enthusiastic about my department, which is so encouraging as nothing like this has been tried by the Gallery before.

Somehow my work has given me self-confidence, something I've had precious little of. Being part of a team rather than sitting at home by my own desk has also made me realise that work creates a social network and there's always the Friday night wine before we close the doors. Everyone joins in and it is very much a family atmosphere. We all want to achieve something for the Gallery and work hard hoping to reach our goals. Money is always short but we find new ways of pulling in cash; classes, lectures, film shows, a crèche and even coffee mornings for the over – 65's.

"Could you come in and see me after your lecture today. There's something I want to discuss with you," Dr. Jordan asked. It had been a friendly request but Nina immediately started worrying and she found it hard to concentrate as she rattled through the advantages of art as a medium to reach difficult teenagers. She had given this talk to so many school administrators by now that she had it pat off. Even her gestures were part of the unwritten manuscript. Nina had learnt to engage by asking questions that drew them in, making them smile and feel part of the team.

It always amused her to find how people reacted to a bit of flattery or a thoughtful question. So many good people were driven to education by a desire to do something for the children and then got trapped by targets and bureaucratic tangles, that left them with less and less time for the children themselves.

She rushed from the lecture through the dark corridor behind the main gallery and stood outside the double doors to the director's office. "Go straight in, Dr Jordan is expecting you," said his secretary, now a firm supporter of Nina's, as she felt that she had been instrumental in securing Nina's promotion.

"Nina, wonderful to see you, sit down." He gestured towards the chair and again Nina found herself admiring his elegant almost balletic movements.

"I have a proposition and I hope you will say Yes. I found this drawing on the board in the classroom studio and I was told by Martha Jones that it's one of yours."

Nina looked at the sketch. It was a drawing done in dark grey ink of the Gallery covered in snow. She remembered how excited she had been to see the formal yews outside the entrance laden with snow, changing these funeral obelisks to something softer and more graceful. Nina had never liked the tough pruning of trees that turned them into un-natural shapes and topiaries abhorred her. The Gallery with its dome-topped roof hidden under cloudlike drifts had appealed to her and she had done a quick sketch of it with frozen hands. Martha had seen it and asked if she could use it in her class. Nina had not given her sketch a single thought and here it was held between Dr.Jordan's long fingers.

"I find it a charming drawing and I wonder if we may use it for our annual Christmas card? We can't offer you a fee, but we will, of course, accredit you as the artist. What do you say?"

Nina swallowed. She had never been complimented on any of her artwork since she left university. And here was Dr. Jordan, a renowned art historian, finding her ten-minute sketch "charming".

"I'd be delighted, thrilled actually," Nina said and after discussing printing methods, message and paper quality, she left the director's office, skipping like a five year old.

She was still on a high when Edward phoned.

"You're never at home, I leave messages, but you never phone back, so I'd thought I'd try at the Gallery. Could we meet for lunch? I think we need to discuss the children."

They had not met since the party for Sophie's 21st. Soon after Paul and his young family returned to Ecuador and although Nina missed her son, she was happy that he had settled down and that he enjoyed fatherhood in a more hands-on fashion than Edward had ever done. Little Cristina was photographed at regular intervals and reams of photos were sent to Nina by her proud son. Their weekly phone call dealt mostly with Cristina's progress. Once home, Maria had recovered quickly from the exhaustion and maybe having her own mother around had helped. Nina could only imagine how confusing it must have been for Maria to become part of the Riverton tribe. Edward's mother was aloof, not through unkindness but due to her Edwardian upbringing. Nina remembered it had taken almost ten years before she had suggested that Nina might prefer to call her mother-in-law by her first name. Maria also had to deal with a father-in-law, who himself had a child only months older than his grandchild and "then there is me," thought Nina, "worried about my son and his future in a strange country."

"What's on your mind? Has something happened? Is Paul all right?"

"Nothing has happened. Why can't we just meet to talk about our, I stress *our*, children? Is that so odd, Nina?"

They met at an anonymous restaurant near Victoria Station, a barn of a room with no charm at all. The waiters all seemed to be Eastern European and were as gloomy as the surroundings. Nina could not understand why Edward had chosen this place.

"Have you been here before?"

"No, I picked it from a restaurant guide. The blurb said it represented good value for money. They forgot to mention that it has the ambiance of a morgue."

Their shared disappointment bridged the awkward silence and they threw themselves over the menus proffered with a surly "still or sparkling?" by a bored blonde.

"Tap, please" was Edward's reply, which was met with tight-lipped silence as the waitress turned on her heels.

A basket of bread was dumped on the table like an unwanted gift and minutes later another waiter arrived with a jug of tap-cloudy water and a wine list with tired corners.

"I think we need some wine to be able to cope with this atmosphere" Edward said and after some lip-chewing picked a Chateau-bottled wine, which certainly did not represent good value for money.

"I really wanted to say how wonderful it was to see you at Sophie's party, so great to see you and the children together. I do miss you all so much."

"Well, you have a new family now to worry about. Our children have grown up and now have lives of their own. Paul has a family and I don't think it'll be long before Sophie gets married. She and Chris seem like an ideal couple."

"And how do you feel now that your nest is empty?"

"If you had asked me some time ago I would have said that I felt as empty as the nest. Now I don't. I love my work and it fills my days. You might not think so, but I feel I contribute something positive for the kids in the area. And did I tell you that a drawing of mine has been picked for the Gallery's annual Christmas card? And if you wonder about the nest itself, well, I know what you probably think; time to move, but I love the house and the garden and Paul and his family need somewhere to stay when they come and see us and Sophie gets into a strop if I as much as try to use her room for guests."

"No, I don't think you should move. As a matter of fact, I like it that you're there. There's precious little left of our old life."

"What do you mean? We're not that old."

"No, I mean of the life we shared. You and me. The family."

"Whatever happens, Edward, we will always be a family."

Edward looked at the wall behind her.

"Sasha is not a happy mother. I think she misses work more than she thought she would and she has not lost the weight she piled on during her pregnancy. I've suggested a nanny, but she doesn't want to return to her office until she's back to her former weight. She sleeps a lot and sometimes I think she hates our son. Her doctor calls it post-natal depression, but it seems to be getting worse and worse. Even her parents are worried. And I feel as if I'm an unwanted guest every time I step inside our front door."

Nina twirled her slice of dried bread between her fingers. She looked up at Edward and felt her eyelids tremble. He looked so unhappy.

"All women go through this. It's not unusual and she will get out of it and."

"and then get pregnant again, no doubt," Edward smiled ruefully.

Nina dropped her bread on the side plate and gently stroked his hand.

"You have a beautiful little son and soon Sasha will be back to normal."

"You know we have our silver wedding coming up next year. Now wouldn't it be wonderful if we could spend that day with the children?"

"Edward, dear Edward. No wonder Sasha gets depressed. You don't celebrate wedding anniversaries after a divorce. That's not done. Now you go home tonight and give Sasha a big bunch of roses and tell her how much you love her and your little boy. Your son needs a proper family around him."

"Don't cut me out, please Nina. You and Paul and Sophie are part of me and it's a part that can't be exchanged."

How easy it would have been to say "You should have thought of that earlier and saved us all a lot of heart ache," but Nina dismissed the idea even before it had fully formed. She pitied Edward. She was free, he was not.

~

The smoke was forming veils of grey and swirled across the table at The Adelphi. Jen was coughing pointedly as the man at the next table lit up yet another cigarette. Nina had arrived earlier than Jen and picked a table close to the window in order to see her coming. The wine bar was packed as it always was on Thursdays.

"It's a shame they don't have smoke free areas here as in some restaurants," Jen said with a louder voice than necessary.

"Well, where would we have been then, all those evenings we've spent here with Tessa and her packets of Marlboro?"

"Tessa, yes. That's what I wanted to speak to you about. But first my good news, well, I think it's good news. Bernhard has asked me to marry him and now as I approach fifty I think it might not be a bad idea to settle down. So I've said yes and we plan to get married this summer, in Brussels. He has family and I have none, so it makes sense, but I want you to be my matron of honour. Please say you will." She looked pleadingly at Nina.

"Always the matron of honour, never the bride." Nina answered with a mock sigh.

"But, of course I will. I'm so happy for you. You were always so against marriage and here you are, planning to marry a judge, and a Belgian at that. So when did you fall in love? You do love him, don't you?"

"What was it Prince Charles said, 'Yes, whatever love is'. Yes, I love and respect him, but we're not talking passionate love, love that burns you and consumes you. I'm happy in his company, we've many interests in common. He's taught me about food and music and I think I've perked him up physically, or, at least, that's what he says. He looks after me and he's a gentleman. I didn't think these things mattered, but they do."

She paused for a while and sipped her wine.

"Nina, I do think that when you come to a certain age, you must go for what you need rather than what you want. I've had all kinds of affairs, happy ones, passionate ones and some real stinkers, but now I'm calm and it is as if my heart is wrapped in cotton wool. I love being cared for, cosseted and it's not made worse by getting a house in Roussillon and a villa outside Brussels. As for the future, I'll keep on working but I'll go freelance so that I can spend more time with Bernhard. He will retire in five years' time and I'm thinking seriously of doing the same then, so that we can move permanently to France."

"I'm so happy for you and he seems such a nice man. How odd, both you and Tessa married and here I am, after some twenty years of being married, living a single life and rather enjoying it."

"Tessa, yes, that's what I wanted to speak to you about. Have you spoken to her lately?"

"No, it was some weeks ago. She sounded fine. She said she was coming to England later, next month, I think."

"I'm concerned about her. Jacques has some rather odd business dealings and she's involved. It seems she's invested part of her settlement in his firm and he's now buying another estate agent and as his partner — and his wife — she's now been asked to invest more. Quite a considerable sum. And she's found out that the house she'd bought is in *his* name. It really stinks, but Tessa seems to ignore all the signs, it's as if she didn't want to know. Can't you speak to her? I'd be happy to help but I don't know French law at all. According to Tessa, this is the way it's done in France. It's not, as I found out from a chap in my office. I think she's being had and it worries me. Will you see what you can do? You're French-speaking, maybe you can talk to a lawyer and find out what needs to be done?"

"Poor Tessa. ", Nina whispered, but in her mind she cursed Jacques, who had abused Tessa's generosity.

"Tessa is tougher than we give her credit for, but I'll speak to the lawyer, who looked after Magda's estate. It doesn't sound right to me about the house. But what does Tessa say?"

"She sounds very calm, it's almost as if she accepts she's been cheated. She says they're very happy and that she loves him and that's the most important thing of all. Money is just money, she said, and pointed out that it was, after all, her settlement from Jack. She thought it very fitting that it was Jack who paid for Jacques."

"Do you remember how the three of us used to sit here over endless bottles of wine and complain about the junk males out there? You know, I think we were wrong. There's junk in all of us. I've spent so much time hating and loving Edward and now I feel nothing but a certain pity for him, but he's *not* junk. And Tor, well *he* was screwed up, not me. Jacques, well, maybe he has his way to love and if he makes Tessa happy that is all that matters. There's a price for everything, I've found that out as I came out of my own protective cocoon. If we can only learn to expect less, we'll receive more."

"For God's sake, Nina, you sound like one of those preachers on American TV. No more cod psychology, PLEASE. Now about my wedding, do you think I am too old to have a white wedding? I have always dreamt of one . . ."

"Well, in your case it has to be very off-white."

The two women smiled at each other and raised their glasses.

CHAPTER TWENTY

Derek Jordan

I'm truly happy, happier than I thought possible. I knew from the first time I saw her that she was special. There was a vulnerable side to her in spite of that clear-headed, jolly efficiency. Since my wife died six years ago I have not even thought of a love affair, affairs, yes, but not love. The more I got to know her the more I liked what I saw and one Friday after last New Year, when we all gathered in the Studio for some wine I mentioned a film I wanted to see and she just said that she'd read the reviews and that it sounded very interesting. Without thinking and I don't know how I picked up the courage, I suggested we'd see the film together and that's how it started. After the movie, it was a rather boring Hungarian art film, I suggested an Indian and over the samosas we talked for hours. Her international upbringing has given her an uncanny eye for English idiosyncrasies. She makes me laugh, even at myself, and I have not done much of that these last years.

Love is different at our age, more comfortable. Like a warm fire on a cold night.

We had a very quiet wedding, there were her children and two friends, Tessa Debrel from France and Jen from Belgium with her new husband. There was also George, some old Hungarian family friend, who wept though the service and then got rather drunk. Later we had a separate reception for all our colleagues and my secretary gave a very sweet speech, intimating that she was the one who had brought us together. I didn't have the heart to tell her that I had had my eyes on Nina for quite some time.

Now we have settled in Virginia, where I am on a year's sabbatical, teaching at a middle-sized university. Campus life seems to suit her and we have a very busy life the art faculty; with lectures, exhibitions and we often spend week-ends in small hotels exploring American history. Being away from Wyckham Wood gives us a fresh start and next year we'll return and then we'll sell her house. I don't want to share space with her ghosts.

Acknowledgement

First of all I would like to thank Stephanie Stones, who edited Junk Male with utter professionalism and a toughness that surprised me. She also happens to be my daughter.

Colin Kaye, a seasoned reader for one of London's most famous literary agents, and his wife Gay encouraged me and insisted on a happy ending.

Andrea Higham read Junk Male at its first stage and provided moral support and friendship.

Minda Despard pushed me not to give up. Sue Reardon Smith made me laugh instead of crying when I got my first rejection slip and so did Vivien James.

To Georgina Rabor, Faith Allen and Kathy Lorenzo at AuthorHouse I have nothing but thanks and admiration for their professional yet friendly assistance all through the publishing process.

And thanks to Dulwich Picture Gallery, which always inspires me and also plays an important role in Junk Male – gently disguised.

Last but not least to John, my husband, without his help and support I could not have written this book. Which just goes to show that, in spite of the many women who helped and encouraged me, not every man is a Junk Male.

London November 2011

About the Author

Pia Helena Ormerod grew up in Sweden. She studied Economics at Stockholm University and made her name in financial journalism, first in Sweden and later in the UK. Asked in an interview why she had turned to fiction, Pia Helena answered "In financial journalism the truth is paramount, in fiction I can invent without the risk of being fired or sued."

Pia Helena lives in London and Junk Male is her first work of fiction. She has written several books on trade, one which received a gold award from the Swedish Chamber of Commerce for the UK.

Pia Helena would love to receive your comments and until her website is up and running please feel free to contact her at piahelenaormerod@virginmedia.com

Lightning Source UK Ltd.
Milton Keynes UK
UKOW051804031211

183123UK00001B/11/P